ShadowChild

Mpho LM Mangole

INDIA • SINGAPORE • MALAYSIA

ISBN 979-8-88909-978-9

This book has been published with all efforts taken to make the material error-free after the consent of the author. However, the author and the publisher do not assume and hereby disclaim any liability to any party for any loss, damage, or disruption caused by errors or omissions, whether such errors or omissions result from negligence, accident, or any other cause.

While every effort has been made to avoid any mistake or omission, this publication is being sold on the condition and understanding that neither the author nor the publishers or printers would be liable in any manner to any person by reason of any mistake or omission in this publication or for any action taken or omitted to be taken or advice rendered or accepted on the basis of this work. For any defect in printing or binding the publishers will be liable only to replace the defective copy by another copy of this work then available.

email: onceuastory@gmail.com
Cellphone: +(267) 75-222-524

For my children:

Hashimiou Mbaki – Your wicked sense of humour and commitment to what you love is inspiring.

Asmau Wada – Your creativity, quick wit and zeal for life motivate me daily.

Zaine Modise – You challenge me every minute I am with you, and help me see the world through different eyes.

You all mean the world to me.

Contents

Prelude - A New Dawn...*9*

Chapter One: New Acquaintances..15

Chapter Two: Forging Relationships....................................24

Chapter Three: Closing Doors 35

Chapter Four: Cows and Companions 46

Chapter Five: King...55

Chapter Six: Stalked...68

Chapter Seven: Slither..79

Chapter Eight: A Momentary Truce 88

Chapter Nine: Forging Friendships 99

Chapter Ten: Sparks and Fireworks 112

Chapter Eleven: Misunderstood Again 127

Chapter Twelve: Midnight Terror 134

Chapter Thirteen: Unexpectedness 145

Chapter Fourteen: Crossed Signals 158

Chapter Fifteen: Give it Time 170

Chapter Sixteen: Heartfelt 182

Chapter Seventeen: A Nasty Little Game 193

Chapter Eighteen: Warmth and Fuzziness 204

Chapter Nineteen: Reminiscing and Remembering 212

Chapter Twenty: Shaken 220

Chapter Twenty One: Things That Go Bump 228

Chapter Twenty Two: Weird Becomes Disturbing 240

Chapter Twenty Three: Growing Pangs 249

Chapter Twenty Four: Clawed Creatures 256

Chapter Twenty Five: Snapped 261

Chapter Twenty Six: Sorrow 268

Chapter Twenty Seven: Knowledge and Knowing 278

Chapter Twenty Eight: Concealment Revealed 285

Chapter Twenty Nine: What's Thicker Than Blood? 292

Chapter Thirty: Nowhere to Hide 303

Chapter Thirty One: Saying Goodbye Again 311

Chapter Thirty Two: A Guest in the Night....................318

Chapter Thirty Three: Pain and Darkness....................324

Chapter Thirty Four: Breaking Through....................332

Chapter Thirty Five: Clashed....................338

Chapter Thirty Six: Darkness Comes Calling....................345

Chapter Thirty Seven: Shadows and Light....................352

Epilogue....................*357*

Prelude - A New Dawn

Jake looked outside the aeroplane window and saw the open, blue expanse that was the sky. It seemed somehow funny to him that he could see the approaching darkness that was night. They were heading right into it and within a few minutes the day would be behind them and he would look forward to getting some rest. It never ceased to amaze him; the concept of watching oneself crossing that barrier of daylight and immediately being in the night. Watching the sunset was so different. It took longer and seemed to prepare you for the darkness. Being in a plane was quick. It only took seconds before one crossed the darkness barrier.

He grinned as the darkness enveloped the plane, looking out the window, in the direction from which he had come. His grin widened as he realised that he could still see the daylight even though, technically, they were in the dark now. Another few seconds and he wouldn't see even that. He leaned away from the window and sat back. He felt the tension in his neck and rolled his head to try and ease it. The motion didn't help.

Looking up at the screen in front of him, he recognised the movie that was playing as one he had already seen. He couldn't be bothered to change it as he was too exhausted. That left one thing that he could do and that was sleep. He'd been awake for more than thirty hours, making last minute arrangements for his mother, making sure that she would have everything she would need while he was away. She had laughed and told him she would be fine. He knew she was right but that had not stopped him from bustling over her anyway. After all, he would be away for at least a year.

When the opportunity to go to Botswana had presented itself, Jake had jumped at the chance. It had seemed like an excellent break for him. The job had seemed perfect for him, as though it had been tailor-made just for him. With no ties other than his mother to think about, moving to Botswana for a year or two had seemed perfect. Perhaps he had become jaded by the constant disillusionment he faced within his life in New York City. There was nothing new anymore. Everything was a constant struggle and he felt he had lost sight of the reason why he had become a doctor in the first place. Moving to a foreign country for a while would help him reassess his life and, who knew? Perhaps he would find something that he had not been aware he had been missing.

Jake raised his bottom a little from the seat and pulled his wallet from the back pocket of his pants. He opened it and took out a snapshot. In the picture was a five-year old boy holding an infant. The baby had the boy's left pinkie finger grasped tightly within its own hand. It was a baby girl and she stared myopically at the young boy who held her. Jake didn't remember her well. His memories of the time he had spent in Jackalas II as a boy were distant and almost non-existent. The only things he remembered really were what his parents had told him.

His dad had been a doctor before him and had worked in most of Southern Africa. He and his parents had lived in Botswana for two years and during that time they had moved from village to village, helping the Batswana where they could. His father had loved it and his mother had dutifully travelled with her husband. One of the last villages they had gone to was a small village called Jackalas II. The village lay about sixty kilometres from Francistown, the second largest city in Botswana. Technically, it was the second of two cities, the first being the capital, Gaborone. That was where this picture he held had been taken; in Jackalas II. It had been about thirty years ago now but he barely remembered the picture being taken at all.

When his mother had learnt that he was going to Jackalas II, she had remembered the picture and looked for it. It had taken about three weeks to find but she had been determined to find it. And she had. Jake remembered how she had called him late one night and announced triumphantly that it had been tucked away in an envelope with some letters she had received all those years ago. When she had shown it to him, he could honestly say that he couldn't remember it. All he saw was himself as a boy and a beautiful baby girl wrapped in a baby blue blanket.

Since he had been given the picture, Jake had looked at it innumerable times. He had memorised every element in it, noting the delicate features of the infant he carried. He imagined sometimes, that he could feel the soft material of the blanket he held on his fingers, the weight of the child in his arms. Everything made sense to him in that picture, every warm feeling he experienced as he looked at it, and the sense of peace he felt as he looked at the younger version of himself holding the baby. Everything, that was, except the wall of shadows that seemed to surround him and the infant he held. He frowned as he studied the image again, wondering what had caused the dark shapes and how out of place they seemed. Even now, as he looked at the picture, the faint shadows were visible behind him and the baby, forming a semi-circle with them in the middle of it.

His gaze moved from the greyish forms and focussed on the girl. It was a pity his mother couldn't recall her name. Perhaps she was still living there and they would bump into each other during his stay there. It was highly unlikely though. A lot of things would have changed in thirty years. She would be a woman now, perhaps with children of her own and a husband. It was highly likely that she had held many little ones wrapped in little blue blankets the way he had held her all those years ago.

Again the shadows in the background caught his eye and he pulled the snapshot closer to his face to study it further. He had thought before that the shadows looked distinctly humanoid but the way the light had to have been positioned, anyone who had stood close to them would have been visible in the photograph. Perhaps he was just being a little too analytical. Perhaps there really was nothing to it. Shrugging slightly, he pushed the picture back into his wallet and then put the wallet back into his pocket. He leaned back and closed his eyes. He smiled as he thought of meeting people that he had lived amongst, at least for a while, thirty years ago. He hoped, he really, really hoped, that he would meet that child he had held so close once before. It was something to look forward to anyway.

Within seconds, the smooth slightly rocking motion of the aeroplane had lulled him into a deep slumber.

Chapter One
New Acquaintances

Kuda was furious.

If she never saw another male face again it would be too soon.

How dare he underestimate her capabilities and hire somebody from outside to do the job she knew she was well qualified to do?

How dare he deliberately overlook her? Not only that, but he had deliberately sought out this new person and that irked her even more. He had head hunted someone from over 13 000km away to come take over the clinic; her pride and joy.

Did he honestly think she was a numskull who was inefficient and incapable of running it? Of all the narrow-minded, chauvinistic people she knew, Doctor Aaron Campbell took the cake, and then some.

She was so wrapped up in her fury that she burst through the swing-doors like a miniature hurricane on legs and promptly crashed into nearly two meters of solid male flesh. When strong hands rose automatically to support her she brushed them aside impatiently and glared at their owner. The man who stood before her watched her expectantly, waiting for her to say something. When he realised that the bundle of fury in front of him was not about to apologise for nearly knocking him off his feet, he spoke.

"Good afternoon. I'm looking for Doctor Aaron Campbell. Do you know where I can find him?" he asked, his American accent drawing out his words.

Kuda listened to the man's cultured voice and her anger boiled over. There he stood in his three-piece suit and crocodile skin shoes, with his brown eyes sparkling and his black hair cut short and neat. His chocolate coloured skin was blemish free, his nose slightly flared out at the nostrils. His plump lips would have been alluring at any other time but now they just irked her more despite how kissable they looked. A package deal, complete with briefcase and tie. He was the epitome of everything Kuda despised and for some unknown reason she felt like slapping him.

"Ha o mmatla, rra, mo itshenkele," she spat out. She did not care that he probably did not understand what she had said; how she had not so politely told him to look for the doctor himself.

"I'm sorry, ma'am. I don't speak Tswana," the man said, pointedly disregarding the woman's rude voice.

"Mo ga se mathata a me," she replied even more rudely. *That's not my problem.*

The man's eyes narrowed and his lips thinned. Kuda noted with satisfaction that his knuckles seemed to tighten on the handle of his briefcase. She wanted to laugh like a little child who had pulled the wings off a fly just to watch it wriggle helplessly on the ground. When the man spoke again, his voice wasn't as amicable as it had been before and Kuda was perversely pleased with that result.

"I think it's rude of you to speak in a language I don't understand," he snapped. "Especially when you know I don't speak it."

"Rude?" the woman snapped back. "First of all, it's called Setswana. Because, you know, we *live* in Botswana. Secondly, where were you when we were learning Setswana?" She stressed the "SE" to make her own point and put her hands on her hips, glaring bloody murder at him. "If you resent the fact that I speak a language foreign to you, how do you think I feel about being forced to speak somebody else's language in my own country? You come all the way from America with your fancy ideas and teach us your crazy ideologies without bothering to learn ours. Well, exc-uuse me for wanting to talk in my native tongue, in my own country."

"Kuda! That's enough."

Kuda spun around and ran her eyes over Doctor Campbell as he came through the swing doors. His weather-beaten face was red and he looked as angry as Kuda felt. His thinning, blonde hair, which was now more white than blonde, stood up in tufts on his head, as though he had been running his fingers through it in agitation. Kuda looked away from his green eyes, wondering how he still managed to get sunburnt despite having lived in Botswana for more than twenty years.

She tossed her head defiantly and pushed her hands into the pockets of her pants, the movement drawing the khaki material tightly across her hips and causing her blue t-shirt to tighten over her chest without her noticing.

Jake, despite his annoyance, noticed, however, and quickly turned to face the older man who had walked into the room. Feeling like a grade one pervert he averted his eyes and kept them locked on Doctor Campbell.

"I'm really sorry about this, Jake. She's not normally like this and I don't know what to say," the other doctor said. The man he had called Jake nodded without saying anything. He was careful not to turn away from Doctor Campbell because he didn't trust where his eyes would involuntarily look. He was appalled but kept it hidden by making sure his face was expressionless. Or at least he hoped it was.

"Don't apologise for me, Aaron. I'm not a child." Kuda glared at the doctor and she felt her teeth clamp together as she struggled to hold back some of the things she really wanted to say to him. She so badly wanted to let loose and scream at him but it really wasn't the time right now. Not in front of Mr Three-Piece-Suit anyway. He probably thought she was a lunatic; not that she gave two squirrels' ears what he thought about her anyway. Still, she didn't need him looking at her like she was an escapee from the local asylum. Again, not that she cared what he thought.

"If you didn't behave like one then I wouldn't have to," the doctor replied sharply. "Could you please go check if the supplies have come in yet. They should have arrived by now."

"Like I told you before," Kuda replied icily, "I'm not your lackey. Thapelo's the one who's being paid to be at your beck and call, not me."

With that, the woman stormed out of the clinic before either man could say anything, disappearing around the corner of the building.

A muscle jumped erratically in the tightly-clenched jaw of Doctor Jake Dawn and he held onto his temper with an extremely thin thread. The flight had been long and tedious and he had been desperately tired when he had arrived in Gaborone. The flight to Francistown had been short, only an hour, and hadn't afforded him the rest he had so badly needed. Once in Francistown, however, he had been hit by an unexpected second wind and now he seemed to be on an adrenaline high. Jackalas had just been a breath away and instead of spending the night in Francistown as originally planned, he had driven down right away. He had been anxious to see Aaron and the place he had been away from for so long. Not even driving on the left side of the road had been a deterrent.

He just hadn't bargained on the spitfire. Or perhaps the "The Little Demon from Hell" might have been a more apt description.

"Why do you let her speak to you like that?" he asked grimly. Aaron sighed.

"She's upset about something," he mumbled. "She'll be alright though. Besides, it was partly my fault."

"That is no excuse. No matter what you said to her she has no right to talk to you that way," Jake insisted. He loosened the tie around his neck, barely aware that he was doing it. "Who is she anyway?"

Aaron smiled with something like sincere and unexpected humour. The wrinkles around his eyes deepened and genuine mirth flashed across his face.

"That," he told Jake, "is Doctor Kuda Chilume. My daughter. And your new associate."

* * *

Although Kuda was upset, she knew that Aaron had really been thinking about her welfare. She felt ashamed as she thought about how she had spoken to him and she knew it had not been justified. She groaned out loud and covered her face with her hands momentarily, appalled. Aaron deserved more respect than that and to deny him that respect had been unnecessary, no matter what was going on personally between them. It galled her though, how he had called in an outsider; an American for crying out loud, to come take over the clinic.

"*'I think it's rude of you to speak in a language I don't understand. Especially when you know I don't speak it.'*," she mimicked disgustedly in his American twang. "Rude, my butt," she mumbled to herself and swiped at the leaves of a *mophane* tree which was growing to her left. For just a moment, she felt a twinge of remorse and distaste filled her as she remembered how she had behaved. She chewed on her lower lip and scowled at herself. Perhaps apologies were in order.

As soon as the thought entered her mind she squashed it flat. She would sooner be staked in the middle of the Kgalagadi

Desert and have boiling water poured on her for a whole week than apologise. She knew it was childish to think the way she was thinking but if Aaron wanted to treat her like a child then she would behave like one.

Looking at her watch, she realised that she had been out of the clinic for about an hour. Since she had to go back sooner or later, she figured she might as well go back now. Sighing, she headed towards the clinic. She was oblivious to the dusty path she walked on, or to the ankle-high maize and sorghum which fluttered gently in the afternoon breeze. The beauty of the river of greenery which was the softly waving leaves of the growing crops was lost on her today. In a couple of months the crop would be ready for harvest. For now, however, it looked more like a lawn than a crop that would grow to be taller than she was.

The day was hot, as October typically was, but she was used to the high temperatures. The rainy season was upon them but sometimes, like this year, the rain would come and then disappear for a spell. The sun pounded a throbbing beat of heat on the heads of the unsuspecting. Dressing accordingly was one way to keep cool, which was more than she could say for Mr Three-Piece-Suit. She hoped he wasn't in the clinic because she wasn't in the mood for another confrontation.

She was disappointed. She found him at the computer, the one item of convenience that they had in the clinic. She noted with ghoulish satisfaction that he had taken off his tie and jacket and the sleeves of his shirt were rolled up, exposing muscled forearms. Her gaze started to travel unwittingly up those arms to assess the rest of him but her eyes flew from his arms to his face when he spoke.

“So the chicken has come home to roost,” Jake said sarcastically and Kuda bristled like a cornered cat.

“I’m not the chicken here,” she retaliated, “but you will be. You think you’re so great but you’re not. This is Africa, Doctor Dawn, not America, and I give you less than six months before you go back to wherever you came from with your tail between your legs.”

“What is it with you, Doctor Chilume?” Jake snapped. “I’ve only been here a couple of hours and you’re treating me like I have some highly contagious and lethal disease. You knew who I was when I arrived, didn’t you?”

“What does that have to do with anything?” Kuda asked, eyes narrowed. Her hands were on her hips, a glare on her face.

“You wanted to make me feel unwelcome and you’re doing a darned good job of it too. What is it that you have against me?”

“You really want to know?” Kuda asked softly. “I resent the fact that you’re not a Motswana. I resent the fact that you’re male. I resent that Aaron chose you to run this clinic and, most of all, I resent that you came.”

“Ah,” Jake said simply, and went back to the computer. He said nothing more and Kuda was surprised. She had expected an angry retort from him and to say she was disappointed was an understatement. She had really been looking forward to a fight but he denied her. She exhaled sharply and headed for the door. It was late anyway and not many more patients would come in. If anything urgent came up the whole village knew where both she and Aaron lived. They would go to either of them.

"A year, minimum," Jake said clearly without looking up as Kuda was about to walk out the door. She knew exactly what he meant but she didn't believe he would stay in the village for that long.

"Not a chance," she shot back.

Jake finally looked up and grinned, exposing perfectly even and white teeth. He's probably had them capped, Kuda thought nastily.

"You're on," he said, and proceeded to do whatever it was he had been doing to the computer.

Kuda watched him for a few seconds, wondering if she should start celebrating now or wait for the six months first. She opened the door, a small smile hovering on her lips. She would be gracious in her victory when the time came. For now, she couldn't resist a last retort as she headed out the door.

"You're in my world now. Bet you can't handle it. Remember, doctor, twilight will still be there after the dawn."

Chapter Two

Forging Relationships

Friday morning dawned the same way Thursday morning had. The rays of the sun warmed her face as they alerted her to the fact that it was time to wake up. As soon as she opened her eyes, Kuda wondered why she wasn't looking forward to the day. Realisation came soon enough and she scowled, kicked back the bed covers and got slowly out of bed. She stretched lazily, like a tired cat, and then wrapped a towel around herself and went to the bathroom. She never wore a nightgown or pyjamas to bed and October was too hot for either of them anyway.

She stayed in a modest little house about a kilometre away from the clinic. Despite its size, she loved the small building. It was minuscule when compared to other more extravagant places in Francistown for example, but in Jackalas II it was "comfortable." It had five rooms; two bedrooms, a living-room/dining-room, a kitchen and a combined bathroom and toilet. All the rooms were large and spacious and Kuda had managed to turn the house into a cheerful home.

She loved the colours orange and yellow, and although the walls were painted white, she had splashes of colour scattered around the room. A picture of a bunch of hibiscus on a wall, a yellow vase on her brown coffee table, orange curtains at the windows, green scatter rugs around her black leather sofas.

The house had running water although it had no electricity. That little luxury belonged to the clinic and Dr Campbell's home. She used a gas stove and fridge, and paraffin lanterns and was satisfied. She wasn't bothered by the lack of modern utilities. Rather than making her feel as though she was missing out on anything, it made her feel like she truly was home. Always home.

She grinned suddenly, wickedly, as she pictured Doctor Dawn groping around in the dark because he didn't know how to light a lantern. It was a cheering thought and her mood shifted immediately. She sang gaily as she turned on the bathroom taps and started to get ready for the day.

* * *

Nearly an hour later Kuda stopped abruptly when she opened the clinic door. She stared in surprise at the man who was looking through their filing cabinet with a frown on his face. She took a moment to really look at him this time. He was tall and well-built without being bulky, with broad shoulders, narrow hips and long legs. She couldn't see his face properly at the moment but she knew now that his eyes were, well, nice to be honest. His face was manly without being too chiselled and his lips were wide and firm. He was clean shaven and his hair was cut very short. As she watched him, he rubbed the back of his neck, as though to remove a kink there which had crept into his muscles overnight. She closed her eyes for a moment, took a deep breath, slowly let it out and opened her eyes.

"I don't believe this," she mumbled as she walked into the room, grabbing her coat off the stand and pushing her arms into the sleeves violently. "You've been here one day and already you're in the office. Don't you have anything else to do until Monday at least?"

Jake looked up when he heard her enter. He eyed her from the crown of her dark haired head to the tip of her sandal clad toes before he turned his attention back to the filing cabinet. Despite the churlish attitude, he had to appreciate her physically. She was a tall lady, perhaps a meter seventy-five. Her hair was cut short, almost cropped close to her scalp. Her forehead was wide, her eyebrows delicately shaped without the benefit of additional grooming. The pert nose above a mouth that looked like it loved to frown and lips that were twisted in irritation sat delicately above a firm chin. Her brown eyes were wide and large, despite how they were now narrowed in exasperation.

Her blue-jeans were not tight, but were fitting enough to give an idea of long and limber limbs. She looked physically able to run a marathon with ease. The open shoes and loose white shirt she wore completed her attire and added contrast to her smooth, coffee coloured skin.

"Nope," he said cheerfully. "My stuff is arriving later and I'll be unpacking the whole weekend. Until then, I'll be right here."

Kuda scowled. She walked past him, making sure that she didn't brush up against him, and leaned over to turn the computer on.

As she walked past him, he noted how her lowered eyelids were framed by long, thick lashes which hid her eye colour from his gaze. He hasn't really had an opportunity to see them during her tirade during their previous encounter, but now, he was suddenly extremely curious to know what shade of brown they were.

With her back still to him she said, "Go paint your house or something, but please stay out of the clinic until after the weekend."

"Why? Do I make you uneasy?" Although she couldn't see him, Kuda felt Jake's grin in the intonation of his voice.

"No, you irritate me," Kuda told him sweetly, turning to see what effect these words would have on him.

"I guess that makes us even," Jake said, "And no, they are not capped."

Kuda had the grace to look sheepish but was saved from further embarrassment when an old woman walked into the clinic.

"*Ta pinda*!" she called out in Kalanga, the local dialect of the region.

"*Pindani*," Kuda said to her as she completely ignored Jake and walked over to her. A young boy of about ten was behind her. The woman stopped and looked curiously at Jake who stood looking back at her. She was an older woman, perhaps in her late sixties. She wore a brown, German print skirt, leather sandals and a light blue t-shirt. Her weathered face was smiling and her eyes twinkled beneath the loosely bound scarf she wore on her head.

"Who is that?" she asked bluntly as she pointed a finger from the hand that wasn't holding the walking stick she held. Kuda laughed.

"His name is Jake Dawn. He's the new doctor here." Kuda spoke in the local dialect that the woman had used.

"Where is he from?" the older woman asked again.

"America," Kuda answered and stole a peek at Jake. There were no Kalanga words for English names, America included, and she knew that Jake knew they were talking about him.

"He's skinny. Did they starve him before they shipped him here?" the woman said good-naturedly. She cocked her head as though expecting Jake to respond to her query.

Kuda bit her lip to stop herself from smiling. "He's not skinny, he's buff."

"Well at least you noticed. Now I know for sure that there's nothing wrong with your eyes. Don't just stand there," she clucked. "Introduce us."

This time Kuda's smile escaped.

"Doctor Jake Dawn, this is Manini Chipo," she said in English. Jake smiled, walked over and held out his hand for Manini Chipo to shake.

"Hello, Manini Chipo," he greeted, but only the "hello" came out without difficulty. The rest came out sounding like

"Ma-nay-nay Chee-po" which was nothing but a confusion of jumbled noise. The owner of the name burst into laughter.

"He talks like a goat which has put its nose into a pot full of pepper and can't stop sneezing," she chuckled.

Kuda giggled and the boy behind Manini Chipo grinned.

"What did she say?" Jake asked quickly.

"I said," Manini explained, speaking fluent English, "that you need to practice your Kalanga before you speak it in public. Maybe Kuda here will be able to help you with that."

"I don't have time," Kuda cut in quickly. Physically moving away from the old woman and Jake, as though the distance would dispel the suggestion, Kuda took a step back.

"Oh, you should have time to help a fellow doctor," Manini said calmly. "Especially one as handsome as this one. Who knows, you might get married and it's about time you had children. Imagine, unwed and childless at your age."

"Manini!" Kuda scolded and was too appalled to look at Jake. She agitatedly twisted a corner of the shirt with her left hand. However, from the strangled noise Jake made, he must have been as appalled as she was.

"What? Am I wrong? Don't you want a man and children in your life? Do you want to be alone forever?" The twinkle in the old woman's eyes was unmistakable. She was virtually shaking with glee.

"Manini," Kuda warned, and the old woman shrugged. Turning her face towards Jake she eyed him thoughtfully.

"*Nyalala ka*!" Kuda scolded again briskly, telling Manini to keep quiet. "I'd better take a look at you before you decide I'm losing my touch. Shall we go to my office?"

"Of course. Lead the way and I'll follow. As usual," Manini sighed with a wink.

"I heard that," Kuda told her.

"You were meant to," Manini shot back as the two walked into Kuda's office, still talking good naturedly.

As the door closed behind them, Jake turned to Una, the young boy who had come in with Manini. He wore khaki shorts and a white shirt, perhaps a uniform from the local school.

"What standard are you in?" Jake asked.

"Six," the boy said shortly.

"Do you play any sport?" Jake asked. A silent nod was his only response. "What sport do you play?"

"Football,' Una said without hesitation and Jake smiled.

"Ah, football. Who's your favourite football player?"

"Doctor Khumalo," Una answered enthusiastically, turning to face Jake for the first time since Kuda and his grandmother had left the room. "He's very good. Better than a lot of other players, even Americans."

"Really? What about Zinedine Zidane?"

"He's alright, but Doctor Khumalo is much better than he is," Una asserted and the two football fans launched into a discussion of which player was better and why.

Twenty minutes later when Manini and Kuda came out of Kuda's office, the man and the boy were still engrossed in their topic.

"Inside every man is a little boy just dying to come out," Kuda said sarcastically to Manini who looked at her and said,

"There's nothing wrong with that. It is a lesson you should learn and put into practice every once in a while."

"I don't have time," Kuda said shortly, folding her arms in front of her chest.

"That statement is going to be the death of you, child," Manini told her and shuffled over to where Jake and Una were talking. "It has been a pleasure meeting you, Doctor Jake Dawn. I hope you enjoy yourself in our village and never let the attitude of some of us get you down." She threw a meaningful look in Kuda's direction. Kuda scowled. "Come, Una, let's go home."

As the two moved out of the clinic, Kuda went up to the computer to enter Manini's condition.

"Whose idea was it to use a computer?" Jake asked as he peered over her shoulder.

"Aaron's. We both have our own patients but sometimes one of us isn't here and the other looks at the patient. We still fill out the patient's medical card but cards restrict what you want to write; how you feel the patient looks or if you're worried about them. Sometimes when Aaron isn't here, I make a note about something I wanted to ask him and when he gets back, or if we miss each other, he responds. In that case all I have to do is go to the computer."

"How does it work?" Jake asked and Kuda spent the next fifteen minutes giving him the key codes and explaining how the files were arranged. Kuda noted with a lack of surprise that Jake was computer literate and didn't really need a lot of explanation. She was impressed but didn't show it and when she was through, Jake clearly understood what she had shown him. He asked a few questions which Kuda clarified and which he understood immediately.

"So," he said afterwards, "What's wrong with Manini?"

Kuda paused a moment and then sighed.

"She's got cervical cancer," she told him. Jake frowned.

"How bad is it?" he asked.

"Bad. Stage four."

"Why isn't she in the hospital?" Jake asked, trying to make his voice neutral. Kuda heard the accusation in it anyway and a slow anger started to simmer in the pit of her stomach. She switched off the computer and turned to face Jake. She took a deep breath, trying to dampen the simmer and when she spoke her voice betrayed none of the heat in her belly.

"She's over eighty-five years old, even though she looks much younger than that. I know that's not a reason but she feels she's lived her life and lived it well. She's as fine as she'll ever be and you'll soon find that Bakalaka have an attitude of 'it's not broken, don't mess with it.' I don't know how much longer she'll be alive but it's not long and there's nothing I can do to change that."

“You could have started off by taking her to a fully equipped hospital with sufficient facilities to help her,” Jake said and his voice was now fully accusatory. He stood up and glared at Kuda, his brow drawn so tightly it looked like it would bleed.

The simmer in Kuda’s belly burst into flame and she too stood up. She felt the blood rush to her legs and arms and knew that if she didn’t walk out of there soon, she would slug Jake on the lip.

“How? By hitting her over the head with a club and dragging her to the hospital in Francistown? And then hitting her again and pulling her by her hair to South Africa? Believe me, Doctor Dawn, that’s the only way you’ll get her to go,” Kuda snapped back. “And before you get self-righteous with me know that I care for my patients and try to do my best for all of them.”

The two doctors glared at each other and neither was willing to back down. Although Kuda’s head stood nearly thirty centimetres below Jake’s, she was not intimidated. The dark-brown eyes of Doctor Kuda Chilume collided with the lighter brown eyes of the African-American doctor. Finally the lighter shade of brown relented.

“I’m sorry,” Jake apologised. “I had no right.”

“You’re damned right you didn’t,” Kuda shot back. The flame was not about to be extinguished with a single admission of fault.

“Give me a break here. I’m trying to apologise.”

"You know that little prayer? 'Oh Lord, help me to keep my big mouth shut until I know what I'm saying.' Well practise it a bit more and you'll never need to apologise."

"What is it with you?" Jake said through gritted teeth. He was holding onto his own temper with difficulty and the effort made the vein at the base of his neck pulsate furiously. "You never let up, do you?"

Kuda said nothing. She stared at Jake's collarbone, hypnotised by the throbbing of his vein. For some reason, she wanted to reach out and touch it. Shaking her head fiercely she roused herself from her semi-trance like state and stared at Jake. She saw his lips moving but she didn't hear anything he said. He abruptly stopped talking when he realised she wasn't paying attention. She looked dazed, like she had had too much sun or something. Jake frowned.

"Are you alright?" he asked. This time Kuda heard him. His vein wasn't pulsing as furiously as before and she could concentrate now.

"Fine," she lied. "I felt a little dizzy just then. Excuse me. I need a drink of water," she mumbled then almost ran out of the room.

Jake looked after her with a puzzled expression on his face, wondering what had gotten into her. One minute she was a regular fireball and the next she was a dazed bag of jelly. If women around here were as confusing as she was, it was going to be a long year.

Chapter Three
Closing Doors

Kuda was in her consulting room when the door opened and Aaron came in. She could see at once that he had something to say to her. The lines on his face were deeper than usual and the mouth that was usually so quick to smile was drawn down in a frown. His thatch of greying hair, which had once been so thick and corn-coloured, had receded slowly over the years, leaving behind a baldness that made him look as homely as a farmer on his ranch rather than the distinguished doctor he was. He pushed his glasses back onto the highest part on the bridge of his nose and then scratched his left ear, almost as though he wasn't aware he was doing it.

She waited.

"Kuda," he began. "I know that you and I haven't ever been friends but I always hoped that we could be."

She waited.

She wanted to let him know how what he had said wasn't true. Once, a long time ago, they had been close. As close as any father and daughter could ever have been but that had changed. So many things had changed. Too many for them to ever go back to the close relationship they had once shared. She wanted to say all these things to Aaron, but she kept quiet. It was too late now.

Aaron continued to speak. His voice was low and quiet. He spoke as though he was trying to force the words out of a throat which refused to cooperate with him.

"I know you don't like me and I know why. I also understand why but it's hard for me not to treat you like my daughter." Kuda looked away and as always Aaron knew nothing else he would say to her on this topic would get through to her. He sighed. "Anyway, I just wanted to tell you that I'll come to work for another week before I hand the reins over to Jake. I'll stay in Jackalas for another three weeks, sorting out my things before I go back home."

"Home where?" Kuda asked as she turned to look back at him.

"I want to go back to America."

"Why now after all these years?"

Aaron smiled crookedly. It was a small, sad smile.

"I'm old, Kuda, and call me sentimental, but I want to be buried at home."

"At home, huh?" Kuda said softly, and Aaron knew he had said something she had taken the wrong way. Again. "And Botswana has never been your home," she continued just as softly. "I guess I always knew that but to hear you confirm it doesn't improve the way I look at you, Aaron."

"Kuda, you know that's not what I meant." It was a silent plea for her understanding. Kuda dropped her head and rubbed her eyes. She couldn't be angry at him anymore. She just couldn't. Aaron seemed to sense some of what she was feeling, perhaps because he was feeling some of it too. He wanted to reach out and console her but he knew her well enough to know that his gesture would add fuel rather than water to the fire. Instead he clasped his hands behind his back, as though they might reach out to her on their own volition.

"Anyway, I'll be under your feet for another month and you'll get more tired of me than you already are," he told her.

It was meant to be a joke but it came out all wrong and Kuda felt a tug of remorse in her heart.

"Aaron –" she began but the knock at the door cut into what she was about to say. Angelica put her head around the door without waiting for a response and Kuda wanted to throw something at her. Something heavy and hard that would cause permanent damage.

"Kuda, there are some patients here to see you," she informed her before closing the door again.

The man with the droopy eyes and pale skin looked at the young woman who sat before him and she looked back at him. For a moment the animosity that had existed between them for so long, breeding and expanding until it had become almost tangible, seemed to dissolve and disappear. For just a moment, they were once again father and daughter. For a moment, they were family again.

"You'd better see to your patients before they get tired and leave," Aaron mumbled as he moved to the door. Kuda nodded slowly and watched him as he left the office.

It was a sad situation, she thought unhappily. A very sad situation indeed.

* * *

Four thirty came quickly enough and Kuda tidied up everything and covered the computer and printer with the plastic cover. Everybody else had already left, leaving her the sole occupant of the small clinic. They had gone to help Jake with his furniture. Imagine lugging furniture all the way from South Africa to Botswana. It must have cost a fortune and the money he had used would have been enough to buy new furniture in Francistown anyway. What had he thought? That Batswana still used animal skins and that the women sat on the ground at their "master's" feet? Botswana may not be New York City or wherever the heck he came from but it had its share of comforts and it was one of the better places to live in the whole world.

Sighing, she made sure all the windows and curtains were closed, noting that the rooms got immediately darker. She noted a thick layer of flies on the windowsill as she did so. Funny. She hadn't noticed them before. She turned the lights on and went back to the window sill.

For a moment she stared at the layered insects, knowing that they represented something that she should have been aware of but which her brain was failing to grasp. A frown formed on her brow but she smoothed it away with a shrug after a long minute. They were just flies after all. Not cockroaches or some other skin tightening insects. Still, the pile was really thick. She walked from window to window, and on each pane a layer of flies, about a centimetre high, lay by the window. She didn't remember there being so many flies in the clinic that day. If she had seen so many flying around she would have noticed and remembered.

Strange. She would have to ask Tapiwa to do something about it.

She stood gazing at the flies for a little longer, her face creased in thought and a persistent niggling in the back of her mind.

Something was not quite right. This did not make any sense. Walking slowly, she went and stood by one of the windows. She lowered her face until her eyes were level with the window sill. How was it possible that all of these flies were dead; that a layer of flies this thick would have escaped everyone's attention over the course of the day? Although she could not clearly reconcile it in her mind, there was an element of wrongness that would not go away.

Turning her head a little to her left side, she took a closer look at the dead insects, their fat little abdomens and their compound eyes creeping her out in a way she hadn't anticipated. With a little shudder, she stood up and quickly left the clinic, turning the lights off and closing the door behind her.

The weirdest part was that there wasn't a single fly amongst all those flies that was alive. Not one. That was not logical. Shaking her head, she tried hard not to think about them as she pulled the door closed.

Only two other people had the key to the clinic; Aaron, who would undoubtedly give his to Jake, and Tapiwa, the cleaning lady who swept and mopped the floors twice a day and came in on Saturdays to polish them. Two of her daughters, who worked at the local primary school, came in to help on Saturdays and they were paid for it. They always did a good job and Tapiwa had reason to be proud of them.

Kuda turned to lock the door and as she did so she caught a glimpse of a shadow from the corner of her eye. She whirled around and there was nothing there. She was as alone as she should have been but suddenly fear beat its way steadily down her back. Despite the heat the sweat dried on her brow and pinpoints of goose bumps pricked their way across her arms and legs. She looked frantically around, searching for something, anything, to explain her sudden irrational fear. There was nothing there. There couldn't be.

God, the flies. The *dead* flies. Something must have happened. Something really bad. There were never that many flies in the clinic at one time. Something was here. Something had caused their death. Something had followed her to work.

Another shadow, or maybe it was the same one, caught her eye again and this time, without waiting to examine it, Kuda bolted. She flew from the clinic and had to force herself to stop when she remembered that she had not locked up. For a long time she stared at the door, steeling herself to go back and lock it, wondering if she would have the guts to do it. She must have stood there for a good eight minutes, perhaps an eternity, waiting for another glimpse of the dark shape that had terrified her into bolting from the clinic like an unsettled calf. Nothing else happened.

Finally she moved slowly towards the door, the keys in her hand, arms outstretched. She slowly moved forward like a rusty robot with unbending knees. Then, as though afraid that if she stalled for too long her courage would desert her, she ran forward, locked the door, tugged at it to make sure the bolt had slid home, then moved quickly away. She stood a few meters away from the door, trying to understand what had happened to her. When revelation did not knock on her door of her mind she backed away and headed for home. Although the goose bumps had retreated from the surface of her skin she still felt cold. She rubbed her arms to try and dispel the icy feeling but it did not seem to work.

Backing away from the door, she took a few steps, her eyes still locked on the building. The keys were clenched tightly in her hands like a much needed weapon that she wasn't aware she wanted. She continued to back away until she felt safe enough to turn and walk away. With a little shake of her head, as though she was waking up from a night terror, she turned and walked away.

Having moved away from the unsettling, unseen presence that had scared – no, terrified her – in the clinic, she started to feel a little better. Maybe it was the pleasant heat of the early evening sun that chased her fears away, or maybe it was being physically away from the source. Whatever it was, Kuda welcomed it. The further away she moved from the clinic, the more the feelings of unease she had felt disappeared, like ice left on the sand in the middle of the desert. Before she had walked half-way home, the memory of it had all but disappeared.

It was almost as if the incident had not happened at all.

The occurrence in the clinic had made her completely forget about Jake Dawn but thoughts of him entered her mind again as she kept walking. On her way home, Kuda had to go past Jake's home and she decided there and then that from now on she would find an alternate route, even if she took longer to get home. The exercise would do her good anyway. Aaron lived about half a kilometre from the clinic and Jake's house was half a kilometre from Aaron's, with the three places forming an almost equilateral triangle. Kuda lived about another half kilometre from Jake's, those three places forming a straight line. Choosing another way to get to and from work really would be a hassle, but if it meant not having to see Jake after hours, it would be worth it.

As though thinking about him had conjured him, Jake appeared on his front door and spotted her. He grinned. Barefoot, he was dressed in shorts and a t-shirt.

"Hello, Kuda," he shouted to her. "Why don't you come in and give me a hand." It wasn't an order, just a neighbourly thing to say really, but Kuda didn't like it. He looked too comfortable, like he had been there for ever. Like he was now a part of her village. As it was, he had been there for too long already. He didn't belong there.

"Why should I?" she asked coolly.

"Many hands make light work," he answered, undaunted.

"And too many cooks spoil the broth," she retaliated.

Jake's face tightened.

"I'm sorry I asked. Please forgive me for assuming that you'd come off your pedestal long enough to come to the aid of us mere mortals," Jake shot back before striding back into the house. He slammed the door behind him.

Kuda was so shocked by his unexpected sarcasm that she stood there glaring after him for a few moments after he had disappeared, unable to move.

"Of all the cheek," she muttered to herself before stalking off towards her own home in quite a bit of a temper. Suddenly, without warning, she laughed because she knew she had absolutely deserved what Jake had said to her. Her laughter sounded rusty because she hadn't laughed like that in quite some time but it felt good all the same. In fact, it felt so good she tried it again and this time it came out sounding much better, much more natural.

"It's good to see you in such a good mood," a male voice said behind her and she jumped, her short-lived humour shattered. She spun around and glared at the man who had startled her.

"What do you want, Timile?" she asked harshly. Timile smirked.

"Why, you of course. Haven't I made that obvious enough? If I haven't, I should try harder."

"Go take a nap on the railway line," Kuda suggested sweetly.

The smile on Timile's face disappeared and was replaced by a scowl. There was something off-kilter in Timile's eyes that Kuda had seen before but couldn't identify. It made her uneasy and it was there now. Involuntarily, she took a step back. He saw that he had unsettled her and the smirk came back.

"You should be very careful what you say to me, little girl. I don't like to be insulted," he warned.

"You seem to do that alright by yourself," Kuda said coldly and Timile grabbed her arms. Hard.

"I told you not to insult me," he snarled, and the fear came rushing back into Kuda's heart. She hid it well, grinding her teeth together to square her jaw.

"Get your hands off me," she snarled right back, "or you'll be sorry."

"Oh, yeah? What will you do? Force me to?" He laughed but he did let her go, pushing her backwards so that she nearly fell.

Kuda glared at him. As usual his clothes looked as though they had come fresh from the dry cleaners. His shoes were well polished, as though dust and dirt had been warned not to land on them. The crease in his pants was razor sharp and looked as though it could slice a hair in half; long ways, not across. His hair was cut short and brushed; his nails clipped and remarkably clean. His shirt was whiter than a brand new cloth diaper. Yet, despite his immaculate condition, Kuda wanted him nowhere near her.

"If you ever touch me again I'll go down to the District Commissioner's office in Francistown and have you arrested for assault. Do you understand me?" she said between her teeth.

Timile attempted a smile but it came out looking like a leer.

"You don't scare me with your big talk, Kuda, so save it for someone who will appreciate it because I don't," he said to her.

"I'm warning you, stay away from me."

She spun around and continued her walk home. Timile stood watching her for a long time before he turned and stalked away. Neither he nor Kuda were aware that they had been observed.

Jake had seen the whole episode from his doorstep.

Chapter Four
Cows and Companions

When Kuda got home she was still feeling very uneasy. She was not surprised when she saw that her hands were shaking. Timile did that to her and to be quite honest he terrified her. There was just something not quite right about him and it gave the impression that if he was pushed, no matter how slight the push, he would lose whatever little balance he had left and go berserk. It was really scary on occasion and Kuda prayed fervently that when he finally became unbalanced she would be nowhere near him.

Changing out of her pants and shirt she donned a once black oversized t-shirt, which had been in the wash too many times too often, and a pair of Khaki shorts. Pulling on a large floppy straw hat she looked at herself in the bedroom mirror. It wasn't exactly the latest in fashion but it was comfortable and she was happy with it. On her way out she grabbed an apple from the kitchen. She closed the front door behind her, locked it and called to her dog. He had not been home when she had arrived but she was sure he was back now. She was right. King came lumbering up to her and she had to bend only slightly to cuddle him. King was a huge dog and Kuda loved him dearly. He tried to lick her face and Kuda giggled, moving back quickly.

"Come on, boy," she said as she straightened. "Time for our walk."

The dog barked once, as though in agreement, and the two started off to Manini Chipo's, where they went almost every day at this time of the day. Kuda walked slowly, keeping a lazy eye on King.

Manini Chipo lived about twenty minutes' walk away from Kuda, walking really slowly as she was doing now. She could make it there in seven minutes if she needed to but today she was just enjoying her walk. She knew almost everybody in the village and she stopped quite often to greet people or just waved to them and continued on her way. She loved this time of the day, watching the children play and the older boys bringing in the cows.

It was a lot cooler now than it had been an hour ago. The sun was making a slow retreat behind the rose-coloured sky and the colours made her feel secure. There was such beauty in the defined lines of the horizon that it was at times like this she so badly wanted to believe in the existence of a higher being; a being that could explain the pain that had been such a constant part of her life. However hard she tried, she could never quite make that leap to belief in a higher power, no matter how many signs may have been pointing her in the right direction. She shrugged, pushing the thought aside. There was no use in thinking about something which you had no proof existed.

Around the time that she would get to Manini's, Washington would be bringing in the cattle. She would talk with Manini for a while before they went down to the *kraal* to help with the cow milking. This was their usual routine.

"*Ta pinda,*" she called out when she got to Manini's yard. King barked once and galloped off to one of the three huts in the yard. A sudden scream seared the air and Kuda's heart seemed to leap from her chest to her throat. She ran towards the hut that King had disappeared into and was in time to hear Manini chuckle in a self-defacing manner. Kuda's heart settled and she breathed again.

"What on earth is the matter?" she asked when she came to a stop beside the door. "I thought you were being murdered or something."

"This big, gangling mutt of yours startled me, is all," Manini muttered. Kuda noticed that Manini was pushing something under her skirt and was about to tease her about it when she noticed the shuttered expression on her face. Instead she asked where Una was.

"He has already left for the *kraal.* He said he'd wait for Washington there," Manini murmured.

"Shall we go?" Kuda asked.

"In a moment," Manini hedged. She wasn't looking at Kuda. "Can you wait outside for a minute? There's something I'd like to do first before we go."

Kuda nodded, not bothering to hide her curiosity. Besides, Manini knew her too well. She took King by the collar and waited for Manini by the wooden gate. The old woman came out of the hut about two minutes later and, grabbing a pail, she followed Kuda. They set off down the well-used path to the kraal. Both women were preoccupied. Kuda was thinking about the menace she had seen in Timile's eyes and heaven alone knew what was going through Manini's mind.

The cattle *kraal* was about a hundred meters away from Manini's yard and they heard the lowing of the cattle long before they saw them. Washington's whistles and shouts merged with the cattle sounds and King, deciding that the two women were taking too long, ran on ahead. Kuda heard Una calling to King and she saw the dog run towards him. They made such an odd pair, those two, with the huge animal almost as high as Una was tall. Una was a small ten year old and King could have knocked him down with his tail if he had wanted to. Kuda, however, was not worried that that would happen. King was as gentle as a butterfly and had never bared his teeth to a soul, except Kake and Timile, and that wasn't surprising.

Kake was the local witch doctor and his evil surrounded him like the mangy hyena-skin coat he liked to wear around his emaciated shoulders. He smelled like it too. He was a tricky one and his and Kuda's paths had crossed once too many times. She kept out of his way as much as possible and avoided him at all costs except for the times he deliberately sought her out. Kake could be as deadly as the cobra he had called himself after.

She had thought often about the hyena-skin he wore, having heard the stories about men being able to turn themselves into the animals whose skin they wore. The thought both fascinated her and terrified her. The possibilities of it being probable defied all logic and raced hard into the supernatural.

"Kuda!" Are you going to help me with the milking today or do I have to do it all by myself?" Washington yelled at her, drawing her sharply from her thoughts. She looked at the tall, thin man with no hair on his head, his toothy grin aimed at her.

"I'm a volunteer, Washington, so if you don't ask politely I'm taking my services elsewhere," Kuda yelled back.

"Get your butt over here, woman!"

"Politely."

"If you're not in this *kraal* in thirty seconds I'm coming to get you! What is it with women nowadays? When I was in Washington D.C...."

Kuda and Manini looked at each other and rolled their eyes heavenward. When Washington started talking about being in the United States' capital nothing could put a lid on him. Kuda, with Manini's empty pail sitting squarely on the top of her head, sauntered over to Washington and gave him a big cheeky grin.

"If I was given five thebe for every story that you tell me about Washington DC I'd be a multimillionaire by now," she said. Washington aimed a swipe at her behind but Kuda easily avoided it. "Your reflexes are getting worse by the day, old man. What you need is a good dose of Mmantshadi. She'll have your reflexes back good and proper in no time."

Washington chuckled, his old sun-wrinkled face crinkling until he looked like a grape that had been left in the desert for decades. His white teeth gleamed in the sun and his eyes almost disappeared as his mirth continued.

"If you sic Mmantshadi on me I'll close the two of you alone in the *kraal* for a whole day and you'll be sorry," he laughed. Kuda grinned with him.

She loved this man. He had been there for here in the hardest days of her life. Him, Manini and Aaron. But, she didn't want to think about Aaron now so she focussed on Washington.

"Where is she now?" she asked, looking around.

"Behind the *kraal*," Washington told her. "She'll come in when she's good and ready."

Washington, Kuda and Una entered the *kraal* and went about their daily task of milking the four cows that were part of Manini's herd. All in all she had twelve head; two bulls, five cows and five calves. It wasn't a lot but it was enough and Manini was satisfied with what she had. The *kraal* was built of tree trunks dug into the ground in a circle. They were about a metre sixty high and the cows slept within it, reducing access to them by possible predators. The down side of this was they pooped in there as well and it was always interesting playing "skip the cow patty", especially during the rainy season.

Una helped Kuda while Washington milked alone. Una had once watched a documentary about cattle, the light brown and white dairy cows, and how they were milked without having their back legs tied together to stop them from moving or kicking the bucket, literally. He had told Kuda about it and then had added,

"Maybe I should take Mmantshadi to them and see if they can milk her, tied legs or not."

Kuda had laughed until tears had gushed from her eyes and a stitch had formed in her side. When she thought of anybody trying to milk Mmantshadi, fresh tears had poured from her eyes and she had laughed more than Una had ever seen her laugh before. Finally she had wiped her tears away and had taken a deep breath.

"Yeah," she had said and nothing more. Una had grinned.

"Yeah," he had said back and the two had grinned at each other.

Mmantshadi was the most stubborn, recalcitrant, temperamental cow that had ever been born and it was just sheer bad luck how she had been born into Manini's *kraal*. Nobody touched Mmantshadi. Not to milk her, not to treat her for ticks – which probably stayed away from her anyway – not to do anything to her. She was the meanest, most hot-tempered female to have ever been born in Jackalas II and nobody was in a hurry to take the title from her. The first Mmantshadi had been Washington's wife. Now there was a woman who could have given the bovine a run for her money. Washington's wife had been as ornery as they came and her disposition had not been improved by the thirty-eight years she had been married to Washington.

Washington loved to tell the story about how, one time, a couple of herdsmen had been negligent and their cattle had eaten quite a bit of the wheat in Mmantshadi's field. Instead of apologising to her they mocked her anger because she was a woman, and not a very large one at that. Furious, Mmantshadi had hiked the bottom of her skirt into the waistband and folded her hands into fists. She had grabbed the man closest to her and rained fists on him as though he had suddenly found himself in the middle of a meteor shower. The man had been caught off-guard and as the fists pounded him the second man had tried to pull Mmantshadi off him. This had seemed to infuriate her even more and before he knew it, the second man had joined the first. Finally, unable to tolerate the fury of the woman they had disparaged, the two men had taken off and run as though a band of hyenas was on their heels.

She had died, fifteen years ago, childless, from a traffic accident and despite his tough guy veneer, Washington had mourned his wife. He liked to joke about how he missed having someone chase him from his hut with a flaming piece of firewood and this was probably more than just a joke. When the cow had been born five years ago, on Kuda's birthday, and had proved to be trouble from day one, Washington had declared that it reminded him of his wife; with all due respect to the dead.

Now, as Manini stood watching the three people as they milked the four docile cows, she frowned. She knew she didn't have long to live but there was still so much to do. Yet she was so tired. Not only was there Una to look out for, but there was Washington and Kuda as well. And now, Jake too. So much work, so little time. Her beads had started to talk again and there was something brewing.

She could feel it in the air and on the ground. Whatever it was, it was coming fast and it would soon be here. A feeling of dread had been germinating within Manini and over the last couple of weeks it had grown fast. And now, Manini was as restless as Mmantshadi got when the clouds on the horizon were pregnant with the promise of a mean thunderstorm.

Yet there was so little time...

Chapter Five
King

After the milking had been done and Mmantshadi had decided that she was going to spend the night in the *kraal* after all, the four set back to Manini's home. They chattered easily together, with the assurance of being old friends, with no discomfort between them. While Washington and Una did most of the talking, Kuda was subdued. Manini noticed it but said nothing until they got back to her compound. Shortly after their arrival, Washington said his goodnights and set off for home with half a pail of milk. Una started a fire. When it was burning sufficiently he put a pot of water on it after which he went to have his evening bath. It didn't take long for the water to boil and when it did, Kuda set about preparing the evening meal of porridge. She loved helping Manini and this was one thing she did for her as often as she could.

King stood not too far from where the two ladies sat, looking out into the darkness. There was a stillness about him that Kuda noted but quickly dismissed. He was intense like that a lot of the time, like he could hear something that only he could catch and he was deciding whether to go investigate or not. His ears were up as straight as they could get and he stood as still as a statue.

As Kuda was stirring the porridge with half an eye on King, Manini spoke.

"What happened to you to make you so subdued today, Kuda?"

Kuda continued to stir.

"Nothing much," she said quietly.

"Let me rephrase that. What did Timile say to you to upset you this time?"

Kuda's lips twisted wryly and she looked away from King and at Manini.

"Sometimes I think you're a mind-reader or some kind of mental magician and I wonder why I bother to hide anything from you." She sighed. "Anyway, it's not what he said, it's how he said it. It scared me and I hate feeling afraid of anything. Especially Timile. He's dangerous and I hate that he scares me," she said grimly. Today, something else had terrified her more than Timile ever had but she was not about to tell Manini. Funny though. She couldn't quite remember what it was. Just a feeling that she had been afraid. She frowned. Not understanding the feeling that didn't seem to have anything associated with it.

"I've told you to stay out of his way, Kuda. I know it's difficult –"

"You're right about that and it's not as if I go out of my way to deliberately bump into him," Kuda cut in, miffed.

"I know, I know," Manini soothed placating her. "What you really need is a masculine figure in your life."

"I have King, remember."

Manini rolled her eyes and Kuda caught if just as the fire flickered higher. She rolled her own eyes.

"That's not what I'm talking about and you know it," Manini said with a sigh.

"Who do you have in mind? Washington? All the 'masculine figures' I know in this village are either too young or too old. I'm not going to be a cradle-snatcher or marry someone old enough to be my grandfather's granduncle."

Having heard his name leave his mistress' name, King came bounding up to her. He sat next to where she was and then laid his huge head on her lap. Kuda absently stroked him with her one free hand and scratched behind his ear. King gave a content sigh and then gazed up at Kuda adoringly. Kuda smiled at him.

"There are eligible men here," Manini told her.

"Yeah, right. Like who? And don't tell me Chose and Thapelo."

"Well, what's wrong with them?" Manini asked calmly.

"I'll tell you what's wrong with them. If you put Thapelo's brain on the sharp end of a pin, you'd have enough room left over to hide an elephant. As for Chose, he and I grew up together. He's too good a friend for me to jeopardise that friendship just to get rid of Timile. I respect him too much for that. Besides, his heart's already spoken for."

"Jake?"

“He’s not even in the counting.”

“Why not?” Manini asked lightly. “He’s a man –”

“Really? I hadn’t noticed,” Kuda said smartly as she stopped stirring the porridge. She put a cover on the pot and looked at her mutt where he now lay at her feet. Manini continued as though she hadn’t spoken.

“– He’s handsome, he’s got more than his fair share of brains and he’s here. I repeat, why not?”

“Because,” Kuda ground out between her teeth. “I don’t want him.”

“Hmmm,” Manini murmured and Kuda glared at her. She loved Manini dearly but sometimes, like now, she wanted to throttle her. To just wrap her hands around her throat and squeeze slowly.

“What’s that supposed to mean?” Kuda asked.

“What’s what supposed to mean?” Manini asked in turn, a smug look on her face.

“I give up,” Kuda said in exasperation. “I can’t win with you.”

“That’s because I’ve had more experience. Don’t feel bad about it, dear. You’ll get even one of these days,” Manini consoled and Kuda could almost see her tongue lolling around in her cheek.

“You can count on it,” she replied, then grinned cheerfully.

“What are you grinning at?”

"Oh, nothing."

"Is this your way of getting back at me? By rousing my curiosity and then letting me hang there?"

"Curiosity killed the cat."

"To quote Una, 'satisfaction brought it back.' Now shoot."

Kuda chuckled and uncovered the pot in which the porridge was cooking. All was well and she covered it again.

"I was just thinking about a bet I made with the good Doctor Dawn. I told him that he wouldn't last six months here and he took me up on it. By the Easter Holidays next year I doubt he'll still be here. Why are you looking at me like that?"

"Something just occurred to me."

"What?"

"You don't want to know."

"Yes, I do."

"What were you saying about curiosity and cats just now?" Manini grinned wickedly and Kuda rolled her eyes.

"Are you going to tell me or not?" From the lusty chuckle that emitted from Manini, Kuda knew that her curiosity would not be sated tonight. "Fine, let it never be said that I was one to beg for a few words from anybody, even if it's you, Manini."

"Okay with me. But it has something to do with the lady protesting too much. Your porridge is boiling over."

Kuda jumped to stir the porridge again and also to reduce the amount of heat by pulling out some of the wood from beneath the pot. She left just enough to provide a nice, simmering heat.

When she eventually sat back down, Una had come to join them. From then on they talked about trivial things until Kuda left at about six thirty. It was time to feed King and he was giving her soulful looks with his big browns that Kuda could no longer ignore.

“Bring Jakc with you tomorrow when you come,” Manini said to her as she was leaving. Kuda gave her a sharp look.

“He’s not like King, Manini. If I whistle he won’t come running.”

“Smile and say please and he just might do that.”

Kuda shook her head in exasperation but said nothing more. Manini had not made a request. It was an order and Kuda knew that if Jake was not with her tomorrow when she came she would be in trouble. She waved goodbye to Manini and Una then set off down the road with King by her side.

* * *

When she got home she fed her beast and stood watching him for a while. He always ate with gusto but sometimes he wolfed his food down a little too fast and got hiccups. His bowl of water, as usual, sat by his plate and when the hiccups were bad enough, lapping up the water seemed to help.

King's head was covered mostly by white with grey and brown coloured fur over his forehead, ears and the top of his head. From his shoulders, over his back and down his hind legs, his fur was a mix of black and light brown while his legs were mostly a light brown colour. He stood about a meter twenty at his shoulders and his head stood higher. He was a huge animal by any standards and he looked more intimidating than he actually was. Kuda swore there was quite a bit of wolf in him although she didn't know how. After all, there weren't any wolves in Botswana.

King had actually appeared on her doorstep one miserable, rainy night three years earlier. She had been asleep, strangely enough, having a dream about a white lion touching an African Ridge-back, a large dog which was known for its fierce loyalty. As the two touched, a light shone between them and a cub-puppy hybrid lay on the ground between them when the light finally faded. She woke up at that point and it was then that her ears caught the sound of whimpering. She had opened the door and found him shivering on her doorstep. Her heart had melted on the spot and she had picked him up immediately. He had been a huge bundle of fur and big beautiful brown eyes. They had been inseparable ever since. She had tried to find out where he had come from but none of the villagers seemed to know. This had seemed to cement her belief that he was meant to end up on her doorstep that night.

"Hey, Chilume. Catch!"

As Kuda looked up a white object came flying at her. She put her hands up in time to catch the ball and to keep it from slamming into her face. She grinned when she saw Chose strolling over to her in his gym outfit of worn sneakers, worn track-suit bottoms and worn tee-shirt. She threw the volleyball at him. He caught it and threw it back.

"What do you mean by sneaking up on a helpless little lady like me? Don't you know that I could have had a heart-attack?"

Chose snorted rudely and King looked disgustedly at him before going back to his food.

"Hey! I'm the one who should be looking at you like that, King. Just look at the way you're eating." Chose knelt down and ruffled the back of King's neck. King made the same sound that Chose had just made and Chose tweaked his ear.

"Love me, love my dog," Kuda said.

"As you're so fond of reminding me," Chose sighed. "Although how somebody could love you, never mind your beast, is beyond me."

"Hey!" Kuda shouted, feigning insult, and King barked once. She threw the ball at Chose's face but he caught it easily, laughing.

"I'll sic King on you if you don't behave," Kuda warned and Chose laughed outright.

"This coward? He wouldn't know how to hurt a mosquito if it landed on his nose and stung him infinitely. All he does is bark, one bark at a time, mind you, and look loveable. And despite his intimidating size he's nothing but a country mouse at heart."

King barked once as though in agreement and Chose and Kuda laughed. He finished eating and went round to the back of the house.

"Would you like to come in for a drink?" Kuda asked.

"I thought you would never ask," Chose breathed and Kuda sniffed the air delicately.

"I do declare, sir, what is that perfume you're wearing? Eau de Stinky Sweat? It must be new in these here parts of the world and it's one scent I'm never going to buy."

Chose lunged at her and Kuda turned to run but Chose caught her easily and they tumbled to the ground. Kuda was one very ticklish woman and Chose knew it. He pinned her to the ground and dug his fingers into her ribs, tickling her mercilessly. She squealed with laughter and tried to escape but Chose was practically sitting on her. He tickled her until tears rolled down her face.

"Stop, please!" she screamed, laughing at the same time.

"Apologise."

"I'm sorry," she gasped. She rolled about in the dirt, trying to get Chose off her. All to no avail. Her sides felt like they were ready to split and her bladder was dangerously close to relaxing.

"That's not sincere enough. Apologise." His fingers played her ribs like a master piano player and Kuda's hands flailed helplessly, trying to stop them.

"I'm sorry, Chose. I won't say it again. I promise. I'm sorry!" she screamed.

"Not enough," Chose growled.

"I'm wetting myself!"

Chose chortled but he did stop the finger movement. "Now that's what I like to hear."

"You'll pay for that and that's a promise."

"Oh, really?" Chose asked with a playful leer, wiggling his fingers above her dramatically. "We'll see who has the last laugh."

He was about to tickle her again when a loud cough came from the gate. Both Chose and Kuda looked up. Jake Dawn stood there with his face as emotionless as a computer monitor.

"Excuse me for bothering you, but I need to borrow the key to the clinic." His voice was as blank as his face.

Chose got up from his awkward position and pulled Kuda to her feet. She dusted herself off and asked,

"Why didn't you get it from Aaron?"

"He's not at home."

"Come on in. I won't bite," Kuda said with mild sarcasm.

"Said the spider to the fly." Kuda dug her elbow into Chose's stomach when he said this and he groaned loudly. Jake watched all this patiently, not saying anything more after he had come into her yard.

"Before I forget the reason why I came," Chose said to Kuda in Kalanga. "We're having a little session for our doctor friend here tomorrow night at my place and you're to come."

"I don't know," Kuda replied hesitantly in the same language. "You know I don't like parties."

"It's not really a party and only a few people are coming. Come on, you'll enjoy it." Kuda gave him a doubtful look then looked at Jake. "For me," Chose coaxed in English and Kuda gave in without enthusiasm.

"Oh, alright," she grumbled gracelessly.

"Fine. See you tomorrow at seven thirty, then." He smiled before grabbing his ball from where it had fallen during their tussle. He said goodbye to her and Jake and ran off before Kuda could change her mind. "I'll take a rain check on that drink you offered me," he yelled.

"I changed my mind," Kuda yelled back. Chose waved and continued with his run. Kuda looked after him with a soft smile on her face. Jake did not miss it.

"The key, please," he reminded her. The smile dissolved. She raised her hand in a snappy salute, stood at attention and said, "Yes, sir!" in a brisk voice. She marched into the house and came back a few moments later with the key in her hand. She handed it to him, holding it high on the key-ring as though afraid to touch him because he was contaminated or something. He snatched it from her, muttered a thank you and was about to leave when King came bounding from around the corner of the house. Jake's eyes almost popped out from their sockets when he saw the large animal which came running over to Kuda.

"Good heavens," he whispered in amazement. Kuda took one look at his face and pursed her lips slightly, a sure sign that she desperately wanted to laugh and could just, barely, control herself. King looked up at Jake curiously and the subject of King's curiosity looked ready to run if King moved any closer to him.

"Doctor Dawn, this is my pooch, King," she introduced.

"You named him that because of his size didn't you," Jake said uneasily. He glanced behind him, probably to see how far away the gate was from where he stood.

"No actually. I named him after the author who was my favourite in high-school. Stephen King, the horror writer."

"Why didn't you just call him Cujo?" Jake asked.

"I thought about that but then two things came to mind. One, Cujo was a purebred Saint Bernard, King isn't. And, two, Cujo went mad and started killing people. I didn't want King to have that hanging over him so I called him King."

"The case of give a dog a bad name, huh."

"Yep. He's really as gentle as a lamb. Aren't you, baby." King barked once and Kuda cheerfully said, "Say hello to the nice doctor, King."

Without warning King got up on his hind legs and put his front paws on Jake's chest. Kuda could almost see his heart stop beating and her lips pursed even more. King came almost up to his shoulder and Jake stood as still as a lighthouse in a thunderstorm.

"No, not that way, King. Down, boy." King grumbled, the sound coming from his chest sounding like and approaching train, but put his paws down. "Now, shake."

King got down onto his haunches and raised his right paw. When Jake made no sign of accepting his shake, King barked once.

"Go on and shake his paw. He'll be insulted if you don't and I'd hate to see that happen. King is part lion and sometimes that comes to the surface. If it does I won't be responsible for what he might do." Jake gave her a withering look but he bent over and took King's paw in his right hand, shook it twice and let go. "Now say, 'Pleased to meet you, your highness'," Kuda smirked and Jake gave her a dirty look.

"Thanks for the key. I'll bring it back as soon as I finish," he said stiffly, then turned around and stalked out of the gate. Kuda thought she might have gone too far and thought about apologising but he was already too far to call back. She stood looking after him thoughtfully before she moved indoors.

Chapter Six
Stalked

After making sure her gate was closed to stop the cows, goats and sheep from entering her yard, Kuda turned on her radio and put Kenny G into her CD player. Sinking into the inviting sofa she lay back and closed her eyes. She was tired. For some reason she was feeling more strung out than usual and she wondered if this feeling had anything to do with the most recent addition to the clinic. She shook her head mentally in denial.

Jake may be cute – Cute? Alright, gorgeous, but that didn't mean that he had to radically alter her life or anyone else's. After all, he would be here for less than six months anyway and it wouldn't do if anybody got too involved with him. If she did, she would end up with the short end of the stick. So, all in all, it would be safer to keep their relationship professional and nothing more. That way it would be easier to shake off the dust and carry on with one's life. Not that he had made any indication that he was interested in her in that way, anyway…

All the same, it meant no heartache at all for her. None at all.

She must have dozed off for a while because when she opened her eyes the huge shape of a man was standing above her, leaning over the back of the sofa. She uttered a strangled scream and scrambled to her feet, her heart beating as though it wanted to dig a hole out of her chest. For one terror filled second she thought it was Timile and the thought of murder actually entered her mind before she clamped it down. In the fading light her fear was evident in her eyes and the man was aware of it.

"It's only me," Jake said softly, not wanting to spook her any more than was necessary. He heard her take a ragged breath, the sound harsh in her throat. He frowned. He might have startled her but it wasn't as though he was Quasimodo or the wolf man or something hideous. Why was she so afraid?

"What are you doing here?" she demanded and her voice was tight, still scared. His frown deepened.

"I brought back your key," he replied easily. "I'll put it on your table. I knocked but you didn't answer. And the door was open," he explained.

He laid the key on the table and was about to leave when she spoke again.

"Don't go."

Her voice had lost most of its fear but there was still a note of underlying tension in it that she was visibly trying to throttle. The light was fading fast and Jake wished he could see her face more clearly.

"Please sit down while I turn the lights on. I'd like to say something to you." She sensed rather than saw his raised eyebrows and she sighed. "Don't worry, I won't scream again."

He moved around the couch and sat down, his eyes never leaving her as she reached for a box of matches on the table and lit one. She put it to a gas lamp which had been sitting in a corner and suddenly the whole room was washed in bright light. She shook the match out and went around the room, closing the curtains. Jake admired the way her sleek muscles stretched beneath her clothing when she moved; he would have to be blind not to. Kuda finished and turned to face Jake, only, she looked at his left ear and not his eyes.

"I want to apologise for this afternoon," she began. "I know the reaction most people have when they see King for the first time and I shouldn't have made fun of you about it." She stopped and Jake continued to look at her expectantly. When he realised that that was it, he bit his inner cheek to keep from smiling.

"I had a very bad experience with a dog as a child, actually," he said solemnly. Kuda looked interested.

"Really? What happened?"

"I got bitten by a one-eyed, three-legged dog," he answered soberly. Kuda knew he was pulling one over on her and she was amused.

"Really?" she said dryly.

"Yep, but it's a long story and I'll tell you one day if you're nice to me," he replied, still sober.

"When dogs lay eggs," she muttered under her breath.

"I heard that," Jake told her.

"Good," she shot back. Their short truce was over. Jake got up to go. "Before you leave, Manini would like to see you tomorrow at around five and she's given me the honour of escorting you." The way she said it made it sound like something distasteful she had to get off her tongue in a hurry.

"Why?"

"I don't know but I promised her I'd bring you along." It wasn't exactly the truth but Jake didn't need to know that. "I'll come by at about quarter to."

"Did it ever occur to you that I might have plans for tomorrow and might not be able to come?" he asked with a raised eye-brow.

"No," she replied gaily, fake toothy grin and all. "Do you?"

"That's not the issue here," he said and Kuda saw that his breathing was very measured, very deliberate.

"Fine." Kuda flopped onto the sofa nearest to her. "If you want to break a little old lady's heart, far be it from me to point it out. Besides, she was so looking forward to seeing you but I guess I'll just tell her you had better things to do." She gazed surreptitiously up at him from under her lashes and saw a muscle work in his jaw. She tucked her lower lip into her mouth and sucked on it, hiding her grin.

"Fine," he said. The muscle jumped harder. "I'll be there." He turned and stomped to the door.

"Ah, doctor?" she called sweetly. Jake whirled around. "Bring a hat."

He didn't even bother to reply to that and marched out of the house, slamming the door behind him and leaving Kuda grinning hugely like some idiot on drugs. For some reason getting under Jake Dawn's skin had been thrilling. Something she could get used to.

She got up and walked to her spare bedroom where she lit another lamp. There was a double-bed inside the room which was pushed to one corner. What dominated this room was the painting and drawing equipment scattered all over it. A large easel stood near the window with a table nearby which was filled with brushes and paints. She studied the partly done painting on the easel with a critical eye, finally deciding it wasn't half bad.

It was a portrait of Manini Chipo. The old woman was standing, looking up at the sky with a thoughtful expression on her face. It was dusk and the colours of the evening clothed her like a warm coat and embraced her, making her look serene and content. She looked worry-free and a half smile lingered on her face, making it seem as though she had seen something wondrous in the distance that nobody else could see.

Kuda had tried to get the painting just right but hadn't quite managed to portray the wisdom, the sense of tranquillity that ought to have been there. She had tried over and over again but had failed dismally each time. She was her own worst critic and had not been happy with anything she had done so far. She had put the painting on the easel each night since she had started it, hoping that every evening when she came into the room she would be able to finish it off. So far it hadn't happened although it didn't stop the nightly ritual of putting the painting on the easel. She finally took it down and set it carefully on the bed before putting a fresh piece of paper up on the easel.

Kuda had never been to art school, well not in the true sense. In primary school there had been lessons but that had been it. So when her talent showed itself the only person who had encouraged her had been her art teacher. When she went to high school there had been no art classes but she had still scribbled a bit in her spare time or when she was bored. She had doodled in class and her books always had sketches on practically every page. Drawing live subjects was tricky so she didn't do it much. What she did was draw from memory, like the partly done portrait of Manini Chipo. Her mind was a camera, able to store even the most minute of details, and bring them up later when she wanted to draw them. It was a trick she had acquired as a little girl and she had practised it and honed it to perfection, until she could close her eyes and see whatever she wanted to see and then put it on paper.

She had many pictures of King, for example. King chewing his first bone; King barking for the first time; King chasing a mother hen; King being chased by the mother hen. She had lots of others too. Una taking his first step; Manini yelling at Washington; Mmantshadi chasing Washington after he had drunk enough beer to render him courageous enough to try and milk her. He had gotten over that idea in a hurry. There were lots of other paintings and each one told a different story.

Picking up a pencil, she started to sketch, all the while thinking about all the possible things that could have upset Manini. Of all the ideas she came up with, Una came repeatedly to mind. But what was it exactly that she was worried about? When Manini had a problem she usually confided in her. Why was it different this time? Kuda knew Manini very well, and two reasons came to mind: either Manini didn't want to worry her, or she was afraid Kuda wouldn't approve. Either way, Kuda was worried.

Her hand stopped abruptly in mid-stroke when she suddenly realised what she had drawn. It was Timile as he had looked when he had grabbed her arms earlier that day. His lips had been curled in a snarl and in his eyes had been insanity, pure and simple. This is what had scared her so much. She sat there for a long time, just looking into Timile's pencil drawn eyes and without warning a picture burst into her mind before it just as quickly disappeared, leaving a bad sensation in her conscious memory.

She had seen herself doubled up in agony, lying on the floor, with Timile standing over her. In his hand was something sharp. Kake had been watching, there yet not there somehow.

It had been preposterous really, so why had goose-pimples broken out on her arms? Why had a cold finger scrubbed itself all the way down her spine? She shuddered and threw the pencil onto the table. She didn't feel like drawing anymore.

Getting up, she put the sketch-pad on the floor, against the easel, and went to the bed to get the painting of Manini. She carried it carefully back to its place of honour and set it down gently. She looked it over slowly, gazing at the well-known features tenderly, at the woman who had been more of a mother to her than any other woman, including her own mother.

She switched off the lamp and left the room, leaving the door slightly ajar. It was quarter to nine and she didn't feel like sleeping yet. She thought about visiting her friend Susan but decided against it. She walked outside and sat on the doorstep before whistling softly for King. A few seconds later he came trotting up to her, the outline of his body huge and muscular in the twilight. He sat next to her and rested his head on her lap, waiting for the scratch she always administered to the back of his ears. King sighed dreamily as Kuda began to scratch his neck and Kuda thought, if he were a cat, he'd purr. She smiled in the darkness, feeling at ease.

Kuda looked towards Aaron's home and she could hear the humming of his generator. His lights were still on and she found herself wondering what he was doing. Probably reading one of his medical journals, she thought. He used to do that a lot when he was still married to her mother. The two of them would sit on the sofa, her feet on his lap as she read a novel or knitted. Kuda would have her own book to read while she either sat between them or on the floor, with the sounds of the village gently permeating their home.

Shaking her head to dispel the memories, she looked across to Jake's place and saw his silhouette in the window of his bedroom because his curtains weren't drawn. She looked away quickly when she saw him pull off his shirt, feeling like a peeping-tom. However, her eyes seemed to act upon their own accord and strayed back to the window.

She saw him do a few upper body stretches and her hand stilled on King's neck. After a few seconds King pushed at her other hand with his nose but when Kuda paid him no attention he snorted, got up and curled himself into a huge ball where he promptly fell asleep. Kuda's eyes stayed glued to Jake's dark shape so when he stopped, went to the window and snapped the curtains shut, Kuda felt as though she had been given a slap on the back of her hand for doing something naughty. She felt like the kid who had been caught with her hand in the sugar-bowl, complete with sugar dust covering her mouth.

She got up abruptly, only now realising that King had moved away, and went back into the house. She locked the door before she stripped off and prepared to take a long, cold shower. This was followed, nearly forty-five minutes later, by bed.

* * *

After King moved away from Kuda, he moved around to the side of the house. Raising his head, he smelt something familiar but it was not a smell he liked. A slow rumble like an approaching freight train started in his chest and he padded to the fence, his ears standing straight up, his head high. The rumble stopped and he sniffed the air.

His eyes scanned the darkness but he could not see what it was that his nose had caught the scent of. He squatted slightly and then pushed off with his hind legs, jumping over the meter three high fence without any strain. He put his nose to the ground then raised it after a couple of sniffs and started moving in the direction of the smell. His large frame moved quickly in the darkness, surprisingly lightly for a creature so large. After running for a few minutes, he started to sprint, for he had caught sight of the reason for the smell.

* * *

Timile stared at Kuda's house. He saw the lights go out and the anger that had been boiling within him all day nearly consumed him then. How could she? She continually rejected him yet she allowed Chose and that new man to be around her. How dare she?

He had been standing in these woods for over six hours, watching her for most of the day and then well into the night. He had seen her frolicking with that boy in the sand. In the sand, for goodness sake! Didn't they have the human decency to do whatever they were doing in the house? Away from the sight of moral people? And she had enjoyed it too. She had laughed as that boy had put his hands all over her body. She had begged him not to stop. And as if that wasn't enough, that other man had come to her. Not just once but twice. *Twice!* What kind of moral message was she passing onto her patients?

Well, he'd just have to teach her that that kind of thing just wasn't done. It wasn't acceptable. Yes, he would have to teach her a lot of things. He had the time. He would just wait until the two of them were alone. If that didn't happen, he would have to arrange it. That was fine, too. He liked arranging things. He liked fixing things too. Yes, he would fix Kuda. She definitely needed fixing. It was just a matter of time.

As the lights went out in Kuda's home, he started to pack his binoculars into the front of his shirt so he could set off for home. As he lowered them, however, he caught sight of a large shape moving swiftly away from Kuda's house. Startled, he tried to catch sight of the rapidly approaching mass and gasped when he realised that Kuda's Goliath of a pet was making his way rapidly in his direction.

Without even bothering to pack his binoculars away he started sprinting. One minute he was standing and the next he was moving so fast that Bolt would have been envious. There was no way he wanted to be here when that creature reached the spot he was currently standing in. After a while, he slowed down, realising that he could not hear any sign that the dog was following him. Just to be sure he took out his stalker glasses and frantically searched the area he had just come from. He caught sight of the dog, but it had stopped and after a second or so it turned and walked back to Kuda's yard.

With a sigh of relief he put his binoculars away and started walking home. As he walked, his thoughts drifted back to all the other times he had fixed things. Nobody had ever known just how well he did that and it seemed as though he would have another chance soon. He really looked forward to that. It would give him great pleasure.

In the darkness, his teeth shone through in a grin which would have made Kuda wish for death right then if she had seen it.

It was the smile of a man without a conscience.

Chapter Seven
Slither

When Kuda awoke the next morning she and King went out for a long run. It was always cooler in the mornings and not many people were out and about. The sky was a clear blue and not a single cloud marred its perfection. There was a slight breeze which kept her cool on her jog, and the full heat of the sun would not be felt for another couple of hours.

Depending on her mood or the weather, she jogged between ten and twenty kilometres. It was a liberating experience and she enjoyed the freedom her moving limbs seemed to have as they pumped effortlessly through the air. King seemed to relish the motions as much as she did, padding along beside her most of the time, but often going off into the brush to investigate something that caught his attention. This was how they usually spent their run.

Usually. Today, however, her mind was not at peace the way it normally was when she was out jogging. And the reason?

Doctor Jake Dawn.

The man was insufferable. Not only was he annoying but he was also self-righteous and… and annoying! He had only been here a short minute and he had already made himself judge, jury and executioner in her life. He had jumped feet first into her arena and was determined to be a daily nuisance. Or so she thought anyway.

So caught up was she in her mindless anger that she didn't realise that she had run much farther than she usually did. Her head turned as she heard the persistent sound of the go-away bird in a tree to her right. Looking around, she realised she was close to a bridge that was built over a river which was more sand than water at this time of the year. The bridge was a concrete structure which hadn't developed any potholes yet. Surprising, really, for the typical workmanship in the local villages. It was still relatively new, so there was still hope for the potholes.

To her right was a hill which was full of rocks and trees, surrounded by hillocks with similar rock cover and foliage. She had passed this area so many times but had hardly ever taken the time to study it. She was usually in too much of a hurry to get to where she was going. Now, as she took it in, she noticed the thick trunked trees that grew along the road. Mophane trees were scattered everywhere and would become food for the worms in a few months. The rocks leading up the hill were mainly white but there were darker grey ones which looked like they had been thrown down by a giant hand playing dice with a thousand stones.

She stopped abruptly and looked around for King. She didn't see him anywhere but wasn't worried because he would show up eventually. He always did. Besides, no one messed with him so she hardly ever worried about him. She was a bit out of breath and decided to start a slow jog back. As she turned, however, she caught sight of something which glinted about thirty meters away from her. She stopped and looked at it for a while. The shimmer repeated itself and her curiosity got the better of her. Many years ago she had heard stories of people disappearing in these hills after they had gone looking for gold and diamonds. She hadn't heard the stories in a while but for some reason the flicker called to her. She didn't know what the glimmer was but she knew she was about to find out.

Knowing that it probably wasn't a good idea, she decided to go and investigate anyway. The glinting item could have been anything and she was determined that she would try and get a closer look. Watching her step, she carefully made her way up the hill, being careful to watch where she put her foot and, where she had to put her hands to help her up as well. Making steady progress, she was quite chuffed with her pace until she stepped wrong and her foot slipped. She didn't fall right then though. It was her next step which she got wrong and sent her slipping and sliding to her left. She grabbed at the undergrowth around her, pulling the grass and shrubbery out by the roots, and scrambled desperately with her sneaker clad feet, trying to get a foothold on anything that would stop her rapidly increasing descent.

Panicked now, Kuda took a calculated risk and, bending her knees, she then straightened them quickly and jumped, trying to land on a group of rocks that looked relatively stable. She miscalculated, however, and missed the outcrop, hitting her head against a large boulder that was to the left. It wasn't a debilitating knock, but it was hard enough for her to see a flash of light which forced her to close her eyes for a couple of seconds. She landed hard and fell to the ground, flat on her back.

She lay there for a moment, trying to get back the wind that had been knocked out of her when she landed. She took in a few deep breaths and tried to calm her racing heart. Her blood sped through her veins and she felt like her inner organs would implode because of the pressure. While she was trying to gather herself, she quickly did an assessment of her body. Nothing seemed to be broken although her left ankle felt a little sore. Her sigh of relief seemed loud and she chuckled softly to herself. What she had just done had probably been one of the most stupid stunts that she had ever pulled; and there had been many over the years.

She opened her eyes and her short relief died a sudden death. One part of her primitive brain realised that the go-away bird was no longer calling and the only sound she could hear was the rustling of the leaves as the wind blew through them.

The blood seemed to freeze within her body as she saw the four metre long black mamba that stood with half of its body off the ground, looking directly at her where she lay. Its olive skin looked like it had been polished by a veteran shoe-shiner and the scales seemed to have been placed together by an accomplished puzzle maker. The eyes of the serpent were grey but the pupil was so large that the oil-black colour covered most of its eye.

She felt her eyes widen and her breath catch in her throat. Its eyes were fixed on her and it opened its mouth slowly to reveal the inside of its mouth, reminding her why it was called the black mamba, for the interior of its maw was darker than tar. It flattened out its neck like the hood of a cobra and swayed its raised body slowly from side to side. For a moment it stopped swaying and then moved slowly back as it prepared to strike.

Kuda closed her eyes, not breathing, not wanting to see one of the most venomous snakes in Africa as it got ready to kill her. She felt like her goose bumps had goose bumps and that her skin was recoiling, shrinking in on itself as it anticipated the lethal shot from the strike of the mamba. Had she been a praying woman, she would have offered a prayer to her creator right then but instead, she took a deep breath and made peace with her universe. She tensed her body and got ready to feel the repeated bites that she knew the mamba was capable of delivering. All it took to kill a human was one dose of venom and she knew that she would die a painful death. No one knew where she was and no one was coming for her. They would probably find her body in a few days for they would only start looking when she failed to show up for work on Monday.

"Will anyone miss me?" she asked herself, the small voice in the back of her mind unbidden. She wasn't sure and that was a hard pill.

It was then that she literally felt the breath lock in her lungs. As she released it, it felt like she was exhaling it a molecule at a time. Every beat of her heart thundered through her body like a pulse and she almost felt each goose bump as it seemed to grow on her skin. The throbbing in her foot beat along with her heart and the same pounding pulsed in her ears, a symphony of pain and fear in a body that was about to breath its last.

Suddenly, she thought of her mother; of her smile and the light that she always seemed to have glowing in her eyes. The way she had sang to her at bedtime every night until she was eight and insisted she was all grown up and didn't need a lullaby anymore. Of how she had comforted her whenever she had been upset and how *she* had never seemed to get angry. She thought of how much her mother had loved her and her heartbeat sped up.

She thought of Aaron. Of how he had made her mother happy in the eleven years of their marriage. She remembered every minute of their wedding day, of how she had felt sad, felt like he was replacing her in her mother's life, despite her mother's reassurance that she had room enough in her heart for both of them, as did he. The fear was only dispelled when Aaron had called to her after he had said his vows to his new wife. He had made his own promises to her, telling her that he would be there for her when she was ill and when she was well; when life was hard and she needed an ear for her to vent into. He would be her point of contact when life got hard and she needed support, for her to always remember that he would love her no matter what.

It was then that she opened her eyes.

The mamba still stood in front of where she lay, still flat on her back, but for some reason it was not striking. A loud hissing sound like a boiling kettle came from its mouth and suddenly it looked first left and then right. Then, it slowly dropped its body to the ground and started crawling towards

Kuda. She wanted to move but she dared not. She felt the heat of the earth burn through her clothes, like she was lying on a bed of fire with the heat slowly licking her body. A sob caught in her throat as she tried not to move, not to jump up off the ground and run like a mad man, because had she done that, the venomous creature heading in her direction would have chased her down and killed her for sure.

The large black mamba slowly crawled over Kuda's left foot and then under her slightly raised knee. She wanted to jerk her foot back but knew that was certain death waiting to happen. Not stopping there, the mamba crawled over her thighs and then under the small of her back, in that curve that never quite touches the ground when one is lying flat, and then over her chest. Kuda could feel every movement of the large reptile as it slithered over her body, from her feet all the way to her chest. It made a second roll around her chest, its thick, muscular body curling itself around her shaking body. Then, it brought its face close to hers and hissed again. She saw its fangs as they curled backwards into the cavern that was its mouth and the venom drops that hung off the end like lethal teardrops. All it took was one drop of that poison to kill her.

Around her, a myriad of shadows seemed to suddenly appear; like she was driving under a canopy of trees. A kaleidoscope of black and white danced in front of her eyes, as though she were standing in front of a whole lot of Rorschach inkblots that were being flashed too quickly for the eyes to make out. The shadows got denser and thicker and they moved around both her and the snake, surrounding them in a circle of blackness that seemed impenetrable.

The viper seemed to look at her for an eternity before it slowly crawled off her again. Kuda felt its body uncoil itself from around hers as it moved away. It felt like a huge hose pipe was being pulled off her. Where its scales touched her bare skin it felt like sandpaper was being pulled slowly over her; dry, rough and terrifying.

She dared not move after its tail had slid off her neck. She hadn't realised it before but her cheeks were moist from the tears that had escaped her eyes as the beast had crawled over her. Just as suddenly as the black and white coloured images had appeared, they disappeared. She still lay in the dirt, where the heat was almost unbearable now, until, for some reason she knew that it was okay to sit up. Wary of doing so quickly, however, she turned her head slowly and rolled her eyes, trying to catch a glimpse of the Herculean serpent that could have killed her with a single bite. It was nowhere to be seen.

She shakily got to her feet and tested her tender ankle. It was fine. Without even trying to dust herself off, Kuda started to beat a hasty retreat in the opposite direction to which the snake had gone. Her legs were wobbly and almost failed to support her but she was determined to get the hell out of there. Her ankle started to throb again but she had no time to listen to it. She had to get out of there before the mamba decided to come back and finish what it had started.

She didn't understand what had just happened and she wasn't about to stick around to question why she was still alive. What the snake had done was contrary to everything that she heard or read about black mambas. There was no explanation for why it had not attacked her.

Not knowing how she got there, she found herself at the main road once again. She started jogging back to the village. It was more of a sprint but who was keeping tabs? Her lungs burned and her throat was on fire but she pushed herself harder than she had ever done before. She would not stop until she got home.

There was no way in hell she was ever going to talk about this to anyone. No one at all. Not Manini. Not Aaron. NO ONE.

She was alive and there was no logical explanation as to why she was. Black mambas had a notorious reputation for being vicious, aggressive killers. How then, had this one not only left her alive but had seemed to be deliberately letting her know that it could have killed her if it had wanted to?

She swore that she would never talk about this incident or dwell on it again. It was enough that she had literally been missed by the serpent's fangs.

Who was she to question fate?

Chapter Eight
A Momentary Truce

She arrived home just over an hour and a half after she had headed out and, after making sure that King's bowl of water had been refilled, she went inside and took a long, cool shower. Already the day's events were disappearing from her mind like morning mist in the Kgalagadi Desert. By the time she finished her shower, she had no recollection of what had happened to her earlier in the day.

When she was done, she wrapped a huge yellow towel around herself and padded to the kitchen in her bare feet. Along the way she switched on the radio. They were playing a song she knew and she sang along cheerfully as she poured cold milk into a pot then set it onto the stove to warm up.

There was a knock on the door and she put the heat down before going to answer it. The towel covered her pretty well, from her armpits to below her knees and it really was decent. Besides, it could only be either Manini Chipo or Chedza, both of whom were okay. So when she opened the door with a smile on her face and saw Jake standing there she didn't know whether to invite him in or slam the door in his face. Jake also stood there, blinking owlishly at her as she stood there with the door open wide and her hand on the handle. Finally he opened his mouth to say something but Kuda's towel chose that particular moment to slip. She let go of the door handle and made a mad grab for the slipping towel. She grinned sheepishly and took a couple of steps back.

"Excuse me. I need to get dressed." She stopped suddenly and a look of comical dismay appeared on her face as a loud hissing came from the kitchen. "My milk!" she wailed as she spun around on her bare heels and ran to the kitchen, displaying a bare back to Jake.

Jake heard the cluttering dishes and muffled curses and frowned. He followed the blistering language into the kitchen and allowed himself a peek inside. Kuda whirled from where she had dumped the pot onto the kitchen counter, towel held precariously in one hand. When she saw him her face went darker than it had been and she held out her hand accusingly.

"There!" she yelled. "Are you satisfied? I burnt my fingers and it's all your fault."

She stuck her hand under the faucet and bit her lip to try to stop from crying out.

"Let me see," Jake said, suddenly by her side.

Kuda stubbornly shook her head, keeping her head averted. Jake had, by now, realised that to get through to her by rationalisation was a lost cause. Talking was merely a waste of time with Kuda and reaching for her hand he pulled it out from out of the flowing water. Kuda immediately curled her hand into a fist.

"I'm a doctor, too, Jake Dawn, and I am perfectly capable of assessing the damage to my hand," she snapped rudely.

"If you don't uncurl your fingers right now I'm going to forcibly do it and I might just break a finger in the process." Although Jake's threat was said amicably enough, the anger in his eyes was real.

Kuda bit her lip again, this time to keep it from trembling. She slowly relaxed her fingers. She realised just how big Jake was, all of a sudden, and this time she couldn't keep her lip from trembling.

"Does it hurt much?" Jake asked, and there was concern in his voice.

Head still down, Kuda shook it quickly. She didn't trust herself to speak at that point and didn't want to betray her emotional state by saying anything. At least with her face averted he couldn't see her reaction to his being so close. She stared at her hand where it lay in Jake's and marvelled at how large his looked when compared to hers. It looked strong and very male. However, it still held hers with gentle tenderness.

"I'm alright," she finally said and was proud of the steadiness of her tone. "I just overreacted." She looked up at him. "What did you want?"

"I didn't have any coffee at my place and Aaron wasn't home. You're the next neighbour I have. Do you have any to spare?"

Kuda sighed. She jerked her head in the direction of a cupboard, her uninjured hand still holding her towel tightly to her chest. When she realised that her other hand was still ensconced within Jake's, she pulled it away.

"Look in there. I'll go put some clothes on."

She moved past him, careful not to brush against him, and practically ran to her bedroom. She changed into a pair of shorts, a shirt and sandals, then shook her head with a little chuckle as she realised the towel had covered more of her than what she currently wore. She thought about changing then decided against it. It was too hot. When she finally left her room she saw that Jake was standing by the main door.

"I found it," he said, shaking the bottle in her direction. "Should I leave you some?"

"No. I hate coffee. I only have it for when Chose comes over."

"I see. Well, I best get going. Thanks for the coffee."

Kuda nodded, not saying anything. Jake turned and walked out of the house. He did not look back and for some perverse reason she felt like throwing her shoe at him. Instead, she closed the door softly behind him and went to her paintings.

Later, at around eleven, Kuda decided she had done enough painting and doodling for one day and started to prepare lunch. *Phaletšhe* and *morogo*; mealie-meal and one of the Tswana vegetables which tasted a bit like dried spinach. As she was putting the water on to boil for the *phaletšhe,* a thought popped into her head. She felt a huge grin bloom on her face as the thought took root. Still grinning, she increased the water in the pot.

* * *

Kuda pounded on the door to Jake's house but there was no answer from within except for the whining scream of some electrical machine. Transferring her bundle from one hand to the other she opened the door and looked in. Jake was in a corner, busy drilling something into the wall. He seemed not to be aware that she was there and continued with whatever it was he was doing. She stood by the open door and looked around the house.

Kuda had been in the house before but she had never seen it in such confusion and she seriously doubted she ever would again. The furniture was pushed to one side and covered in white sheets. A large, thick maroon carpet was folded and lay draped over most of the chairs. Various medical books and journals were scattered haphazardly in two of the corners. Curtains, which should have been up, were lying all over the place like the cocoons of some huge prehistoric butterflies that were ready to hatch. She could also see the kitchen and a bedroom from where she stood and neither sight was particularly eye-pleasing.

Pots, pans, plates and cutlery were all over the kitchen and the fridge was in the middle of it all, with the freezer door half open. In the master bedroom, the bed was unmade and his clothes were everywhere. She was thankful the door to the other bedroom was closed. Who knew what horrors lurked within! At least the mess was not made on top of another mess. Aaron had ensured that the house was swept, mopped and polished before Jake moved in.

She turned her attention to the man himself. He was dressed in a pair of shorts and headphones, which explained why he hadn't heard her knock. In his hand was a hand-drill and he was apparently fixing the bookshelf while listening to a Walkman. She thought about turning around and walking out but one look at the kitchen and she knew the man hadn't eaten anything. Suddenly she felt mean and was actually turning to go back home when Jake switched off the drill and looked over his shoulder. When he saw her standing there his brows shot up to his hairline.

The silence was immediately very loud to Kuda after the shriek of the drill and she stood there uncertainly for a moment, not sure what to do or say.

"This is a surprise," Jake said as he pulled off the headphones and turned to fully face Kuda. She felt her eyes widen involuntarily as she caught sight of his bare chest. Feeling uncomfortable, she raised her eyes and looked instead at the shelf that stood behind him.

"What's the matter? Cat got your tongue?" Jake asked smoothly. His saccharine tone got through to her and she shook her head.

"No, I just couldn't hear you after all the commotion you were causing in here. What are you doing anyway? Massacring the bookshelf?"

Thankfully, Jake ignored her nonsensical statement and turned his gaze down to her hands instead.

"Fixing a couple of broken shelves. I'm done now anyway. What's that?" he asked, pointing at the covered dish in her hand.

"It's..." She was suddenly embarrassed.

"Smells like food," Jake said helpfully. "Did you bring me lunch?"

"As a matter of fact..."

Jake laughed incredulously, not believing it. However, when Kuda avoided his eyes he knew she had and it knocked him back for a loop.

"Are you serious?" he asked.

"Yes," she answered, and she knew she sounded annoyed. She didn't care.

"How sweet of you," he said. He sounded touched.

"Wait until you see what it is before you go all sentimental on me," Kuda warned and Jake shrugged.

"I'm sure if you cooked it, it's edible," he told her. Then he spoiled it all by saying, "If it's not, don't worry, it's the thought that counts."

Kuda pushed the warm dish into Jake's stomach and spun around, feeling as though he had slapped her in the face. Jake caught her by the arm before she could march out of the house and whirled her back to face him. The dish was now safely in his other hand.

"Has anyone ever told you," he said amiably, "that you have a hair-trigger temper and that if you don't control it, one of these days it's going to get you into a whole lot of trouble?"

"I'm not going to tell you where to stick your words of wisdom but you had better get your hand off me. I don't like being man-handled." Her voice was tight, like a cello string about to snap.

Jake let her go but she didn't move. Instead she took a deep breath. Nobody spoke for a moment.

"I'm sorry –" Kuda finally said at the exact same second that Jake said it. They both stopped speaking. Another uncomfortable stretch of time passed between them before Jake laughed quietly.

"Is it my imagination or do we keep apologising when we're together? It's becoming a compulsive habit, don't you think?"

Kuda almost smiled at his words.

"It's not very healthy either," she said.

"Truce?"

"Why bother? It won't last very long."

"Ah, the world's greatest optimist. Putting my idea down before we even put it into practice. Now, why is that, I wonder?"

"I'm not going to apologise for the way I am, Dr. Dawn –"

"Jake."

"What?"

"Call me Jake."

Kuda blinked like a myopic owl and stared at him, asking herself what her calling him Jake had to do with what she was about to say and, on top of that, making her lose her train of thought.

"This is crazy," she said, shaking her head in confusion. "This is really crazy. All I did was bring you lunch to prove a point and now everything's going haywire."

"Must be something they hypnotised into us in med-school. Do you think we can sue?"

She almost smiled again and so she shook her head instead.

"Find a spot and have your lunch. I've already eaten."

There was a sudden twinkle in her eye which made Jake uneasy and he wondered if maybe she had put arsenic into the food. He sat down warily and invited her to do the same. After she had found a small unoccupied spot, she set herself down.

"What point were you trying to prove?" he asked. Was that a hint of a smile? Why the pursed lips? She shook her head without answering and Jake's suspicion grew. Dread was a hard little ball in the bit of his stomach and he wasn't sure he wanted to uncover that dish.

"Don't worry. It won't bite," she said, and for some reason that only made him sweat a bit more. He had an idea that whatever it was she wanted to prove started in that dish and he gave her a sour look. He uncovered it. And breathed a sigh of relief. Then frowned.

"What is it?" he asked.

"*Phaletšhe*, or pap, and *morogo*."

His frown deepened. "Like I'm supposed to know what that is."

"The pap is a traditional meal," she explained. "It's a staple, actually. You prepare it by boiling water and adding ground mealie-meal to the water until it becomes a solid but smooth lump. Then you leave it to cook for a while, stirring it occasionally, until it's ready. Then you serve it. The *morogo* is actually leaves from a small shrub and you prepare it much the same way as you would prepare spinach or cabbage. You'll probably be eating a lot of both while you're here."

"So you gave me the first dish –"

"So you'll know how to eat it when somebody invites you home and you won't embarrass yourself."

"Meaning that you want me to humiliate myself in front of you."

"You said it, not me. Eat. It's really not that bad."

Jake studied the white lump, which was still pleasantly warm, and the spinach-like substance for a moment. Kuda looked steadily at him.

"At the risk of sounding like an absolute idiot, how does one eat this?" he asked. There! That was definitely a smile, no matter how small it was.

"Take a bit of the *phaletšhe* – careful, it's hot – with a bit of the *morogo*, raise your hand, put the two into your –"

"Thank you. I think I can take it from there."

"Go ahead," Kuda encouraged with a fake, sweet smile. After glancing at her briefly, Jake did.

Using his thumb and forefinger he pinched a little *phaletšhe* off the larger lump, pinched a little *morogo* and popped the resulting mass into his mouth. He tasted it carefully. Kuda scratched her nose to hide her smile but Jake caught a glimpse of it anyway.

"It's really not that bad," he said.

"I hate to be a wet sock but you hardly put enough in your mouth to satisfy a sugar-ant, much less taste it. Try again. Take a little more this time, though."

Jake did and to his surprise it was okay. Besides, he was hungry and food was food, right? He tucked in and this time Kuda's smile was obvious. Jake stopped eating and stared at her.

"What is it?" she asked, smile dissolving.

"It's just that you haven't smiled at me since I got here and I was surprised."

Kuda stood up abruptly. Jake was prepared for her flight from his new home but she confused him again.

"Need any help in sorting out your house? I thought the guys who came over yesterday would have done something but I see I was wrong. What were you doing?"

"Talking. Getting to know one another."

"Ah." The sound of infinite wisdom. "Where should I start?"

Chapter Nine
Forging Friendships

Jake stared at her. "You're going to help?"

"I asked didn't I?"

"Sure. How about the kitchen," he said quickly, afraid she might change her mind.

"No problem," Kuda said and walked there, minding the items lying on the floor. Jake looked after her thoughtfully, not knowing what to think. Kuda was definitely one confusing lady. He went back to his meal. After he had finished eating he went to the kitchen. Kuda was kneeling by the cupboards, packing his pots neatly and efficiently. She looked up as he came into the kitchen and there was a smudge of dirt on her cheek.

"Do you need any help in here?" he asked her.

Kuda looked slowly around the kitchen. It was relatively large but still not big enough to have Jake as well as her working side by side in it. There would be too much brushing up against each other and that was something she definitely didn't want. Jake at a distance was fine. Jake close-up was a different story altogether. Especially Jake without a shirt on.

"No. Why don't you go do your bedroom while I finish up in here and then we'll tackle the sitting-room together?"

"Okay," Jake replied. He put the plate on the counter and then looked at Kuda.

"Don't ask," Kuda said as he opened his mouth to speak. "Sometimes it's better not to know why a woman changes her mind."

Jake thought about pressing it but he minded her words anyway and went to the bedroom. A few minutes later the strains of Kenny G floated out of his room and Kuda was pleasantly surprised. It took about an hour for Kuda to put everything away. When she was through packing everything she stood back to admire her handiwork. Neat. Very neat, if she did say so herself. The fridge and stove both used gas and they were hooked up so there was nothing to do there. She was all done. She wondered how Jake was doing. She didn't have long to wonder because as soon as she walked out of the kitchen Jake walked out of the bedroom.

Their eyes met.

Jake had thrown on a short-sleeved shirt but hadn't buttoned it up and Kuda eyed the beads of sweat on his chest with decided interest. Jake, on the other hand noted that the smidgen of dust that had been on her cheek had been joined by its cousins. He felt a sudden urge to wipe it off with his fingers but he wasn't sure how Kuda would react to that so he stayed put.

"Ready to take on the sitting-room?" Kuda asked. Jake nodded. "Where should we start?"

"I think we should get the carpet on the floor and then we'll take it from there. We'd be better able to decide how to place the furniture. What do you think?"

"It's a good idea," Kuda agreed. So they set to it.

The sitting-room was a lot tougher than the kitchen had been. There was much more bending, lifting and moving things around and by the time they were done Kuda's back felt as though a herd of cattle had danced on it. She plopped into one of the chairs and groaned.

"Next time I volunteer to help you, talk me out of it," she moaned.

Jake chuckled. "Why do I seriously doubt that there'll ever be a next time?" he asked and Kuda smiled.

"With that attitude there won't be," she said to him.

Jake's eyes were drawn to the curve of her lips. It was a genuine smile this time, not one of those cynical little mouth twists that he had quickly come to know and wasn't too partial to. It startled him with its unexpectedness and he wasn't sure of exactly what it was he had said to make her smile at him. He wouldn't think about it right then though. He wanted to enjoy the curve of her lips without any distractions.

For a while they sat in silence, neither of them saying anything. Kuda leaned back, closed her eyes and took a deep breath. Jake did likewise and all was quiet save for the melodic whistle of Kenny G's saxophone as it flowed through the house. Kuda finally raised her arm and looked at her watch.

"Heavens! It's nearly five thirty. Manini's expecting us." She looked at Jake and there was an apologetic expression on her face. "I know I bulldozed you into it but she is waiting."

"It's not like I had anything better to do but I would appreciate it if next time you would consult me first," he said reprovingly. Kuda grinned.

"To quote, 'Why do I seriously doubt that there'll ever be a next time?' "

"Stranger things have happened," he chuckled.

Kuda nodded, then laboriously stood up. She felt as though her back had been broken in a dozen different places and the bones hadn't been set properly.

"If we want to get to Manini before the cattle come home we'd better leave now," she said as she stretched her aching back muscles. Jake stood up too.

"What time do they come in?"

"Around six. They have their own in-built timing system and they come home at exactly the same time every day." Jake gave her a sceptical look and Kuda looked back at him earnestly. "I'm serious. Haven't you ever been on a farm? They're like birds which go south for the winter only the cattle do it every day. Like Pavlov's dogs."

"Talking about dogs, where's yours?" Jake asked, deciding not to press the dubious topic of the cattle.

"King? He's probably on his way to Manini's as we speak."

"He's a clock-watcher too, huh?"

Kuda nodded solemnly.

"You got that right. He's a watch-dog. One of the best."

* * *

The two people walked slowly in the direction of Manini's home, not really talking much but for once, comfortable in each other's company. There was a slight breeze blowing and it helped with the heat a bit. Not by much but Jake wanted to believe that it was slightly cooling. Still, he had never been so hot in all his life and he longed for the cool convenience of an air-conditioner. Funny enough, Kuda looked as cool as lettuce dipped in ice water and he envied her. He supposed the heat took a lot of getting used to. Adaptation was a long process. Look how long it took the ape to evolve into modern man and in some, the process wasn't even complete yet.

So absorbed in his thoughts was he that he didn't hear the person who was calling out to Kuda until Kuda stopped and turned to face the young girl who was now running towards them. Pleasure lit up Kuda's face when she recognised the girl and Jake was astonished at how much Kuda's face changed when she allowed her composure to slip a little. She was a beautiful woman and he couldn't take his eyes off her.

"Chedza. What are you doing here?" Kuda asked the young lady.

"The Debate Team got an exit for the weekend. We're going up against St. Joseph's College next week Friday and we're supposed to get something 'presentable', according to our headmaster, to wear. Unfortunately when he says presentable he means old-fashioned, boring, and stodgy. Kind of like him."

"Chedza!" Kuda laughed, pretending to be shocked.

"Well, it's true," Chedza defended earnestly. "If he got any more old-fashioned he'd become so square we could fit him into a box with exactly the same length, width, and breath."

"Sounds like my old high-school teacher," Jake said, speaking thoughtfully, finally taking his eyes off Kuda's face. "I bet he wears the same style suit to school every day but in different colours and you could tell what day of the week it was by the suit he's wearing that day."

"That's him to a T," Chedza confirmed. "Know him?"

"No, but I see headmasters are the same throughout the world and they don't seem to change from generation to generation."

"Don't encourage the child, Doctor Dawn. She's bad enough as it is without you adding to it," Kuda scolded.

Chedza and Jake looked at each other and grinned.

"You know what they say," Chedza sing-songed.

"Yep," Jake agreed, nodding gravely. Kuda looked at them both suspiciously.

"No, I don't. What do they say?" she asked.

"Should I tell her?" Chedza asked Jake over Kuda's head.

"Be my guest," Jake said. Kuda frowned.

"Birds of a feather defend each other," Chedza informed her solemnly.

"Meaning what?" Kuda demanded.

"Meaning," Jake added, "That a square is a square is a square."

Kuda snorted rudely and tossed her head.

"I will have you two know that I am not old-fashioned and that I wore the third shortest skirt to my high-school leavers' party," she told them. "Besides, do you two know each other? From some previous life perhaps?" Chedza chuckled.

"No," she said, "but I heard my mother talking about the new doctor and you must be it."

"His name is Jake Dawn and he's a medical doctor. So if I drop dead tomorrow you know who to turn to. Dr Dawn, this is Chedza Maphorisa. She goes to school in Mater Spei College in Francistown and she's our hope for the future." Kuda introduced them and put her arm across Chedza's shoulders, giving her a quick hug.

"No pressure," she said with a smile as she looked at Jake. "Anyway, I thought you weren't from around here. Your accent's quite genuine, not like some people's, whose names we won't mention."

"We love her anyway," Kuda grinned and Jake laughed.

"Pleased to meet you, Chedza."

"Likewise, Doctor Dawn. How long are you staying?" Kuda gasped at the impudence of this question but Jake took it all in stride.

"As long as it takes."

"To do what?"

"To win a bet."

"What bet?"

"Chedza," Kuda chided softly and the girl minded her manners.

"Sorry. I guess it comes from being on the debate team –" Chedza apologised.

"From being nosy, you mean," Kuda interrupted.

"But," Chedza finished with a quick look in Kuda's direction, "I have to run. However, there's something that I need to talk to you about. Later. Is it alright if I come by tomorrow morning?"

"Of course it is, you know that."

Chedza nodded. "Yeah. Anyway, I've really got to go. It was a pleasure meeting you, doctor. Bye, Kuda." And she was off, disappearing like ice on a hot stove.

"Nice girl," Jake said and watched that pleasure light up her face again.

"Yes," she replied. Then, "Manini lives over there."

At first he could not see anything except the rippling green that was her farm. The thigh high maize was a carpet of green that rippled with the slight breeze. Then, slightly off the field, he saw three or four thatched roofs that undoubtedly belonged to huts. After walking a few more minutes he saw the whole yard and not too long after that they were at Manini's.

"*Ta pinda*," Kuda called out but there was no answer. "I guess they left without us."

Jake looked around. There were three complete mud huts and then, what seemed to him, one with a whole chunk missing from near the top. Then there were two others with half the bottoms missing. Actually, they were built on top of wooden stilts and stood about half a meter from the ground. Jake looked at them quizzically, wondering, also, at the way the "windows" had been filled up with mud.

"How come those two there are elevated and that one there doesn't have the wall all the way up to the thatch?" he asked.

"Because those two are storage huts, where Manini keeps her harvest and that third one there is a *segotlwana*, a cooking area slash kitchen, if you like. The reason why its wall doesn't go all the way up is so that the smoke has an exit while we're cooking."

"A ventilator?"

"Of sorts. See, even we backward Batswana knew about that before we were taught it in school," Kuda said.

"I didn't say anything," Jake replied.

"Sorry. Anyway, if you're observant you'll notice that even in the other huts the wall doesn't go all the way to the thatch. Except in the storage huts and that's to keep out bugs."

"How long does it take to build one of these?"

"Depends on the builders. Some take days, others take weeks."

"Who builds them? The men or the women?"

"The women."

Kuda was dying to make a crack about that question, something witty and scathing about male dominance but the whole afternoon had been something of a cease-fire and she didn't want to throw the first knife. So she bit her lip and took a deep breath.

"Let's go down to the *kraal,*" she said instead. They left the yard and took a back trail, both walking briskly, neither talking.

Jake heard the lowing of the cattle before he saw the *kraal.* He also heard shouting, barking and loud whistles mingled with the *moos* of the animals. The cacophony of sound was new to him and it was pleasing in a way he hadn't anticipated. When he finally saw the kraal he was surprised. It was made completely of *mapako* in the shape of a rough circle and attached to the large circle was a smaller circle. Inside it stood Manini Chipo, Una and an old man who he did not know.

"Why isn't that cow inside with the rest?" he asked Kuda.

"We let her do as she pleases. She won't have it any other way." At Jake's uncomprehending look, she chuckled. "It's a long story, doctor, and I'm not sure I want to go into it right now."

Jake was about to ask another question when Manini looked up and saw them.

"It's about time, you two. Jake I can forgive, Kuda should have known better. What did you think? That the cows were going to milk themselves?" she bellowed.

"Lay off the kids, Chipo. Can't you see that they're enjoying each other's company?" the old man said and Kuda rolled her eyes.

"Washington, Washington, Washington," she chided. "You still have a lot to learn about my tastes. No offence intended, doctor."

"None taken," Jake replied although Manini noticed that Jake's face tightened a notch.

"She didn't mean that the way it came out, Jake. Take no notice of her and come meet Washington. He's always more enjoyable company at this time of the day than Kuda is. I think it has something to do with the sun going down. It takes away her better half and leaves behind her dark, sinister, evil twin." Manini eyed Kuda with disapproval and Kuda wondered what she had said this time.

Ignoring the two people who now glared at her, she called to King and to add insult to injury, King ignored her and lumbered up to Jake instead.

"Of all the cheek," she muttered crossly. Washington heard her and grinned.

"Don't worry, sweetheart. You've still got me," he told her.

"Yeah, right," Kuda mumbled back and grabbing a pail from near where Manini stood, she marched over to where Una was watching the whole thing with interest. She got a leather thong that she would use to tie the cow's back legs with while she was milking it. She washed her hands with the little bit of water that was left in the pail and prepared to milk one of the cows that she usually milked. Suddenly she grinned, feeling as though the motion would split her face in two. She looked over to where the trio of Jake, Manini and Washington were chatting amicably.

"Hey, Doctor Dawn," she called. "Ever milked a cow?"

"Hey, Doctor Chilume," he yelled back. "Ever been to the moon?"

"What is all this 'doctor' talk?" Manini asked in real surprise. "Has it suddenly been declared illegal for doctors to call each other by their first names because if it has, nobody told me."

"It's difficult to call somebody by their first name unless you've been invited to do so," Jake said meaningfully.

"Then I'm granting you that permission," Manini replied neatly. "Now, to get back to Kuda's question, have you ever milked a cow?" Jake groaned. Manini grinned. "Thought you would get out of it that easily?"

"Are you going to give it a try, doctor?" Kuda asked.

"No, thanks. I think I'll give it a skip for today," Jake replied uncomfortably and Kuda chuckled.

"Very well. I'll let you off today but I don't forget easily and you'll milk one of these cows before the end of the week. Maybe I'll give you Mmantshadi."

Washington guffawed until tears ran down his weathered cheeks and his stomach hurt. Una joined him and Manini sighed sufferingly. Jake merely looked puzzled and when

Washington saw his confused look he laughed even harder, if that was possible.

“What’s the joke?” Jake asked, sounding a bit miffed.

“It’s a long story, Jake. Come walk with me while they –” she looked back with a sniff, “– laugh themselves to death. There’s so much I want to learn about you and there’s no time like the present. Shall we?”

Chapter Ten
Sparks and Fireworks

"How do you find our village?" Manini asked Jake as they headed away from the group in the *kraal.* As usual she walked with her back as straight as a bamboo shoot. Her step was sure and Jake wouldn't have believed that she was as old as Kuda had said she was if he hadn't known. He felt himself shrug as he answered her.

"It's alright. It's just a lot different from where I come from," he told her. He noticed that he had shortened his stride so that she could keep up with him. Manini nodded.

"And back home you have a woman?" she asked.

Jake should have felt irritated by her intrusion into his personal life but for whatever reason he wasn't. He didn't really know this woman but there was something about her that reassured him. He felt comfortable with her, the way he had felt with his own grandmother. Perhaps she was one of the people who had been in the village when he had been here as a boy. He must remember to ask her. For now, he had to answer the question she had posed to him.

"No. I have no woman back home. I had a woman a couple of years ago but things didn't work out between us," he said.

And that was something that had always puzzled him. Sharon and he had been so perfectly matched it was incredible. She had been an accountant and they had enjoyed all the same things in life. Their relationship had been perfect and that was why it had been an awful shock for him when she had broken it off. He had never been able to explain it and neither had she. It had been the weirdest thing. She had just said she didn't want to be with him anymore and left it at that. They had remained friends though and soon after that she had started dating someone else. The strangest thing of all was that he was sure she still had feelings for him. When he had finally swallowed his pride and asked her to come back to him she had regretfully told him that she just had this feeling that they had never been meant to be together.

He had gotten really angry then and yelled at her, accusing her of throwing a perfectly good thing away. She had broken down and confessed to him her fears then. That she was afraid. She'd explained that she'd been having some really bad dreams. Dreams of her impending death if she didn't cease her relationship with him. She had described the dreams in vivid detail and he had called it rubbish, that together they would get through it. She had been so hopeful, so willing to trust him. He had convinced her to give them a second chance. She had wanted it as badly as he had. They had even set a date for their wedding.

Less than two months before the wedding, Sharon died in a horrible accident.

He shook off his memories and listened to what Manini was saying to him.

"I think you will like it here. It is a nice little place but there are many things that will happen here that did not happen in America, Jake. You must learn to be patient, especially with Kuda."

Jake smiled slightly as he realised that Manini was giving him her approval to go after Kuda if he so desired.

"She is a difficult woman," he said to her.

"My! Whatever gave you that idea?" Manini asked with a big toothy grin. Jake guffawed his laughter. Manini chuckled and shook her head. "She is a wonderful person, Jake. She just needs a lot of patience and understanding from all of us. She has shut the world out for such a long time that it has made it difficult for her to trust anybody. Even I have had a difficult time getting her to open up to me."

"What made her that way?" Jake wanted to know.

Manini shook her head. "The time will come when you will know all the answers. It is just not now."

Jake wasn't happy with her cryptic answer but he knew he had to let it be. He sighed. It seemed as though he would have to be patient with everybody if he ever wanted to learn anything in this village. Patience wasn't his strongest trait but he had a feeling he'd need to make it so if he was going to get anywhere with anyone in Jackalas II.

He and Manini continued their walk in silence.

* * *

Kuda, Washington and Una finished the milking with no sign of Manini or Jake so they headed back to her home with the pails of milk. Mmantshadi opted to spend the night outside the kraal and who were they to persuade her otherwise? They found Jake and Manini drinking tea in the *segotlwana*.

"Who are the loafers then?" Kuda asked mildly.

"Don't be impudent, young lady," Manini said and Kuda grinned at her.

"Sorry, but I can't seem to help it. It must be something in the air, something in the fading rays of the sun," Kuda said dramatically, raising her hand to her face, tilting her head to the right and closing her eyes.

"Uh-oh," Una groaned. "She's getting all poetic and once she starts she never stops."

Kuda aimed a swat at his bottom but Una jumped deftly out of the way. He took the milk and put it away, giggling as he went.

"Manini, I have to get going. King's making those eyes at me again and I can hear his stomach rumbling from here. Doctor Dawn, are you coming?" Manini gave her a reproving look and she shrugged. "It's something I have to get used to," Kuda justified.

"Yes, I'm coming." Jake stood up and smiled at Manini. "Thank you," he said simply and Manini smiled back.

"Pop in any time, Jake. Don't wait for an invitation," Manini said to him.

"I will."

He waved goodbye and he, Kuda and King set off for home. They walked in silence for a while before Kuda's curiosity exploded from within her and she asked.

"What were you two talking about?"

Her answer was a warm chuckle from Jake. "I was wondering how long it would be before you asked. See? I even set my watch." He showed her and she scowled. "Manini warned me about your unequalled curiosity.'

"So you were talking about me?"

"Hardly."

When nothing more was forthcoming she tried again.

"Well?"

"Well what?"

"What were you talking about?"

"Nothing that would interest you."

"I asked, didn't I?"

Jake stopped and faced her. He studied her face intently then shook his face, pondering.

"My mistake. I thought your nose would be about as long as an elephant's trunk by now but I'm mistaken. Yep. It's still the same size."

Kuda swirled around and marched off in a huff, said nose stuck in the air in indignation. Jake's rich laughter followed her all the way home and rebounded in her head the way an echo would resound in a large, empty hall. Lingering long after the source of the sound had gone.

Chose found her in practically the same mood when he came over nearly three hours later. She hadn't changed and she was lying on her sofa reading a novel.

"I can't believe this," he muttered. "I waited for you and you didn't show. Why?"

"Simple. I'm not going."

"You can't not go, Kuda."

"Why not?"

"For starters, you promised. I was counting on you and you can't just let me down at the last second," Chose scowled.

Kuda looked up at him and grimaced. She had promised after all. It was only fair that she went. She got up from the chair and put her novel aside.

"You're right. I did promise.'

"Gee, you don't have to sound so enthusiastic about it," Chose said sarcastically and Kuda shook her head in disgust.

"What's the world coming to? You do a guy a favour and he doesn't appreciate it. I know why you want me at your little party tonight, Chose, and you'd better not forget that I'm doing you a favour. Anyway, I'm not Cupid. I shoot a different type of arrow."

"Barb is more like what you shoot. And that's when you're not busy shooting off your mouth."

"That does it!" Kuda glared at him as she threw herself back on the sofa. "I'm not going."

"Aw, come on, Kuda. I need you there tonight. You're the only one who can blow my horn and make it sound like music. You know that you're the only one that Susan ever really listens to and I need all the help I can get."

"The reason why Susan listens to me is because the only thing that ever comes out of your mouth is crap, Chose."

"I know," Chose replied despondently but the twinkle in his eyes refused to hide. Kuda threw her hands in the air and got up from the sofa again.

"Why do I bother?" she cried. "I'll go change."

* * *

There weren't that many people at Chose's little get-together. When Kuda and Chose arrived, there were, in fact, only six people. Thapelo and Angelica were there, including Susan who was a teacher at Jackalas II Primary School. On the other side of the room, Susan was talking to Jake and they appeared to be deeply enjoying their conversation. Susan was smiling and Jake was laughing at something she had said. Kuda frowned.

"The cavalry's here," Angelica said spitefully when Kuda came through the door.

"You should bottle your nastiness, Angelica, and sell it for five Pula an ounce. You'd be rich beyond your wildest imagination within a week," Kuda retaliated.

Angelica scowled and opened her mouth as though to reply then just as quickly shut it. She looked like a fish that had been suddenly ejected from the water by some unseen hand. Kuda smirked in a completely unladylike manner. She looked up just as Susan chuckled then whispered something in Jake's ear. Jake grinned dashingly at her and Kuda's eyes narrowed.

"You came to pick me up while your guest of honour was here?" she asked Chose incredulously. He shrugged sheepishly and gave a helpless grin. Kuda muttered something under her breath that Chose couldn't hear. He had a pretty good idea of what it was, however.

Kuda looked around. Chose's modest home had been transformed to cater for this little group gathering which Kuda found hard to call a party. The sofas had been moved back against the walls to make room for dancing and a dining table had been stacked with various types of food, including biltong, *pap* and various salads. It wouldn't be a do without braaid sausages, steak and *vors* and Kuda suspected that the meat was marinating somewhere. Pop music was blaring from a stereo and Thapelo was the acting DJ.

"Where'd you get the dining-table?" Kuda asked Chose.

"Susan lent it to me," he said nonchalantly but Kuda saw right through him and gave a big "Aaw!"

“It’s nothing like that,” Chose muttered. “She had a table which I needed and she allowed me to borrow it, that’s all.”

“Right.”

“Anyway, this is a *braai* too. The fire should be ready just about now.”

Kuda noted the not so subtle change of topic and allowed him to escape... *this time.* She wasn’t through with her ribbing yet and Chose knew it just as much as she did. After Chose had made quick his escape, she hesitated a moment before walking up to where Susan and Jake were sitting.

“Hi, Susan,” she started amicably. “I see you’ve met our new doctor.”

“Yes. Jake and I were just talking,” Susan replied. Her pretty face wore a cheerful smile and she looked as though she was enjoying Jake’s company well enough.

“Hello, Kuda,” Jake said, watching her very carefully.

“I don’t recall giving you permission to use my first name, Doctor Dawn,” she replied immediately, saccharine sweetness in her voice.

“Oh, come on, Kuda,” Susan protested. “You’re going to be working practically hand in hand with Jake. Surely you’re not going to call him Doctor Dawn all the time.”

“Try me,” Kuda said dryly and Susan frowned.

“I don’t know exactly what it is you two had a fight about but I’ll leave you to sort it out while I go help Chose. I do believe, however, that Kuda must have started it and –” she went on, ignoring Kuda's gasp, "– I expect you both to have sorted it out by the time I get back."

Susan gave Kuda a pointed look and then stood up, going outside before either of them could say anything. Kuda flopped into the space she had just vacated.

"I don't believe this," she said crossly. "Betrayed by my best friend and to top it all off, she goes and deserts me."

On the stereo Thapelo had put on a *kwasakwasa* cassette and he and Angelica were gyrating furiously in the middle of the room. Jake watched with interest.

"What music is that?" he asked, ignoring her griping. Kuda sighed and briefly educated him on the style of the music. They watched the dancers in silence, Jake because he was interested, Kuda because she wanted to untangle her confused thoughts. Being in Jake's presence made her uneasy and she couldn't figure out why. It was unnerving and it made her feel extremely irritable.

Fortunately Susan came back just then.

"Everything solved?" she asked.

"Do you want me to tell you the truth or do you want me to lie?" Kuda said. Susan shook her head and then smiled wryly.

"I should have known better. Especially where you're concerned, Kuda. You're a lost cause."

"Thanks for the vote of confidence."

"Is that what that was?" Susan asked, tongue in cheek, and Kuda chuckled. "Would you like to dance, Jake?"

Jake glanced ruefully at the dancing couple on the floor.

"I'm not sure I can," he laughed.

"Don't worry, I'll teach you."

"You talked me into it then."

Susan held out her hand and Jake took it and got up. She led him to the dance floor and started to demonstrate some of the simpler moves, moving gracefully and lightly. Kuda watched.

Susan was dark in complexion, a lot darker than Kuda, and her skin was clear of blemishes and smoother than a baby's bottom. She was really a tiny little thing but padded in all the right places. She was also the exact opposite to Kuda in almost every way. She was the thinker while Kuda tended to leap into places where angels had second thoughts about entering. She was sort of a mother figure but her tongue was quick and sharp, able to draw blood if she was crossed, which was rare. Susan was slow to anger but she tolerated nonsense about as much as dogs tolerate cats. Everybody knew this, especially her standard seven class.

And Jake? Jake was tall and beside him Susan looked extremely delicate. And well protected. Something stirred in Kuda's chest and she wasn't sure she liked it.

She stood up and went outside to Chose, who she found staring moodily into the fire. Kuda felt sorry for him.

"How's it going?" she asked softly. Chose looked up. He looked back down without saying anything. Savagely he stuck the end of the stick he was holding into the fire.

The flames flared up and the flaming red underbelly of the charcoal was revealed. For a moment it looked like the huge bloody gash of a wounded animal that refused to heal before the flames died down and the coals settled. "Come on. It can't be that bad."

"I don't understand," he said hoarsely, pain an oozing throb in his voice. "I've loved her for as long as I can remember and she's never ever given me any encouragement. Then pretty-boy over there comes and she's all over him."

"That's not fair, Chose,"

Chose sighed. "I know. I'm sorry."

Kuda moved closer to him, put her arms around him and hugged him, comforting him. He wrapped his arms around her and hugged her back. They sat like that for a moment. One giving, one receiving comfort.

"Sorry to interrupt you two but we brought out the meat. We figured the fire was ready," Susan said behind them. Chose and Kuda let each other go.

"Give it some time," Kuda whispered to Chose and gave him a quick kiss on the cheek.

She turned around and the first person her eyes collided with was Jake. For some reason he was looking at her with what seemed to be extreme disapproval. She looked back at him, not understanding his tenseness.

"I'll go call Angelica and Thapelo and we can start *braaing*," Kuda said.

“Don’t worry. I got it,” Susan said as she walked back into the house.

Jake and Chose watched her as she entered the kitchen. Then, Kuda turned towards Jake and she saw that his eyes were narrowed and he still looked angry. Shrugging, she turned back to Chose. Susan came back with the others in tow and Thapelo headed to the *braai* stand. Putting the meat on the grill, the others continued to dance as they chatted about this and that.

When the food was finally ready, Susan dished out for everyone and handed them their plates. Jake sat next to Susan, Kuda next to Chose and Thapelo next to Angelica. The food was delicious and they all enjoyed the grilled meat, corn on the cob, pap and other delectable foods. Angelica brought everyone a round of drinks and they all sat around the dying fire and passed time.

During a lull in the conversation, Angelica asked Jake a question. “Is this what you thought you would find when you got here?”

“Not at all,” Jake said with a little chuckle. “It’s different but a good kind of different. And I’ve loved meeting you all.” He cast a look in Kuda’s direction. Kuda pointedly looked away. Chose shook his head and Kuda wrinkled her nose at him.

“You must have heard a whole lot of stories about Africa though. You know? ‘Where the ‘savages are’ kinda stories,” Kuda said.

“There are stories like that everywhere, Kuda,” Susan chided. “And we do have stories. Boy, do we ever!”

"Like what?" Jake asked.

"Well, there was the lady who turned herself into a monkey while she was hitchhiking," Thapelo said.

"And the lady who used a sewing needle to transport her boyfriend from Maun to Gaborone while he slept. It's alleged he went mad but who knows for sure?" Angelica chuckled.

"Or the large snake that lives in a field. You can go in and eat what you want but you can't take anything out of that field because of the snake. You never see it but you see its trail. And it's huge," Susan told them.

Jake listened with wide eyes, wondering if he should believe them.

"There are darker stories, however. Of people who could change themselves into wild animals." This was from Chose. "Of evil men and women who dappled in the dark arts and wove a web of magic so mysteriously sinister that they crossed the bridge between being human and being beasts."

"Like werewolves?" Jake asked, intrigued.

"Worse than werewolves," Chose told him. "Much worse."

"More beer anybody?" Kuda asked as she stood up suddenly.

Her question was greeted by a round of laughter, as though the atmosphere had gotten too serious for a moment and needed to be diffused.

"Hansa for me, thanks," Chose said.

"Drink, Susan?" she asked her friend.

"Coke, please."

"Doctor?"

"I'll come with you and see what you've got," Jake said.

"Why? Don't you trust our African brews?" Kuda's attempt at humour fell flat as Jake failed to respond appropriately.

"You said it, not me," he told her.

"Fine."

The two went back into the house, leaving an uncomfortable silence between Chose and Susan. Kuda looked back uneasily and saw Susan's face. Susan looked sad and unhappy about something and Kuda was actually turning back to go ask her about it when she caught Jake's eye. She looked away quickly, unsettled and a little startled by the anger in them. Now what had she done?

Chapter Eleven
Misunderstood Again

Jake and Kuda entered the house, the sound of the music so much louder than it had been from the outside. The beat throbbed through the entire building and thumped a tattoo that had Kuda's heart seeming to pound along with the sound. The walls of the house seemed to vibrate to the music and Kuda decided she would probably have a headache by the time the session was over.

"Guys," Susan called to them. "*Braai's* ready."

They nodded their acknowledgement and Kuda and Jake walked into the kitchen.

Immediately they were inside Kuda felt intimidated by Jake's size. The kitchen was practically stunted by his bulk and she began to feel claustrophobic. Not to mention that she seemed to be dwarfed by said bulk, wanting to hug his torso for some odd reason. Some *really* odd and alien and unwanted reason.

"Beer's in the fridge," she said but when Jake made no move to go towards it she turned to face him. The spark of anger was still flaming in his eyes and even though she wondered what that was all about, she was not going to ask. That had been the plan, anyway, but her being her, she put it out there.

"Are you going to tell me what I did wrong or do I get to play twenty-questions with you?" Kuda asked Jake. She took a can of Fanta from the fridge, closed the door and pulled the tab, raising it to her lips for a sip.

"Do you seriously get a kick out of hurting people you call your friends?" Jake began in disgust. "Can't you see they're in enough pain?"

Kuda was stunned. The hand lifting the can to her lips stopped mid-air and she stared at him over the top of the can. She felt her jaw working for a moment, trying to help her say something. Nothing came out until she took a deep breath and started afresh.

"Could you please explain that to me because I honestly don't have a clue as to what you're talking about," she said calmly, the can still in the air.

"Try another one, Doctor Chilume. You're so shallow I can see right through you. The sad thing is that you're only going to end up hurting two very nice people."

Kuda stared at Jake for a moment before she slammed the can on top of the counter, opened the fridge again and started pulling out drinks in silence. She slammed each one on the counter as she took it out, afraid that if he said another thing she would throw a cold beer at him.

"Aren't you going to say something?" Jake demanded.

"Say what? You've already decided you're my judge and jury and you've convicted and found me guilty of something I know nothing about. So how could I possibly have something to say?"

She slammed the fridge door shut and put the canned drinks, one by one, on a tray, keeping her back to Jake.

"I've seen how you twist Chose around your little finger and he does whatever you want because he's in love with you."

Kuda laughed incredulously then turned to glare at Jake. Her hands were balled at her side, a new side-effect of being around Jake, and she gritted her teeth in vexation. She felt her eyes narrow and tried to keep her breathing even. So much for having wanted to put her arms around his waist earlier. Now she wanted to put her hands around his neck; and squeeze.

"Chose is not in love with me, you idiot." She was about to tell him Chose was in love with someone else but Jake broke in.

"And poor Susan. She was miserable every time she saw you and Chose together and to top it all off we found you necking in the back and it's so obvious you don't love him the way he loves you."

Kuda was shocked but Jake went on, disregarding her state. She was appalled that Jake would imagine that she was using Chose and that she would do so at the cost of hurting Susan. Yes, she and Chose were close, but he was like a brother to her. Susan too was like a sister. Perhaps the reason she had never seen that the two of them were into each other was because they were like the Three Musketeers. Always together and always having fun. She had sworn never to interfere with either of their love lives and she may have overlooked Susan's feelings for Chose but she would never intentionally hurt her friends. Jake needed to understand that.

"Susan was upset but you went on ahead and twisted yourself all over Chose like bubble-gum on a hot plate. As for Chose, if he's too blind to see that a woman like Susan is crazy about him, perhaps he doesn't deserve her."

"Jake Dawn, you're a pig-headed, egotistical, jackass who doesn't know what the hell he's talking about," she yelled at him, small hands fisted at her sides. So much for her trying to get to a point where she could explain the real situation to Doctor Stupid.

"Do you love Chose?" he asked suddenly.

"No. Yes. Not in the way you think!" she spluttered.

"See? You're nothing but a manipulative –"

The slap, when it came, had a lot of power behind it, power lent by the injustice of the accusations that were cast at her. It was quick and landed squarely on Jake's cheek. With the speed of a striking viper Jake caught Kuda's hand in his and glared down at her. A muscle worked in his jaw and on seeing just how furious he was Kuda's own anger dissolved and was replaced by sheer terror.

When he saw it, Jake let her go and she stumbled back blindly and crashed into the wall behind her. She covered her face with her hands and stifled a sob which locked in her throat and made it hurt.

"For goodness' sake, Kuda. What did you think I was going to do to you?" He took a step towards her and she shrank away, holding her hands out in a warding off gesture. Her eyes were open so wide it looked as though the balls would pop out of their sockets and her face was haggard.

"Stay away from me," she cried out hoarsely and Jake stopped. A pulse jumped rapidly up and down in his throat and his teeth clenched. He saw her fear and couldn't understand it. Why was she suddenly afraid of him?

He spun around and marched out of the kitchen, his back stiff in barely controlled anger, his movements cardboard-like. God, he missed being around normal, sane women.

Kuda slid down the wall, her hands back at her face and her eyes closed. Her breath rattled in her throat, coming out as a harsh painful gasp, hurting her. She whimpered. A hurting, desolate sound. What the hell was going on with her lately? She was normally such a reasonable, even-tempered and rational person. She had never, ever, slapped anyone before in her life and she was appalled at her behaviour. Granted Jake had deserved it but she should not have placed her hand on him in anger. Her palm stung like the time she had been caned on the hand in high-school and she could only imagine how Jake's cheek felt.

But something else was beating at the back of her mind like a person buried alive in a sealed casket, wanting to come out, screaming, with no one around to hear them. Memories of something horrific had come to the front when Jake had caught her hand, but they would not fully emerge into her conscious mind, like something has sealed them deep with her. She struggled to remember, drawing nothing, but the feeling would not go away.

Hands landed on her shoulders and she screamed.

"Kuda!" It was Susan's voice. She sounded scared and Kuda opened her eyes and stared at her. "What's wrong?" Susan asked.

Kuda couldn't say anything for a while and Susan looked at her, face full of concern. Her beautiful features were creased in concern and she looked genuinely worried as she knelt next to where Kuda sat.

"Stomach cramps," she lied. "Bad."

"I'll go get Jake."

"No!" Kuda cried a bit wildly and Susan was startled. "No," she repeated a little more calmly. "I've got some medication at home. I'll be fine." She attempted a smile which came out all wrong and actually scared Susan even more, rather than consoled her.

"Still, I'd rather Jake walked you home."

"I feel better now. The cramps are going and I'm sure I can make it home alone. Don't worry about me, Susan, I'll be fine." She got up slowly from the floor and took a deep breath. Susan stood up as well, holding Kuda's elbow to make sure she was stable on her feet.

"Do me a favour, alright?" Kuda said to her.

"Sure."

"Could you take the drinks outside and tell the guys I wasn't feeling too well and had to go home," she asked her friend.

"Wouldn't you rather somebody take you home?" Susan was still worried. "If not Jake, then maybe Chose?"

Realisation fully hit Kuda then, when she saw the shuttered look in Susan's eyes when she mentioned Chose walking her home. She took a deep breath, cursing herself deeply for being such a fool, for not seeing it sooner. Now was not the time to say anything, however.

"I'll be fine," she said instead and twisted her lips into some semblance of a smile to try and be reassuring. Susan didn't look convinced and her frown deepened but she nodded anyway.

"Okay. I'll see you tomorrow then."

"Thanks, Susan." Kuda gave her friend an impulsive hug before turning and heading out the back door.

Susan looked after her, still concerned about her. She would ask Jake to pop in on her on his way home just to see how she was doing, despite her protestations.

Chapter Twelve
Midnight Terror

She was standing alone in the darkness. Above her, the sky was a dark blanket covered with fireflies. The moon was a blazing ball, like a white ball that had been set on fire, offering enough light to allow her to see her surroundings. She stood in a barren landscape, where nothing grew around her. Her eyes had adjusted to the darkness and she could see that she stood in nothingness. There was complete silence around her which lasted for only a moment as, in the distance, she heard it.

It started off as a faint growling sound, like a tractor engine that was miles away. As she stood frozen to the spot, the sound came closer and closer, growing in intensity. Panicking, she looked around for a place to hide. There was nothing. That she could use for shelter. The vast emptiness didn't offer a single place of refuge. Still, that didn't mean she had to stay there and wait for whatever it was that was coming, for indeed, there was something heading in her direction. And it sounded hungry.

Turning, she started to run but stopped almost as soon as she had started. She couldn't tell from where the sound was coming. What if she ran towards it instead of away from it? She stood there for another long moment, her heart beating rapidly inside her chest, her breathing laboured. Whirling around, she glanced futilely in all directions, desperately looking for a place to hide. Not finding anything, she stood still. Listening.

Then. She saw it.

A lone figure walking towards her across the dark sand. Except, walking wasn't exactly the right word for it. Loping was a better description for the way that this being approached her. She couldn't make out if it was masculine or feminine but from its height, she assumed it was male. A dark, tattered cloak-like cloth flowed behind him and the same cloth like material covered his head. She could not see anything more of this figure except the dark shape of it as it continued to move towards her. As it approached, she realised the sound was coming from the approaching being.

The sound stopped and a deep chuckle resounded. The chuckle was more terrifying than the growl. She took a step back and prepared to run.

"Kuda."

Her name as it reached her ears was carried on a breeze that made it sound low and rough. She cocked her head as she heard it. The resonance of it was wrong. Like the sound was being forced through a channel that it had no business going through. She strained her eyes as she tried to get a better view of the approaching creature, for she was sure now that it was not human. She took another step back though, not taking her eyes off of it.

She blinked and when she opened her eyes, in that split microsecond, the creature was gone.

"Kuda."

The name came from behind her now and she swirled around, almost falling in the process. It stood behind her, the hood covering its head. Slowly, it raised its face and looked at her. She wanted to scream but she couldn't. Her voice died in her throat.

She stared, horrified. She couldn't believe what she saw. It was impossible. Yet there it stood nonetheless.

This creature that stood before her was tall, close to a couple of meters tall. Its arms were long and the claws, for they were not fingers, fell way below its knees. Beneath the torn cape, the body appeared to be grotesquely deformed, with what appeared to be a hump on its back. Despite the hump though, there was an aura of such power that surrounded this creature, as though it could tear her apart in an instant if it so desired. There was a breadth around its shoulders that spoke of immense strength and its arms looked like they could tear a buffalo limb from limb.

"What do you want from me?" Kuda asked. Her voice was little more than a whisper in the void. She took another step back.

There was a one word response to her question: "Life."

* * *

Jake cursed himself and called himself all types of a fool for giving in to Susan and promising her he would look in on Kuda on his way home. The time was quarter after midnight and he was so tired he just wanted to go home and sleep.

However, a promise was a promise and he would carry out his promise to Susan.

When he got to Kuda's gate he stopped. He was about to open it and go in when a huge shadow detached itself from the side of the house. For a second he swore his heart froze in his chest before it cranked up again into its regular beat.

King.

Now Jake wasn't a coward by any standards but King was enough to make any man bow out gracefully before he went into Kuda's house uninvited. He stood still and called out softly to the huge canine. King came over to the gate and sniffed at Jake's feet and legs through the wire. Then he sat down as though to say, "Come on in, bud. What are you waiting for?"

Jake did and gave King a quick pat on the head before walking up to the house. The living-room light was on but when he knocked nobody answered. Maybe she had fallen asleep on the sofa. But, if she was really ill, as Susan had said, she might have collapsed or something. He frowned.

"Kuda?" he called. He knocked again, louder this time. It did occur to him that if she was just sleeping she would be plenty mad to see him at this late hour. Especially after all the things he had said to her earlier that night.

A moan came from inside the house and his frown deepened. It came again, this time followed by a loud sob. Jake knocked again but when Kuda started to scream in earnest he threw his shoulder against the door and heard the lock shatter. He rushed into the room where the screams were coming from, afraid of what he would find. He noted that King came in after him, right at his heels.

He didn't know whether to be relieved or amused when he saw, by the light that came from the living-room, that she was having one monster of a nightmare. Her sheets were wrapped around her slender legs and her T-shirt was soaking wet. She writhed about on the bed, her hands flailing in the same warding off gesture that she had used on him at Chose's place.

After a second of watching her, he put out his hand to shake her awake.

* * *

Kuda awoke with a start, the strong hands of Doctor Jake Dawn grasping her shoulders where she lay on the bed. She sat up quickly before standing up, and pushed him off of her in a panic, as she usually slept in the nude, however, as she quickly looked down, she realized that she was still fully clothed from the party. When she had resolved that problem, she moved on to concentrate on the much larger issue at hand.

"What do you think you're doing here?" Her voice was hard and her eyes were a powerful glare, trying to intimidate the doctor.

King whimpered and came up to her, licking her hand as though to comfort her. She laid her hand on his head, seeking comfort as well as giving it.

"I came to check on you," Jake responded, not really shocked that she wasn't happy to see him. "I decided to honour my promise to Susan, despite my reluctance to do so." Kuda frowned even harder, if possible, remembering specifically telling Susan that she didn't want her to tell Jake anything. Her frown softened when she realized that all Susan was trying to be was a good friend and look out for her.

"And who gave you permission to enter my home in the middle of the night? I don't know what it's like in America, but you cannot just enter other people's homes. It's called breaking and entering in Botswana, and you can go to jail for that." A muscle worked in Doctor Dawn's neck, and Kuda could see the power with which he was clenching his jaw. His hands were balled tightly by his side, and his entire demeanour was tense.

"I heard screaming," Jake told her.

Kuda was genuinely confused, her eyes downcast and narrowed, trying to figure out what he was talking about. She looked down at King who was gazing up at her. He whimpered and licked her hand again. For a moment, she felt slightly dizzy, her head swimming alarmingly. Her hand slid off King's head and her body swayed. She wasn't sure how he got to her so quickly but her body failed her and she crashed into Jake's chest. His strong arms immediately cocooned her, holding her up so that she didn't fall. She felt safe where she was, the sound of his rushed heartbeat arousing something in her chest. That unnerved her, however.

"Get your hands off of me," she said this as she slapped his hands away and sat back on the edge of her bed. She hugged King close to her chest and wrapped her arms around his neck. Jake immediately took a step back.

"I'm fine, and I don't need you babysitting me. Now, I don't know what kind of stories you're trying to come up with, but I was not, under any circumstance, screaming." Jake was now visibly pulsating with an anger that he was so desperately trying to reign in. He had walked all the way to her house to see if she was alright, and that was how she repaid him?

"You must have been having a nightmare," he forced out through gritted teeth.

"I wasn't --"

"Listen, Doctor Chilume, you were asleep, and I know what I heard! What do you want me to say? I'm sorry that I was worried about you? I'm sorry that I wanted to check up on you? I'm sorry that I hauled my sorry ass all the way here to apologize?"

"What?" she asked, everything suddenly clear. Her daze was gone, and she was really interested in hearing about this apology that Doctor Dawn was talking about. He sighed and sat next to her on the bed. He buried his hands in his head, rubbing his temples like he was trying to rub away a Kuda-induced migraine. He laughed to himself, thinking about the challenge that he had accepted from the moment that he had seen her. Six months seemed like a lifetime away right then.

"I talked to Chose after the party and he told me everything." He clasped his hands between his legs and stared at them, not wanting to look Kuda in the eye. After a long silence and no scathing remarks, he deemed it safe to look back at her, only to realize that she was already watching him. Her beautiful brown eyes studied him intently, not judging, as was the norm, but genuinely interested in what he had to say.

"You may proceed," she encouraged, obviously not having gotten what she wanted. Sighing, he stood up, shoving his hands in his pockets and stood adjacent to her. That way he wouldn't have to face her, but he wasn't looking completely away from her either.

"I'm sorry for being 'a pig-headed, egotistical, jackass who doesn't know what the hell he's talking about'." Kuda's lips curved ever so slightly at the corners, but it wasn't enough to be considered a smile. When she still remained silent, Jake continued. "I was in the wrong, and it wasn't my place to assume. I should have just stayed in my waters instead of wading in too deep."

"Damn straight," Kuda told him as she stood up quickly and hurriedly walked to the confused looking Jake Dawn. King followed close behind her as though he were her own personal cheerleader.

"Are you going to –?"

"It was nice of you to drop by, Doctor Dawn, but it's late-" she glanced at her bedside clock, "- and you must be going. And I'm sorry I slapped you."

She shooed the doctor out of her house, despite his abundant protests, King following close behind him. It was only after he was outside that she realised with shock that he had broken her lock. She looked around quickly for something that she could use to ensure that the door stayed close. Once the door was firmly shut and barricaded with a chair, she rested against it, listening to Jake cursing her not so quietly. Eventually, when she believed that he was no longer on her doorstep, she made her way back to her bedroom and crawled into bed, clothes and all.

She was so tired. So very tired. It wasn't a physical fatigue though; it was a weariness that seemed to seep into her very soul. As she lay looking at the ceiling, however, her eyes refused to drift shut the way she had hoped they would. After another hour of lying in the dark with no chance of her drifting off, she got up and went to her painting room.

* * *

On Sunday morning, Kuda was up early. She had barely slept and decided to go out for her morning jog extra early that day with King, enjoying the exhilarating feeling of her burning lungs as she sped through the tiny village. As she made her way out and across her yard, she realized that Jake too was up. He was sitting on his veranda, sipping what Kuda assumed was coffee. King galloped over to his yard and stared at Jake, his tongue hanging out and a goofy look on his face as though to ask him why he wasn't joining them,

Jake didn't wave to her or acknowledge her in any way, but she knew that she was being watched. She knew she looked good in shorts and hoped, stupidly, that he was admiring her legs. And enjoying the sight.

Whistling to call King over and away from the offender, she continued to jog with him by her side. As she inched closer and closer to the dam that provided miraculous morning scenery along with all of their water, she started to increase her speed, pushing herself to the limit until she felt as if she were going to fall apart. She sprinted harder, boosting with all her might, and then she started to slow down as she advanced to the water's edge. She bent over and put her hands on her knees, taking deep, cleansing breaths. The oxygen didn't seem to be enough as she tried her best to offer relief to her aching and burning lungs. Her legs and arms were sore, cramping, due to the effort that she had exerted on her body. Once she could properly breathe again, she grinned and cheered.

That was the fastest time that she had ever ran that distance. Or was it? She frowned. She may have run it faster but for the life of her she couldn't remember and she was not normally one to forget. The frown disappeared as she caught sight of her pooch.

Seeing that King was already working his way back, and believing that she was fully recovered, she jogged carefully, and in a controlled manner, back to her house. As she padded by her new neighbour's house, she didn't fail to notice that he was gone. Something fell in her chest and her eyes actively sought him out. She didn't see him anywhere and she scowled. She didn't like the idea of having any sort of feeling towards him. Resentment or otherwise. She padded into her house and immediately guzzled down a bottle of water like a dehydrated baby hippo in the middle of a drought. The cold water dripped down her chin and trailed down her neck, offering some feeling of coolness to her hot body. Her hand swiped across her chin, catching the droplet of water, and she walked back to her bedroom to take a shower.

After her shower, however, sudden lethargy weighed down her limbs and she sat down on the edge of her bed with her towel wrapped around her. Sighing, she decided to close her eyes for just a moment. Just a short, short moment.

Chapter Thirteen
Unexpectedness

Kuda jerked awake when there was a loud pounding at her door. She got groggily to her feet, stumbled to her closet and pulled on a pair of shorts. She grabbed the closest T-shirt she could find, which happened to be wrinkled, but clean, pulled it on and headed slowly to the door.

"Who is it?" she asked around a big yawn.

"It's me."

Kuda immediately moved the chair she had used to barricade the damaged door and opened it. She let Chedza in.

"*Dumilani*!" Chedza greeted.

"*Dumilani, wa muka*?" Kuda responded, asking how she was.

"*Nda muka*," Chedza finished, stating that she was alright. "What happened to the door?" she asked.

"It's a long story," Kuda mumbled and then yawned until her jaw cracked.

"Are you awake enough to give me some advice?" Chedza asked her.

"Hardly. My mouth feels as though something crawled into it and died. I can barely get my eyes open and I'm still not sure if you're really here or if I'm still asleep."

"Way too much detail," Chedza said with a little smile. Kuda chuckled.

"I need to go brush up. I think I feel something moving in there," she said.

"As I walk out!" Chedza said as she headed to the kitchen. "I'll go get King something to eat as you take care of whatever –" she waved her hand at Kuda as she entered the kitchen "– that is."

"Thanks, baby. You're a lifesaver," Kuda laughed as she yawned again.

She stumbled back to her bedroom with eyes that felt as though all the sand in the Sahara Desert had been dumped into them. She went to the bathroom and washed her face with hands full of cold water, hoping it would wake her up. When she was done she brushed her teeth while she tried valiantly to get her eyes open. Nearly ten minutes later she was done freshening up and had donned an ironed shirt with her shorts. She wore sandals on her feet and her hair was combed. She felt almost human and a small smile played on her lips.

"Chedza," she called out. "When are you going back to –" She stopped abruptly.

"Good morning. I came to see how you were."

Kuda was uncertain, not sure whether to go forward or backward so she stayed where she was. In the hard light of day she realised just how surreal last night had been. She had kicked him out after he had tried to be neighbourly and it hadn't been the nicest thing in the world. Granted she was still annoyed at him but one had to forgive, right?

"Dr Dawn just got here," Chedza told Kuda unnecessarily. "He says you weren't feeling well last night so he came by to see if you were feeling better."

"I'm fine," she said shortly.

Jake nodded slowly, not sure he believed her. There were dark circles under her eyes and she looked exhausted. Her mouth, while never really ready to smile when he was around, was more downturned than usual.

"You know where to find me if you need anything," Jake said to her, looking at her very closely. It was because he was watching her so intently that he saw her lips curl into a thin smile. That smile said it all: When hell freezes over, Doctor Dawn. When hell freezes over.

Jake turned away from her, a similar smile playing on his own lips. He turned to Chedza and his smile became more natural.

"Have a safe trip back to school and I hope to see you the next time you come," he said to her.

Chedza smiled back at him. "Ditto, Doctor Dawn."

Jake looked at Kuda again. "I'll come by later to fix your door," he told her.

"Don't bother," Kuda replied through her gritted teeth.

"It's no bother," Jake said sweetly and Kuda's eyes narrowed to thin slits. "See you later." Before Kuda could say anything else, Jake had left.

"What was that all about?" Chedza asked, her voice bloated with curiosity.

"You're not old enough to know," Kuda told her. "Now," she continued, rubbing her hands together. "You have my undivided attention. What's up?"

Chedza didn't say anything for a while. When she finally spoke her voice was low.

"Do you remember that advice I needed from you?" Kuda nodded. "Well, here I am."

"Well, you have until the cows come home."

"The actual cows or the metaphorical cows?" Kuda laughed at Chedza's remark.

"The actual cows, since Manini is expecting me. What is it that you need?" Chedza grinned at Kuda, looking slightly nervous. That was new to her, as she was always headstrong and confident; two unstated requirements of being on the debate team.

"There's someone that I think I like at school." Kuda sat down next to her with excited eyes, encouraging Chedza to keep on going. "But I don't know what to do, Kuda! I feel so bad!"

"Why? What did you do?" Chedza covered her face in embarrassment as she spoke into her hands.

"He's a new student at Mater Spei College, so they asked me, since I'm a prefect, to show him around and help him get settled in. This was three weeks ago, mind you. I helped him meet people and we were becoming good friends, but guess what happened?"

"What!?" Kuda asked, nearly bursting with curiosity.

"He assumed my position as a Prefect! I got demoted to Class Monitor!" Kuda gasped.

"What did you do? You've been a prefect for three years and they just demoted you? How unfair!"

"I know! I was upset so when I saw him next –" Chedza trailed off, her embarrassed look returning once again.

"Don't just stop," Kuda pushed. "What happened?"

"I told him that no one would respect him because he looked like an oversized rodent on steroids." Kuda burst out laughing, not seeing the same gravity that Chedza saw in the situation. The poor girl was mortified, and she felt as though her psychologist was laughing in her face.

"Did you honestly and truly say that?" Chedza nodded, her face bright with embarrassment.

"Kuda, please don't laugh at me! Once I had seen his face, I was completely and utterly devastated! I felt so bad for him, and for myself, because I knew that I had ruined any chances that I might have had." Kuda calmed down enough to let Chedza continue her story, even though she was still laughing on the inside.

"You can go on, Chedza. I promise I won't laugh." Good humour was still very evident on her face, but she swallowed it down, wanting to help the girl in any way that she could.

"Now, all we do is bicker back and forth. As weird as it sounds, I look forward to those moments because it means that I have the opportunity to talk to him, but I wished it would go back to the way it once was. I wish that we could just be friends again. Sometimes we have those moments, but then it all goes sour and we're back to the start again." Kuda thought for a moment, thinking about what she would do were she in the same situation. She would be mad that he got her position, but then again, it wasn't the poor guy's fault. She sighed, leaning back in her chair and crossing her legs.

"How often do these moments happen? The one's where you're not at each other's throats."

"Not very often, but it feels nice to not have a go at each other."

"Well, I would say that you both have to swallow your pride and admit that you like each other."

"What?" Chedza's pure skin darkened as she observed Kuda's calm persona. "He does not like me!"

"Oh come on, Chedza. He would not entertain you if he didn't. If he wasn't even remotely interested in you, he would've tossed you aside like an old nappy ages ago! He obviously is somewhat interested." Chedza was about to protest when Kuda cut in. "Now, listen to me, and listen very carefully. Next time you have a ceasefire, just go along with it. If you like talking to him genuinely, why does it have to stop? Talk to him as you would, and that might become a regular affair! Who knows where it might lead?"

Chedza mulled over what was said, playing with the idea in her mind. A smile graced her lips as she leaned in to hug Kuda, her saviour. She pulled back, a much bigger grin on her face.

"So, are you going to follow your own advice, then?" Kuda looked genuinely confused, and Chedza chuckled. "I'm talking about your situation with Dr Jake Dawn." Kuda rolled her eyes heavenward, an irritated sigh leaving her chest.

"Dr Dawn can crawl into a hole and die for all I care."

"Okay, Kuda. Whatever you say, Kuda." Chedza stood to leave, but Kuda narrowed her eyes at her.

"What is that supposed to mean?" Chedza shrugged, an impish grin on her face, and walked out the door, leaving a frustrated Kuda on the couch to think about what was said.

* * *

When Kuda came back from getting something from the local grocer an hour later, she found her door ajar and heard the whirr of a power tool coming from inside her house. She knew immediately who it was and cursed the man beneath her breath for his stubbornness.

"I thought I told you to leave the door alone," she began even before she stepped into the house.

"And I told you I would come back to fix it," he told her smoothly as he turned off the drill. "You didn't think I would do as you asked, did you?" he grinned.

"Obviously I gave you the benefit of the doubt, Jake, but I see it was a waste of mind power on my part. You must be related to the mule."

"Finally," Jake said with a little chuckle. Kuda frowned and wondered what he was talking about.

"Finally what?" she asked, confused.

"You used my first name. I was beginning to think it would be a cold day in hell before you called me by my given name but I see I was wrong."

"I'm sure you don't want to know what I think of that, *Jake,* so finish what you're doing and get out of my house. In the meantime, I'm going to give my dog some water. Maybe I'll sic him on you while I'm at it." She gave him one last glare before she stormed out of the house. When she heard Jake chuckle behind her, however, her brow furrowed in confusion.

"Men," she muttered loud enough for Jake to hear. "Nature's greatest mistake."

She went round to the back of the house and picked up King's water bowl where it lay like an abandoned cap. King lay in the shade of the house and seemed disinclined to move. His pink tongue lolled out of his mouth and his eyes were half closed. She filled his bowl with water from her outside tap and then went to put it down next to where the big animal lay.

"You're a wise one," she said softly as she squatted next to him and scratched him behind the ears. "I'm the crazy one walking around in this heat and Jake goes beyond all madness. And now, to top it all off, he's driving me up the wall. Why can't males ever listen to anything normal people ever say? Is it something they are taught in primary school? When we went to sewing classes were they pulled aside and taught that particular trait that all men seem to master so well?"

"I don't know if King will answer you," Jake said from behind her. Kuda spun around quickly, her hand fluttering to her stomach. "He looks too hot and bothered to me."

"Jake Dawn! You startled me." She glared at him and wanted to blame the rapid beating of her heart on his scaring her but she wasn't sure that was the whole truth. Maybe it had more to do with the way his lips curled when he wanted to annoy her; or how his eyes crinkled at the corners when he was watching her and he didn't think she was aware that he was looking at her. Or how his hands felt when they touched hers. Whatever it was, she wasn't going to think about it now.

She stood up and faced him. He was leaning against the side of her house with the top three buttons of his shirt undone, exposing the hard muscular chest she had seen before. There were beads of sweat there and Kuda unexpectedly wondered what it would feel like if she brushed her palms over his moist skin. It would be warm. And smooth. And tantalising.

"You don't look startled," Jake said, jerking her out of her wanton thoughts. She looked up at his face and the lazy appraisal she found in his hooded eyes flustered her even more.

"What do you mean by that?" she asked, tossing her head to show she was unaffected by him, and hoping to get rid of the foolish ideas that kept popping into it. Like how it would feel to rub her fingers on the five o'clock shadow that darkened his cheeks. Or to press her lips to his. She blinked owlishly then put her hand to her temple, rubbing gently in an effort to wipe out the silly thoughts.

"Are you alright?" Jake asked with a frown, disregarding her own question.

"I'm fine. I just didn't get enough sleep last night."

"Why don't you go lie down for a while?" Jake suggested.

"I've got things to do," she said curtly. Actually, she had been about to go take a nap, but since Jake had suggested it, she would rather keel over than go do it now. Talk about cutting your nose to spite your face.

"What things?"

Jake said this gravely, but there was a twinkle in his eye that put the sun to shame. Kuda did some more glaring in his direction.

"I'll think of something," she said through gritted teeth and a completely forced smile.

"Ah," was all Jake said as he pushed himself away from the wall and went to stand directly in front of her. Kuda immediately felt like too much maleness had invaded her personal space but refused to take a step back. She refused to acknowledge that the threat was more to her hormones than to her physical being. She blinked furiously for a second and then frowned hard up at Jake.

"I think," he began softly, "that you were going to take a nap. But because I suggested it, you wouldn't close your eyes if your life depended on it. Am I right?"

"Oh, please," she said with a sniff. Jake grinned and moved closer to her.

"I'm beginning to know you pretty well, Kuda. More than you would like to admit."

"Get real."

Jake reached out and outlined the rim of her left ear with his right hand, making the gesture oddly intimate. Kuda shivered involuntarily. Not because she was afraid, but because of something warmer. Much warmer. For a moment she could not say a thing. Jake took advantage of this and leaned in towards her, his eyes locked with hers, his lips moving closer.

Kuda could not move. She could not blink, could not seem to breathe. She lowered her eyes a fraction and all she could see were Jake's lips. They touched hers and it was like coming home. It was just the touching of two pairs of lips, nothing to make the earth move. However, Kuda's universe tilted and she felt decidedly light headed. Jake drew back and looked at her with a funny expression on his face.

"Doesn't it scare you?" he asked.

It did. Much more than she would ever admit to him but it scared her for all the wrong reasons and then some. Once again, however, she would rather die than admit it.

"Why would you scare me?" she scoffed. "Nothing you do scares me."

"Really?" Jake asked softly, dangerously.

"Yeah, really," Kuda replied and prepared to march past him.

She never really figured out what happened next. One second she felt Jake's hand on her arm and the next he had his arms around her. Immediately after that, Jake's lips were back on hers but this time his kiss was long and hard and real.

Kuda automatically raised her hands to his shoulders as he tipped her slightly so that she was pressed against his chest, their lips fastened. She felt her heart jump immediately into overdrive and her mind seemed to lose touch with reality. However, these feelings were mild compared to what she felt at Jake's kiss. She felt warm, wonderful, ecstatic. She wished he would kiss her forever. She wished he would stop. Then, when she wasn't sure what she wanted anymore, he raised his head. Kuda looked up at him, her eyes slightly unfocused. Her lips were parted slightly and her breathing was loud and uneven.

"You should be scared, Kuda. Very scared."

The feeling of euphoria dissipated like a bad smell in a hurricane and she stood still, watching him. Her eyes narrowed and the anger in them made them seem like a storm was brewing within them. She pushed away from him and almost fell over for her efforts. She tried to compose herself but it was difficult and the attempt made her shake.

Jake watched her battle through all of this without moving a muscle.

"You've made your point, Doctor Dawn. Now get the hell out of my yard."

She was furious and doing a very bad job of hiding it. Her eyes flashed and her lips trembled ever so slightly. With her hands balled into small fists at her side, Jake didn't put it past her to sucker punch him if he made a wrong move.

He tipped an imaginary hat at her and gave her a mocking grin.

"Gladly," he drawled before he strolled away from her. Whistling, he disappeared around the corner of the house.

Kuda stared at his departing back and wished her eyes could shoot tiny daggers at him but almost immediately her fury gave way to confusion. She stayed where she was for a moment, her face wearing a frown. What the deuce was going on with Jake? First he was yelling at her and practically calling her a tease, and the next moment he was kissing her like his lips couldn't stay away from hers. He must have had too much sun. What other explanation was there?

Turning, she slowly walked around to the front of the house.

Chapter Fourteen
Crossed Signals

Jake couldn't stop grinning. He had finally gotten the best of the high and mighty Doctor Kuda Chilume. He had gotten her so confused she hadn't known which way was up and whether she was coming or going. He liked that. He liked that a lot. He swung his tool belt in his hand and whistled a jaunty tune as he walked home. Life wasn't bad at that particular moment.

Ahead, someone was walking towards him. The guy did not look like any one of the villagers that he had met. The man came directly towards Jake but as he approached, no worm of recognition moved in Jake's mind. He couldn't place him at all. The man's hands were held stiffly at his side and he wore a scowl on his face. Jake felt a twinge of unease wriggle down his back and he frowned, wondering what could be so disquieting about the approaching figure. When the man came nearer, Jake knew that it was because of the look in his eyes. Jealousy. Pure insanity.

"Stay away from her," Timile hissed like a cornered cat. "Just stay away from her or I will kill you. She's mine. Mine!"

"I don't know what you are talking about," Jake said. He didn't recognise the man at all and wondered why he had so much animosity towards him. He was disquieted by his unusual behaviour, however. Sane people did not behave like this. "Care to elaborate?" he asked him.

Timile's face turned even uglier than it had been a moment earlier.

"You think that just because of your fancy talk and your doctor's degree you can take her away from me. She's mine, you hear. Stay away from her," Timile snarled.

"I take it you're talking about Kuda?" In comparison, Jake's voice was cool.

"I saw you kiss her," Timile accused, murder in his eyes.

"And I bet you were just dying to be in my shoes," Jake retaliated, irritated by this man's behaviour.

Timile's fist came out and it was so unexpected it caught Jake squarely in the mouth. He stumbled backwards and fell. Timile dove at him. He rolled away in the nick of time and got swiftly to his feet. Both men got into fighting positions and circled each other warily, like two cockerels in a box. Each looked for an opening through which they could attack the other.

"Both of you, stop it," Kuda commanded sharply. "If you don't, I'll let King go and I will not be held responsible for who he attacks."

Kuda had come up from behind them and was holding King back by the collar. The big beast was straining against her hold, growling deep in his throat. The sound that came out was akin to that of a tractor that was stuck in a ditch: Powerful. His eyes were on the two men and his body was tense and coiled, ready for attack. Despite her efforts, King was pulling Kuda forward as she dug her heels in the ground and tried to keep him back.

The men stopped moving, not sure whether to take her seriously or call her bluff. King's growling increased steadily in volume and both the men took a step back, eyes still on each other.

"Heed my warning, doctor, because the next time we meet I will kill you," Timile spat. He turned and looked at Kuda. "As for you, you and I will have our time." He turned and walked away. Not once did he look back. It was only after he left that King stopped growling.

Jake raised his left hand to his mouth and wiped away the blood that was still oozing down his lip. He turned and gave Kuda a look so dark it would have turned snow black.

"I'm a man and I like to fight my own battles," he told her icily.

"And I see you have the battle scars to prove it," Kuda shot back. She let go of King's collar because he had calmed down. "A word of warning, Jake. Stay out of Timile's way." She turned her back on Jake and she and her pooch started walking back home.

"Kuda," Jake called. She didn't stop or turn around. Jake strode after her and laid his hand on her forearm. She pulled away from his touch. "Kuda, I'm sorry," he said contritely.

She spun round to face him and glowered angrily at him.

"What is it about me?" she yelled at him. "Do I have a sign on my forehead that says 'Kick Me, I Expect It'?"

"I said I was sorry," Jake said.

"Yeah? Well, so am I."

With that, Kuda turned away from him for the second time and walked away from him. This time Jake did not stop her.

* * *

Once home, Kuda lay on the sofa, staring up at the ceiling. Jake had fixed the door and it was as good as new. It wasn't that she didn't appreciate his help. She did. It was just that… well, she wasn't quite herself when she was around him. So they had gotten off on the wrong foot and that had been entirely her fault. She hadn't exactly done anything to fix the situation and she had to admit she had kinda relished the cracks she had been making at him since he arrived. Still, she had to admit that he was a pretty confusing specimen even though everybody – well, almost everybody – seemed to like him.

She remembered the way he had been laughing and smiling with Susan and that same green demon squirmed betrayingly in the pit of her stomach again. In her mind's eye she saw the way he had looked as he had laughed at something that Susan had said. The way his eyes had crinkled at the corners and how his lips had shown a genuine smile.

Then she remembered his anger, unjustified though she knew it had been, when another type of crinkle had affected the corners of his eyes. How a muscle had jumped erratically up and down in his jaw. How his face had changed. The accusations he had hurled at her.

And then last night, when he had tried to comfort her. He had broken the door down when he had thought she was in trouble and that had been surprising. To say the least. That had been completely unexpected. She had never thought he would do something like that for her. He had bent over backwards for her and she had kicked him out.

Kuda's eyes stayed glued on the ceiling. Her thoughts strayed to what Chedza had said to her following their talk. She frowned at the white material above her. Perhaps she should be better at taking advice than at dishing it out. It definitely would help her situation with Jake Dawn.

A soft knock on the door interrupted her thoughts and she called for the knocker to come in. It was Susan. Kuda eyed her thoughtfully, noting the dark circles under her eyes. Susan sat down and Kuda gave her a half smile.

"We have matching luggage," Kuda said to her.

"What?" Susan said, not understanding.

"Giant sized bags under our eyes," Kuda explained. "Seems like neither of us got much sleep last night." Susan smiled wryly and there was a touch of grimness in her expression. Kuda went back to studying the ceiling.

"How are you feeling?" Susan asked her.

"Fine," Kuda replied shortly. Then: "I had a very illuminating conversation with a certain doctor. He pointed out certain things that I have, apparently, been blind to for quite some time now." She took a deep breath, sat up and looked at Susan. "I'm not the most observant person sometimes, though heaven knows that as a doctor I should be. So, instead of waiting to see if time will give me the answer, I'm going to ask you outright. Are you in love with Chose?"

Susan's face shuttered as though someone had drawn blinds behind her eyes. She turned away from Kuda's inquisitive gaze and said nothing. Kuda sighed and looked at her friend reprovingly.

"Why didn't you tell me before?" she asked softly.

"What was I supposed to say to you?" Susan demanded in turn. "Hi, Kuda. How are you? By the way, I'm in love with your boyfriend."

"Maybe you should have," Kuda replied just as softly as before.

"What's that supposed to mean?" Susan asked, and there was anger and a hint of bitterness in her voice.

"It means if you had said something like that I would have corrected you and none of this would be necessary now."

"Now what do you mean?" Susan asked, her brow furrowed in confusion.

"I mean that Chose is not my boyfriend nor has he ever been. He is my friend, period, and I love him as a friend. He knows it, and I know, and I'm surprised that you don't know it, Susan."

"How was I to know? When I came here three years ago, I found you and Chose, and you were so close to each other that I didn't really fit in. You practically spent every waking moment together. Then, we became friends, and I began to spend more and more time in his company. I began to fall for him, and all this time, I couldn't confide in you because I thought you were in love with him and he was in love with you! Can you honestly blame me?"

"Chose and I grew up together. We chased each other in diapers," Kuda said with a little twist of her nose.

"That doesn't mean that you don't find him attractive," Susan blurted out.

"You're right. Chose is a very attractive man. He is one of the most gentle, warm-hearted, kind people that I know, but we don't have that kind of relationship. Besides, it's kind of hard to think of someone in a romantic way once you've seen their diapers being changed."

Susan shot out of her chair and glared at Kuda.

"I'm going home."

"Chose is in love with you," Kuda said softly. Susan stopped dead in her tracks, back stiff, face turned away from Kuda.

"I think that's in very poor taste," Susan replied through gritted teeth, her hands clenched at her sides.

"And apart from those qualities that I mentioned, he's also quite a big chicken where his emotions are concerned. He's been in love with you for some time now, but he wasn't sure how you felt about him, so he made no move towards you. So, now tell me honestly, are you in love with Chose?"

Susan was quiet for so long that Kuda thought that she wasn't going to answer. Then: "Yes. Yes, I love him." Her voice was strangled and tight, and Kuda knew how she felt. Unrequited love was a heavy burden to carry.

"What do you suggest we do?" Kuda asked.

Susan sighed and flopped back into her chair. "I don't know. I really don't know."

The two women looked at each other, and slowly, a thought took seed in Kuda's mind. She started to grin, and as her grin widened, Susan started to eye her suspiciously.

"Now what are you thinking?" She asked.

"Lean a little closer and I'll tell you," Kuda said with a huge grin.

* * *

"Chose?" Kuda called out as she got to his house. "Chose!" She pounded loudly on his door. When it was suddenly snatched open and Chose's puzzled face appeared, Kuda grinned. "I have to talk to you. Aren't you going to let me in?" she demanded when Chose didn't move.

"Am I sure I want to?" he mumbled as he moved out of the way so that he could let Kuda into his home.

"You won't be sorry," Kuda said as she walked past him and made herself comfortable in his sitting room. The room had been returned to its proper order since the party the previous night,

"What are you talking about?" Chose asked with a frown. Kuda merely smiled serenely and then took a deep breath.

"Get me a drink, will you, love?" she said instead. Chose studied her suspiciously, but said nothing more before he went to the kitchen to fix her her drink. He came back with it in his hand and placed it in front of her.

"Sorry, I'm out of ice," he said, not sounding at all like his usual chipper self.

"That's okay," Kuda assured him, and took a slow slip of her water, eyeing him over the rim of her glass. "Sit down. I want to talk to you."

"You've already said that. What's this about?"

"Susan. I want to know exactly why it is that you care so much about her."

Chose looked at her as though she was crazy and rubbed his eyes tiredly.

"Are you crazy?" he asked warily. "She's the stuff my dreams are made of. She's everything that I want in a woman and more."

"Maybe you should tell her that some time," Kuda said softly. Chose gave her a crooked grin.

"The words to strike fear into the heart of poor me. I don't think I could if my life depended on it."

"Come on Chose, it can't be that bad."

"Oh, but it is!"

Kuda chuckled softly then got up. She went around the table to where Chose was sitting and knelt beside him. She cupped his face in her hand and smiled at him.

"Remember last night when you were so afraid that she was interested in Jake that you turned an unbecoming shade of green?"

"How could I forget?" He wore a rueful grin on his face.

"Somebody could zap her up, Chose. You have to tell her you care about her before somebody else does. Are you willing to take the chance that somebody else will tell her before you do?" A pained expression came onto his face. "I didn't think so. Tell her now."

"I can't."

"You can, and you will." Kuda got up and grinned at him like a cat that swallowed a handful of canaries. A look of pure panic appeared in his eyes.

"What do you mean by that?" he demanded.

"I'm getting a little tired of hearing that question," Kuda sighed.

"Well, what do you mean?"

"Susan is waiting outside, and I'm sure the two of you have loads to say to each other."

"Kuda! You can't do this to me!" Chose threw himself out of his chair, as though a blaze had been lit on his bottom, and paced the floor restlessly. He glared at Kuda as though she had betrayed him. Kuda stood up and headed for the door.

"Trust me, I'm a doctor." She ran back to him and hugged him impulsively. "Go with your heart," she whispered in his ear, "and the rest will come naturally." She kissed his cheek and then let him go. "Relax," she advised gently. "Trust me on this." She walked away from him and opened the door. "Susan! You can come in now!" she called.

"Kuda, are you crazy?" Chose squeaked. He looked around as though searching for a hole through which he could disappear. Finding none, he backed up as though he was going to use his sofa as a barrier between him and the incoming woman.

"No, I'm not, but you two are. Totally crazy about each other! Who knew? Give her a chance."

By this time, Susan had reached them, and, try as she might, she couldn't hide the fact that she was as nervous as Chose looked. She kept rubbing her hands on her pants and swallowing hard.

"Hello, Chose," she muttered, her words coming out jerkily, as though she was forcing them out through a constricted throat. Chose nodded like a marionette on the strings of a puppet master. Kuda hid a grin.

"Well, I'll leave you two to talk things over. Come on over to my place when you're through."

"Kuda-"

"No, Chose," she said softly, regretfully denying the plea in his voice. "This is long overdue." She looked at Susan. "You've got to grab onto love with both hands and hold tight, because once you let it go, you may never get it back."

With these words, she squeezed both Chose and Susan's hands and walked out of the door, leaving them alone.

"I hope to high heaven that this works out," she muttered to herself as she closed the door. "I really do."

Chapter Fifteen
Give it Time

As soon as Kuda walked into the clinic, she was greeted by yours truly, attending to Morapedi, one of the many females who had suddenly fallen ill and decided that they needed to be at the clinic every waking moment.

"Dumela mma. O a tsoga?" she greeted her respectfully, asking if she was well.

"Yes, I am fine. I just had a small headache and came to see if everything was alright." Jake just stood there absently as they spoke in their mother tongue, not understanding a thing they were saying and dreading it.

"You know that you could have taken the Myprodol that I had given you when you were here two days ago. And yesterday," she reminded, feeling slightly irritated rather than finding the female population's obsession with Jake to be amusing.

"Since I have not been feeling well for a few consecutive days, I decided to come and see if there was any cause for concern." Kuda was about to respond, but Jake decided to step in.

"I'm not really sure what you're talking about, but do you mind if I finished up here?" Kuda rolled her eyes and turned to the voice that tried to address her coolly, despite the obvious irritation.

"There's no need, Doctor Dawn. Morapedi is well and fine, and there's no need to give her another pack of Myprodol. She just needs to drink some water," she turned back to the patient, "and if the headache continues to persist, she should take the prescribed medicine." Kuda raised an all knowing eyebrow and Morapedi had the decency to look embarrassed. She thanked Kuda for her eye-opening advice, and walked out of the clinic. Turning back to Jake with a smile, it fell off of her face as soon as she saw how stoic he was.

"What?" she asked, not so kindly. He didn't say anything and simply walked to the back rooms to proceed with his work. Not really caring what Jake thought, and deciding not to start then, Kuda sat at the computer, turning it on to see what messages Aaron had left behind. She scrolled through the contents of her computer, going through her files and his own before finally deciding that there was nothing there. Weird. Normally, Aaron had something to say. Actually, the only time he didn't leave her a message was when he didn't come in, and Aaron practically lived at the clinic.

Shaking her head to clear away the niggling feeling that she had at the base of her neck, she proceeded to create Jake's profile, which she had deliberately forgotten to do from the moment that Aaron had tasked her to do it. She worked at the computer, clicking and typing with a frown on her face. Once the dreaded profile had finally been created, Manini Chipo walked in with a banged-up looking Una.

"Well, what happened here?" Kuda asked, looking at the various cuts and bruises that criss-crossed the boy's body.

"This little one decided that he could climb the tallest tree in the village without getting hurt. Now, we know the truth." Una was grinning with all of his teeth still intact. He didn't look like he was in too much pain, but once the adrenaline wore off, he would probably start to feel it.

"We need to get you cleaned up; you look like you went off to fight *Dimo* himself!"

"Kuda, can Dr. Jake fix me so that we can talk about soccer?"

"Everybody seems to want to replace me with Jake these days!" She said it with a smile on her face, but the emotion was real. "I'll go see what he is doing." Walking to the back of the clinic, she knocked on the door of his office. His gruff voice told her to enter, and she opened the door. As soon as she stepped in, the cold air blasting from the air conditioner hit her right in the face. The next thing that hit her was the messiness of his room. Everything was disorganized, and the clutter pained her to see. Being the very neat woman that she was, Kuda had the urge to either straighten everything or leave as quickly as possible.

"You have a visitor."

"Why don't you just diagnose them yourself, since you seem to have taken that liberty into your own hands."

"Oh trust me, I would have if Una didn't personally request your presence." At the mention of the boy's name, he abruptly stood up.

"Is he alright?"

"He's fine, just get out there and see for yourself." She almost left him behind, but she turned to give him some advice. "I would recommend keeping the AC turned off. I know it's hot, but you just have to suck it up: there's not enough electricity to go around for you to spend it all on yourself." Striding all the way back to the waiting area, she allowed Una to go back to Jake's office. Kuda sat at the front desk, resuming her work, but when she felt Manini Chipo's persistent stare trained on her forehead for more than ten minutes, she sighed, put down her work, and addressed her.

"Yes?"

"I didn't say anything," she responded patiently, a cool smile on her face.

"I'm well aware, but you've been staring at me for the past year and a half." Taking her time to respond, Manini Chipo glanced at her old wrinkled hands. Her skin was still vibrant and strong, her nails looking like those of a small child, cut short and clean. Despite the several wrinkles that covered her, she still looked as young and energetic as she had been at sixty years of age.

"You must invite Jake over tonight." Kuda groaned, spinning herself away from the want-to-be host in the swivel chair in which she was seated.

"Why, oh why, do you want to have him there? He's fine when he's in the clinic and in his house. And everywhere else except where you and I will be."

"I think he might be my good-luck charm. I had the most milk I had ever had the day that he came over, so I would like to invite him over once again." After she said that, Una bounded into the room once again, his larger wounds covered in gauze and ointment.

"Look, Kuda! Now I can go tell my friends that I was fighting the hyenas and they'll believe me." Kuda and Manini chuckled, well amused at the wild fabrications of a young child's mind, wishing that they could be as carefree as he is. Manini stood up, her back as straight as the wall to which she was parallel, her head held high in unmatchable poise and grace.

"Jake, as I was just telling Kuda, I expect to see you at the kraal this evening."

"Oh, I'm not sure if I will be able to make it." Manini didn't wait for his response, as she was already out of the door once his sentence was completed. He looked over at Kuda, needing an answer. She leaned back in her chair, her long, shapely legs stretched out before her. She was the image of perfect relaxation, her features soft but slightly bothered, as usual. She swayed slightly in the chair, her entire body moving with the momentum.

"Whenever you're invited somewhere, especially by an elder, you are expected to attend." Kuda spun back around to the computer and continued with her work. Jake headed back to his office, but halfway there, he turned back to watch her carefully. Without him nearby, she was so poised and delicate, looking as innocent as a baby lamb, but whenever she was in his presence, she became the tiger that preyed on that said lamb, vicious and quick to strike. Her demeanour was soft, and watching her work made him want to kick it back and relax.

There was just something about her. Something compelling. Without giving thought to what he was about to do, he walked back to where she sat. There were no patients nearby and the staff had apparently gone to lunch.

"Why do you dislike me so much?" he asked her.

If she was surprised by his question she didn't betray it. Instead, she stopped what she was doing and spun around in her chair to face him. She looked at him as she spoke.

"The thing is, Doctor Dawn, I do not dislike you at all. Au contraire. I find you marginally attractive and your intelligence is a bonus that any woman would find appealing."

"Any woman but you?" Jake asked with a noticeable smirk in his voice.

Kuda made a rude guttural sound in the back of her throat and glared at him. She seemed to be doing a lot of that lately. Slowly the scowl disappeared and her face betrayed the fatigue that was riding her body hard.

"Jake, my life has just settled down again. I don't need any more complications."

"And do I represent problems?" Jake asked her. His voice was soft, his look intense.

Kuda didn't even bother to reply to that one. Instead, she turned back to the computer, only to stare fixedly at the monitor, completely ignoring Jake's question. She knew that he was looking at her but she didn't turn around. She wouldn't turn around.

"What is it that you are so afraid of? A relationship?" Jake asked this when he realised that Kuda had no intention of answering his previous question.

"Yes," Kuda said honestly after a small pause. She still refused to look at him.

"With me?" Jake's voice was softer than ever.

"Especially with you," she mumbled.

"Why?"

Kuda sighed. Why couldn't this stubborn, hard-headed man just leave her alone? Especially now when she was feeling so raw.

"I'm not a young girl anymore and most women my age have a husband and kids, and the men want wives. I'm too old to play games, Jake. I don't want a relationship because they lead to problems and problems are the one thing I really don't need right now.

"You, doctor, don't really belong here. One day you will go back to America and settle down with a nice, normal American lady. If we get involved I will most certainly fall head over heels in love with you and the only person who will get hurt when you leave is yours truly. I am not willing to put myself through that emotional wringer again. I know I'm being presumptuous because you never said you wanted a relationship with me but I feel we would both be better off if we both know where we stand."

Kuda took a deep breath and slowly released it. At some point during her long speech, she had turned to face him. She had been talking, not at him, but at his chest, and now she took a peek at him from beneath her lashes. He didn't say anything for what seemed like a very long time but was, in actual fact, only a few seconds.

"Maybe I can change your mind," he said, his voice low and husky. Kuda groaned before he had even finished his sentence.

"I don't doubt that you could, Doctor Dawn, but please don't try. I need my peace of mind."

"On one condition," Jake said. Kuda eyed him warily. "Nothing big. Only that you stop calling me Doctor Dawn and call me Jake."

Kuda's mouth twisted wryly and she nodded. "Deal," she agreed.

"Truce?"

"Truce."

"Want to shake and kiss on it?" Jake asked, tongue lolling in his cheek.

"I think your word is as good as mine without the shake or the kiss," Kuda told him, rolling her eyes.

Jake chuckled. "Fair enough."

"Still, I would appreciate it if we both kept our distance."

"Don't you think that will be a little difficult to do seeing as how small this village is and how we will bump into each other practically every hour on the hour? I don't know about you but I think it's asking a bit much."

"You know what I mean, Jake," Kuda sighed in exasperation.

Jake studied her, a questioning look in his eyes. Finally he spoke.

"Yes. Yes, I do. I suppose I should be content with us just being friends."

Kuda laughed incredulously and stood so that she faced him directly.

"We can never be just friends, Doctor Dawn." She enunciated her words carefully, as though she needed him to understand a particularly difficult Chemistry equation. "Don't you get it? One minute you are calling me names and the next you're -- doing other things," she stated, waving her hand above her head to emphasise something she didn't really want to talk about. "Then after that you're growling at me, following which you apologise. Now you're assuming we will just be friends? Forgive me for saying so, Jake Dawn, but we can never be just friends. Now, if you'll excuse me, I have the rest of my life to live."

Well, if he hadn't gone and made her mad again. And he wasn't even sure what it was that he had said this time. She tried to walk past him but he stayed her with a hand on her arm. Her skin felt cool and smooth to his touch. He wanted to keep his hand on her arm but in the state of mind she was in at this moment, he didn't want to risk it. He dropped his hand to his side.

"It *does* seem like I'm always apologising to you," he said as she stopped. "But I will try to respect your wishes. No matter how difficult it may be."

Kuda raised her eyes to his. She was grateful and she wanted him to know it. She opened her mouth to speak but Angelica chose that moment to walk into the room.

"Thank you," Kuda said and walked on, past Angelica and out the door. Jake stared after her, wanting to follow her but knowing that the timing was not right.

"Morning, Jake," Angelica said and Jake hid his annoyance at her untimely entrance.

"Good morning. How was your weekend?" he asked her.

"Fine. It would have been better if I had seen more of you," she said, smiling like a barracuda that had just spied a tasty morsel. Jake felt like a piece of meat on the kitchen counter.

Just then Kuda stuck her head around the door.

"Jake, there's a patient here to see you," she told him. Her head disappeared just as quickly as it had appeared. With a slight feeling of relief, Jake excused himself from Angelica and escaped into the examination room.

* * *

Perhaps she wasn't consciously trying to do it but Kuda somehow managed not to cross paths with Jake for most of the morning. They were never alone together and when they were, conversation was minimal at best. Kuda preferred it that way and was not willing to alter the situation if she could help it.

Monday was usually the busiest day of the week. It always seemed as though people waited for Sunday night before they decided to fall sick. In the afternoon, however, the mob subsided and Kuda was able to slow down a bit. She had missed lunch and was starting to feel it in her stomach. She peeked into the waiting room and saw that there were only two more people; a fifteen year old boy and one of the teachers from the primary school. Relieved, she motioned for the next person to come in. The teacher stood up and entered her consulting room. Lunch was just a couple of patients away and she could almost smell it. Just then Chose walked in, presumably from having had his own lunch break.

"Chose, I need to see you later," she told him.

"Sure," he said, a huge grin on his face. "I will come over to your place after work. All I can say right now is that you're the greatest and I love you to bits. If we were alone I would give you the biggest kiss you have ever had!"

Jake chose that moment to call the last patient. Kuda looked up and realised that he had heard what Chose had said. There was the same grim expression that had been on his face when he had confronted Kuda and accused her of leading Chose on. To hell with him, she thought. She wasn't about to go through the hassle of explaining her and Chose's actions to him. If he wanted to think the worst of her again, that was his problem. For some reason this really ticked her off and without thinking she said,

"Give it to me later, baby. I need to work right now but I will see you at home."

Chose, as well as the teacher who was now behind her, giggled. The boy looked embarrassed and hurried into Jake's room. Jake gave Kuda a look that could have made cheese out of pasteurized milk. He went back into his consulting room and closed the door behind him. Chose looked puzzled.

"What's with the doctor?" he asked.

"If you're a good boy I'll tell you later. Right now I have work to do, like I said," she told him.

She entered her room and closed the door. If Jake wanted to believe she was some kind of Jezebel then she wasn't going to waste her time trying to correct him. She didn't care what he thought of her.

Then, she asked herself, why did she go out of her way to antagonise him? That was a question she didn't want to examine too closely. Perhaps she knew that she would not like the answer.

Chapter Sixteen
Heartfelt

When the work day was over, Kuda was tense and frustrated. She had been moving around all day, trying to solve problems while the pretentious Doctor Dawn sat in his air conditioned office like the entitled jerk that he was. The day had been unusually hot, the sun deciding to stretch its rays a little bit farther so as to engulf all who were outside in an unprecedented heat. Kuda's skin was glowing from the slight sweat that had formed on her brow and forearms. She peeled off one layer, exposing her lean arms, sculpted from years of hard work out on the field and in the clinic. She glanced over at the wall clock that Aaron had strategically placed above her desk. One day he surprised her with it after noticing that Kuda always checked her wrist to discover that there was nothing there. She smiled at the memory as she walked back to inform His Highness that it was time to leave.

She knocked on his door and entered without waiting for a response. When she saw Jake sitting before her, his forehead dripping with sweat, she couldn't help but wrinkle her nose at him to cover her mirth.

"You find this funny, do you?" Jake looked unhappy and miserable in his office, like a turtle turned over on its back. Kuda didn't comment as his current state was partly her fault.

"It's time to leave," she simply stated.

"Where are we going?"

"If my memory serves me correctly, you were standing right there when Manini invited you over."

"I told her that I wouldn't be able to make it." Kuda rolled her eyes and hoisted her handbag further up her shoulder. That movement drew Jake's eyes to those toned arms and small hands that had delivered a painful blow to his face just two days prior. His hand subconsciously reached up to rub his jaw, remembering the painful sting.

"I'm going to go home and change, and I'm going to take my time. If you're not on your *stoep* by the time that I pass your house, you'll just have to explain yourself to her." With that, she was out of the door and down the road.

When she was about fifty meters away from her house, she saw King come bumbling up to meet her. She squatted and gave her mutt a huge hug. King gave her a puzzled look, as though trying to understand what was wrong. Kuda smiled, loving the expression on his face. King nuzzled her neck and suddenly things didn't seem so bad.

"Come on, boy" she said as she straightened up. "Let's get you home. You smell bad too. You're due for a bath later this week."

King exhaled with a snort, as though to disagree with her words. Kuda rubbed the back of his head and they headed home. They had been walking for a few minutes when King stopped suddenly. His floppy ears stood as erect as they could and he looked directly at a group of trees about two hundred meters away. Kuda looked at the same trees but could not see anything out of the ordinary. She carried on walking but King stayed where he was.

"Let's go, King," she called. The dog gave her a look and went right back to looking at the trees. Kuda turned to the woods again, wanting to see what it was that had caught her dog's attention. For just a second, she thought she caught a glimpse of something shiny in the trees, but just as quickly as the thought came it disappeared. There was nothing there.

"What are you looking at?" Chose asked as he saw her standing there. He walked up to them and scratched King on the neck.

"King's looking at something out there. I don't know what it is," she told him.

Chose glanced at the trees then grinned at her.

"I told you someone's watching you. Maybe it's someone with a huge crush on you. Or maybe it's the secret police. Do you have any secrets that are worth digging into?"

But Kuda was not smiling. An image of a madman had crashed into her mind and left behind a trail of slime that made her stomach curl.

"Are you alright?" Chose asked, seeing the expression on her face.

"I'm fine," she lied. She was getting rather good at that. "Let's go home."

She started walking but stopped when she saw that King was still staring into the distance. As she watched, he took a step towards the trees. She was about to call him back when for some reason she decided not to. If there was someone there, and that someone was spying on her, then he deserved to get chewed on. Pulling Chose by the arm, she guided him towards her house.

"So what do you have to tell me?" she asked him. Without warning, Chose grabbed her around the waist and tossed her into the air as though she were a sack of confetti. She squealed as he caught her, holding her around her thighs so that she was higher than he was,

"You're the best," he told her, a huge smile on his face. "You deserve to win the Cupid's Award of the Year! If such a thing exists, that is."

"I take it you and Susan got it right, finally," Kuda said dryly, grabbing onto his head so she wouldn't topple over him. "Now put me down before you break something."

Chose laughed. He put her down and then bent to kiss her on the forehead. "You really are the best. Now, since I'm in such a jolly mood, I'm going to race you home. If you beat me there, I'll let you know all the juicy details of what happened last night!"

Before Chose had finished his sentence, Kuda had shot off like a stone from a catapult. Chose raced after her, both laughing because at that moment, something had gone right for once.

* * *

Standing in the grove of trees, Timile had been sure that he had been spotted. When he had seen that dog stop and stare in his direction, he had felt a moment of panic. It was nothing to worry about, however, because there was no way the dog could smell him from there. Never mind see him. He was sure there was nothing to be concerned about.

As he watched, he saw Chose come up to her. That was another person who needed to be taught a lesson. He would take care of him one day too, but only after he had taken care of Kuda and Jake. Definitely after those two. He adjusted his binoculars and saw them more clearly. What was it with those two? They were always so touchy-feely. Didn't they know that certain things were not to be done in public? As though they could hear his thoughts, both Kuda and Chose turned and looked in his direction.

Timile's heart stopped for a beat and he was sure he had been discovered. That he would be caught out before he could put his plan into motion. He lowered his spy glasses faster than an angel could fly and ducked beneath the leaves of the trees around him. When he dared raise his head again, it was in time to see Chose tossing her into the air and catching her again.

A deep rage filled him, and he clenched his teeth so hard he felt it in his temples. He felt short of breath and he knew that if he ever got the chance, he would kill the both of them. He watched as Chose put Kuda down, kissed her, and then chase her to her place. He followed the pair of them with his eyes and only stopped when a dark shape crossed his path. It was Kuda's dog.

More panic raced through him, chasing the fury away as the dog approached. It saw him and started sprinting towards him. Timile fled. He was sure he did not want to be there when that canine got to him. Prudent retreat was always more advisable than hanging around to get the seat of his pants bitten off.

As King approached, Timile ensured that he moved himself out of there faster than King could get to where he was.

* * *

"Do you know what? We talked. It was the first time we had ever really talked and it was amazing."

Chose and Kuda were sitting in her living room. The windows were wide open and a pleasant breeze wafted in from outside. Each had a cold coke in their hands and Kuda sipped intermittently as Chose talked. She studied him, noting how handsome he looked in his white shirt and khaki pants. He sat with an ease that showed how comfortable they were with each other, speaking with an excitement in his voice that Kuda had not heard in a really long time.

"I can't believe it took me so long to approach her," he said.

Kuda coughed pointedly, grinning cheekily at him. "*You* approached her? Correct me if I'm wrong, Mr 'I Can't', but wasn't it my pushing and plotting that did that?"

"You're never going to let me live it down, are you?" Chose chuckled.

"Never!" Kuda grinned.

Sighing, Chose took a sip of his drink. "It was interesting, really. I don't understand how I could have been so blind. She says she's had feelings for me almost as long as I have had feelings for her. It's really incredible how we both missed it."

"Sometimes when you are close to something, you cannot see it as clearly as someone who has a little distance from it."

"You're a fine one to talk," Chose said to her. "We both missed it. When did you get a clue?"

Kuda took a long swig of her drink. "I didn't," she said. She took another swig. She peeked at Chose and saw the surprised look on his face.

"What are you talking about?" he asked.

"Well, it's like this. A certain new doctor, who shall remain unnamed, practically accused me of seducing you away from Susan. He told me, to my face mind you, that I was going to intentionally hurt two genuinely nice people by playing around with your emotions when Susan was so obviously in love with you." Kuda grinned like a maniac.

Chose was quiet for a moment. He tilted his head, puzzled. "After you disappeared last night – where did you go anyway? – Jake and I had a moment together. Susan was looking really unhappy – which I totally get now, by the way – and Jake pulled me aside. He asked me what was going on between me and you."

Kuda's eyebrows shot up but she said nothing.

"I told him you were like the sister I never had – okay well, I have three sisters but you're different. Weird different. And my sisters are as annoying as hell." Kuda burst out laughing. "I told him that you weren't aware of Susan's feelings – which he didn't seem to believe at first – and that had you been, you would have made sure we hooked up. Which you did. Anyway, he pretty much said what you had said and encouraged me to talk to her. He's really not such a bad guy."

"Well, the good thing about last night is that he made me aware of Susan's feelings towards you and he encouraged *you* to go for it. The best part was that it served to increase the animosity between us."

Chose frowned at her. "Why would you want to increase the animosity between the two of you?"

"That's neither here nor there. The important thing is that he served to get the two of you together. That's what we should be happy about."

"I am happy about that, Kuda, but I'm concerned about the two of you. I don't understand your relationship at all. One minute you're chummy, the next you're at each other's throats like lion and hyena. What is it between the two of you?"

"There's absolutely nothing between us," Kuda said vehemently. She stood up and grabbed Chose's empty glass from his hand. "Absolutely nothing," she stressed as she waved the glass at him. She stalked to the kitchen where she placed the glasses in the sink with a thud. It was a wonder that neither of them broke.

"Methinks the lady doth protest too much," Chose said with a little chuckle.

Kuda stormed back into the sitting room. "What language is that? What normal person speaks like that?" she asked, waving a fluttery hand in his direction.

Chose grinned wickedly. "What's up with you?" he asked.

"There is nothing wrong with me and if you are not going to talk about Susan and you anymore then you might as well leave now." Kuda stood before Chose, her hands on her waist, her eyes narrowed, her lips clamped together.

"Do you know what you remind me of?" Chose asked, not bothered by her anger. "Of primary school boys. We would pull the girls' hair and toss up their dresses to get a glimpse of their knickers. But, we only did it because that was the only way we could get their undivided attention. And the girls? Well, the girls would scream at us, chase us and beat the stuffing out of us if they ever caught us. Sometimes we let them catch us because it meant that they did notice us and maybe if we were lucky, we could steal a kiss or two as they were pummelling us."

"You were seriously depraved," Kuda interrupted. Chose ignored her comment and continued.

"What the boys knew, and what the girls didn't get to figure out until much later, was that if you really got under somebody's skin, eventually they would realise that you were more than just a nuisance. Attraction comes in many forms, Kuda."

"All this from someone who has recently discovered love," Kuda said sarcastically. "Get the hell out of my house, Chose, before I throw you out."

"Come on, Kuda. It's so obvious you two cause sparks whenever you meet. Maybe you should have a fling with him or something." Chose was obviously laughing at her, his brown eyes crinkling at the corners as he studied her reaction.

Kuda gasped as though she had swallowed a live wasp. "Out! Out! Out!" she screamed. Grabbing Chose by the wrist, she pulled him from the sofa and then pushed him towards the door. "And don't you dare come back here until your head is screwed on straight. Go harass someone else for a change."

"Kuda, come on," Chose said, openly laughing at her now. He allowed himself to be pushed to the door and out. "Let's discuss this like rational adults."

"Rational? I'll show you rational! If you are not off my property in two seconds, I'll throw something heavy at you!" And she meant it too. Chose saw how serious she was and laughed again.

"You do realise that you are proving my point, don't you?"

Without a word Kuda looked around for something to throw. Finding nothing that could cause substantial harm, she reached for the shoes that she had left behind the door and took careful aim. Laughing like a crazy hyena, Chose ran to the gate. When he was a safe distance away he yelled back, "You can run, but you can't hide. If it's meant to be, it will be, Kuda."

She thought about throwing the shoe at him, she really did. She decided not to because she would be the one to go and pick it up anyway. She thought horrid thoughts about all men in general and then slammed the door as she went back inside her house. As for Jake, he could go to hell. He had been horrid to her ever since he had come to the village and he deserved to get a little payback.

Still feeling piqued, Kuda got ready to go to Manini's.

Chapter Seventeen
A Nasty Little Game

Even though she was in shorts and a tee-shirt, Kuda was hot. She felt the sweat flowing down the small of her back and she gingerly pulled at the tee-shirt to unstick it from her ski. She grimaced and wiped at her forehead with the back of her hand. She looked over to where King lay and felt sorry for her pooch as he panted there with his tongue hanging out. As though sensing her eyes on him he turned to face her and then rolled over with a loud groan.

She rolled her eyes, shook her head and bent down again to pull at the teats of the cow she was milking. Strings of pearl white milk poured into her milking bucket as she pulled all four teats one after the other and before too long she had enough milk to take care of Manini and Una's dinner for the evening, as well as for tea in the morning. She gave one last tug and smiled in satisfaction.

She threw a look in Jake's direction and felt a pang at the easy way he was laughing and kidding around with Una and Washington. Manini was standing just inside the *kraal*, her walking-stick held firmly in her left hand and her right hand shielding her eyes from the sun that aimed at disappearing beneath the horizon shortly. Her old and weathered face was full of worry and Kuda made a mental note to ask her what was on her mind later. Not that she would get an honest answer but it would still be worth a try.

Kuda untied the back legs of the bovine she had just finished milking and smacked it on the rump to get it moving. She straightened her back and pushed her hips forward in an attempt to loosen her muscles and relieve the tension that had been caused by her being in the milking position for so long. She thought about joining the men but Jake hadn't quite forgiven her yet so that wasn't really an option. Turning, she headed towards Manini who still stood by the entrance of the *kraal.*

"Why did you want me to bring Jake?" she asked the older woman as soon as she reached her.

Manini looked at her and frowned, dropping her hand and looking at Kuda with a hint of impatience. Her lips had tightened and her frown had deepened, if that was even possible. Kuda was taken aback. That was a first. Manini was usually the most patient woman on the face of the earth.

"I like him," was the response Kuda got to her question. "Does there need to be another reason?"

Kuda whistled softly through her teeth. She really wasn't the popular one today. Standing uncertainly next to Manini, she caught her lower lip between her teeth and put her weight on her right foot. The pail of milk hung from her right hand and she wondered if she shouldn't go drop it off at the compound and leave. It was kinda frosty in the *kraal* that day, despite the heat.

Una and Washington finished up with the cow they were milking and untied its back legs. Kuda heard a guffaw of laughter from Jake and turned in that direction. His head was thrown back and his laugh sounded out again. He looked carefree and happy and Kuda couldn't help smiling a bit at his uninhibitedness. His shirt had the top three buttons unbuttoned, as per norm, and was tucked into his khaki shorts. His forearms were exposed, as were his long, lean legs; swimmer's legs. His calf muscles were shapely and his thighs looked toned and firm. He wore sandals and his feet were nice looking, with the toenails neatly trimmed and very healthy looking.

He wore a hat and it hid his short hair and half his face as he stopped laughing and looked down at Una. For a moment he faced her direction and she caught his eye. He held her gaze for a spell before he turned back to Una and Washington. As the men finished up and headed towards them, Kuda couldn't help but admire just how attractive Doctor Jake Dawn looked. Too bad he was leaving soon. He might have made a good friend.

She frowned at the direction her thoughts were taking her. She had no desire to be his friend. None at all. He was here for a short time and a short time only. He would be heading back to the USA in no time at all and she had no need for new friends anyway. The few she had were fine. Even if they were all mostly mad at her at this particular time.

"There are two types of people in this world," Washington said, drawing her out of her unsolicited thoughts about Jake's attractiveness. She turned her head to the older man, a small smile flitting on her lips.

“What are those?” she asked Washington. “The old and the young?”

Washington looked at her as though she were crazy. “No,” he told her. “The brave and the cowards.”

“Really?” she asked him. “Wasn’t it the bold and the beautiful last week?” she said with a chuckle.

Washington shook his head, clucking at her like she had lost her marbles. “Whatever gave you that idea?” he asked her. Una was laughing so hard at the exchange that he could barely speak.

“Before that it was the hungry and the fed,” Una hooted, holding his side. “It never ends.”

Kuda chuckled and Manini shook her head as though she was wondering who these people were.

“Come,” she said. “It is getting late. We must get home.”

Washington sealed off the entrance of the kraal as the group got ready to leave. Manini went on ahead with Una and Jake helped Washington seal the entrance by placing cut-off timber across it, effectively shutting it off so that the animals couldn’t go out. Mmantshadi was, as usual, about thirty meters away from the *kraal*, having decided that she wasn’t going to be locked up on that day.

As the remaining party of three headed back towards the compound, Kuda put her pail of milk on the ground and squatted to tie her shoelace. For some reason Jake stayed behind with her. He picked up the pail of milk and held it for her. When Kuda straightened she looked up at him and then at the three people who were now too far away from them to hear anything she would say. She looked sideways at Mmantshadi and then at Jake.

"How did the milking go?" she asked him.

He shrugged. "Fine, I guess. It was my first time."

Kuda nodded and felt a small smile stretch her lips.

"Maybe you should have started with Mmantshadi. That would be something to talk about at the campfires." Kuda spoke seriously, like she had given it some thought. Then she said, "But, I understand. Not many men are brave enough to try to milk her. Come to think of it, I doubt I have ever tasted her milk. Too bad you didn't try. Like Washington said, there are two types of people in this world."

With that, she smiled and followed Manini and her troupe. She had taken a few steps when she realised that Jake wasn't following. He stood looking at the cow that was grazing outside the kraal, the pail of milk in his hand.

"Let's go, Doctor Dawn," she said to him. "Manini is waiting."

Kuda felt a flutter in her stomach as she realised that Jake wasn't listening to her. Like she had swallowed a jar of live moths and they were trying to fly in her stomach. He stood looking at the cow that was slowly munching on that day's grass. Mmantshadi didn't give any indication that she was paying attention to them but Kuda knew from experience that that did not mean that she wasn't aware of what was going on.

"Uh, Jake. We need to go," she said to him. Jake threw an annoyed glance in her direction and then completely ignored her. He started walking in the cow's direction, his intention clear. "Jake!" Kuda hissed at him desperately. "Don't go near that cow!"

When he showed no sign of paying attention to her Kuda shuffled closer to a large tree that grew near to where she stood. It had enough branches to hold onto and climb in a hurry should the need arise. As a child she had climbed it often and she knew it was sturdy. Definitely solid enough to carry two grown people for sure. As for the idiot doctor who was still heading towards Mmantshadi with a pail of milk in his hands, he really needed to turn back.

"Jake!" she called again. "Jake, dammit! Don't go near that cow!"

Again he ignored her and by now he was about fifteen meters away from her. Kuda shook her head and started to panic. There was no way in hell, however, that she was going after him. She carefully climbed up the tree, making sure that the thick branch she eventually sat on had enough room for the silly man to come and sit next to her because, without doubt, Jake was going to need that space. Once she was as comfortable as she could be, she leaned back onto the stem to watch what was about to go down. He wouldn't be able to say that she hadn't warned him.

Jake was still walking purposefully towards the cow which had turned and was now watching him with her big brown eyes. She was still chewing whatever was in her mouth and her eyes steadily followed Jake as he closed in on her.

"For God's sake, Jake. Stop!" Kuda called to him.

Jake stopped, turned and gave her an angry glare. That was when Mmantshadi attacked. Faster than he would have thought a cow could move, Jake turned in time to see nearly a ton of beef with horns charging down at him. He heard Kuda scream and that galvanised him into action. As the bovine lowered her huge head to gore Jake with the large horns on top of it, Jake dove to the side and he swore that he felt his shirt catch in her horn and then give. He landed on his stomach in the dirt and he did not want to wonder about the soft, squishy mass that he landed in. Rolling to his left, he saw that the pail of milk had landed on its side and all the milk had spilt. He would worry about that later because out of the corner of his eye he saw that the cow had turned and was heading back in his direction.

"Get up!" he heard Kuda yell.

Standing up quickly he tossed the pail away and tried to figure out the best route to take to escape the crazy cow. The same cow that was now bearing down at him with her head low and ready to cause him some serious harm. He quickly turned and got his feet moving, running around behind the *kraal.* Mmantshadi followed with a bellow that scared him more than he had thought that a cow's cry could. Tucking his elbows in close to his side he hustled himself out of there, urging his legs to move fast. His feet pounded the earth as he literally ran for his life. He could hear the cow crashing behind him, gaining on him.

He had read somewhere that cows could clock, no pun intended, about twenty kilometres an hour yet he felt that this cow was running a hell of a lot faster than that. He imagined himself being impaled by her large horns, his mother crying at his funeral because she had agreed to his going to Africa, and now, through his own stupidity, he was about to be gored to death, and probably stomped too, by a mad cow!

What probably saved him as he turned was that the cow was not able to make the same sharp turn that he could. Mmantshadi slipped and for a moment she struggled to find her hooves and almost fell. Jake took the opportunity to get to the tree that Kuda was sitting in, her eyes wide and a hand pressed to her mouth. Grabbing the lowest branch he hoisted himself into the tree. As he climbed the tree like a crazy ape on crack he looked over and saw the cow charging the tree. He climbed faster and made it onto the branch that Kuda was sitting on just as Mmantshadi hit the tree with her head.

She let out a snort as she realised that she had missed Jake and Kuda let out a muffled scream. Shaking her head and pawing at the ground, Mmantshadi snorted again, almost as though to say, "That was just a warning. There mustn't be a next time."

Jake was breathing hard and Kuda turned to glare at him.

"What the hell were you thinking?" she yelled at him. "We all told you that cow was dangerous."

"You dared me to go milk her," Jake yelled back, then almost slapped himself for his stupid answer.

"What are you? Six"? Kuda asked him. "You should have more sense than that."

To be honest, Jake had thought that their comments about the mad cow had been exaggerated. He had seen nothing in the couple of days that he had been coming there to indicate that she really was something not to be toyed with. As he tried to calm his beating heart, however, he turned and gave Kuda what he hoped was an icy stare.

"I wonder what Manini would say about what you just did," he said.

Kuda laughed. "Really? You're going to *'report'* me to her?"

Jake chuckled. Then a great belly laugh escaped him unexpectedly. The startled look that Kuda threw in his direction only made him crack up more.

"Oh, great," he heard her mumble. "That fall must have scrambled your brain."

Kuda looked down and realised that Mmantshadi had moved away and was standing at the same spot that she had been standing in before Jake started his shenanigans. She presumed it would be safe to get down in a second or so. The cow looked like it was done chasing dumb people for the day.

"Why would you do something like that?" Jake finally asked her.

"I didn't think you were crazy enough to go and try to milk her. Have you not heard the things that we told you about that cow?" Kuda told him, frowning at him.

"I just thought that if she was as dangerous as you all said she was, she would have been killed or something."

Kuda shook her head. "Manini says she is destined for something big. She won't let anyone hurt her." Kuda looked at Jake and then dropped her eyes. "I'm sorry, Jake. That was really juvenile and I shouldn't have made that dare."

Jake studied her for a moment. For once, her apology sounded genuine and he felt himself responding. Sitting here in the tree with her was probably one of the craziest things he had ever done and it really had been worth it to see such honest emotion in her eyes.

"What am I? Six? I shouldn't have taken you up on it."

Their eyes met for a moment and they both smiled. Something seemed to give between them as they sat in the boughs of the tree, with Jake having cheated death. Finally Kuda spoke.

"Come on, Speedy. Let's get you back. Manini is probably wondering where we are," Kuda said to him softly.

He got down from the tree, casting occasional glances in Mmantshadi's direction. The cow seemed disinclined to continue her murderous stampede and stood calmly in the same spot, not even looking in their direction. He helped Kuda down and as he held her warm body against his, in that one second before he let her go, he felt his heart skip a beat.

She turned away from him and walked over to pick up the pail. She shook her head and giggled. "You're explaining the empty pail, Jake Dawn," she said to him. Jake chuckled

"As long as you keep a straight face and don't spoil it by laughing I will stay as close to the truth as possible. I get the feeling that it is not a good idea to lie to Manini."

Kuda smiled. "It never is!"

As they walked back to the compound in companionable silence with an empty pail of milk swinging between them, Kuda and Jake didn't feel like killing each other for once.

Chapter Eighteen
Warmth and Fuzziness

Jake watched Manini, Kuda and Una as they chatted around the fire. Washington had had to leave and it was just the four of them. They were sitting in the *segotlwana* with the fire burning between them. The sun had set and it was dark outside. The stars and the moon were out, however, and there was enough light to see well enough. King was asleep next to Kuda, his large bulk barely moving. Every once in a while he would sigh and his breath would raise dust up off the ground. He really was a pussy. There wasn't a vicious bone in his body. He wondered why he had ever been afraid of him.

Kuda had cooked *motogo* for supper, soft porridge made from sorghum. It tasted okay but he knew he would have to eat something again before bedtime. There had been no meat in the meal as well and he was craving something salty. He'd probably fry a steak or something when he got home. As healthy as porridge was, it didn't do much to satisfy his need for some hard protein.

Home. It was funny how this place had quickly become just that. There were some challenges, he thought as he cast a glance at Kuda, but for the most part he was happy to be here. She looked content. In her shorts, with her long legs stretched out in front of her, she looked at peace. Nothing at all like the hellion that he knew her to be under the calmness radiating from her now. The sting of her palm on his face would be with him for a while, even if it no longer hurt.

He turned his head and watched as Una got up to wash their dinner plates in a basin. He rinsed the dishes and placed them upside down on a tray after shaking off the excess water. Jake smiled. He'd hated doing the dishes as a kid and he inwardly applauded Una for doing them without being asked. When he was done, Una came back to wish them a good night.

"School night, huh, buddy," Jake said to him. Una nodded.

"I wish I could finish school and not have to worry about it anymore," Una replied. "Being all grown up is amazing. You get to do what you want, when you want."

"Don't be in too much of a hurry to grow up," Jake said. "Growing up has its own set of problems."

He heard Kuda chuckle. "I'm always telling him that," she said. "To enjoy his childhood while he still can but he thinks I'm throwing him a kernel of corn when there's a whole maize field behind me."

"What does that even mean?" Una asked with a questioning shrug. "Speak English, lady!"

"I mean," Kuda said as she stood up, "That I'm not selling you a story. It might look like growing up is everything you want when you are young, but life is tougher when you're older. All you see right now is the larger field but you have to go through one kernel at a time to get through the whole field.

And education, young man, is one of the kernels you have to eat first."

"I like popcorn," Una said randomly and Kuda shook her head in mock pain.

"Why do I even try?" she groaned rhetorically.

"Off to bed, Una," Manini told him. "Otherwise you and I will be fighting in the morning."

With another goodnight, Una headed off to his room, his small body disappearing into the night.

"He's a good kid," Jake said and even in the night's light, he could see Manini beam at his comment.

"Yes," Manini said, "he is. He has never disappointed me."

For a moment no one spoke and then Kuda stood up, stretching slowly. King raised his head and looked at her.

"I'm off," Kuda told them. "It's gotten kind of late. Need to catch up on my beauty sleep."

Manini nodded. "Jake, please see to it that Kuda gets home safely."

Kuda's jaw dropped. As she was about to come back with a scathing reply, Manini spoke softly. "Just this once, Kuda. Please don't fight it."

That snapped her mouth shut quickly again. She ground her teeth together and took a deep breath. Respecting the elderly was hard sometimes. There were so many comebacks sitting on the tip of her tongue but she swallowed them all and all she said was, "Ready, Jake?"

Jake had watched the exchange with interest and was surprised by Kuda's response.

"Um, sure," he said. "Shall we?" He too didn't want to start a fight so he got up and the two waved goodbye to Manini. Kuda called to King who had still been lying by the fire. He came lumbering over to her, licked her hand and then went off ahead of them.

They walked for a few minutes in silence, each in their own thoughts. Despite everything, it had been a good day. The stars shone brightly that night and they easily made their way over the dusty path. It had cooled off nicely over the past few hours and the scorching heat had been replaced by a lovely coolness. While it would still be hot for the next few months, by the time her birthday came around in June, it would be really cold and she would miss the summer, the way she did every year.

As they walked past field after field of growing crops, Kuda smiled. She loved the smell of Jackalas at night. The air was so clean and fresh and there were no impurities in it. They passed various compounds on the way home; homes of people that Kuda had known her whole life. People she had gone to school with, played with, lived amongst. People she had treated for various illnesses. People who she had attended weddings and funerals with. She loved it here and couldn't imagine being anywhere else.

King kept stopping to sniff the air and at a few points his floppy ears seemed to stand up stiffly, as though listening for something that only he could hear. Then he would continue walking only to repeat the process a few minutes later. Kuda looked around but couldn't see anything out of the ordinary each time he stopped. There were many trees around them, however, and she couldn't really see that much. Super dog hearing was not something she was blessed with.

"How long have you lived in Jackalas?" Jake asked her.

She turned to face him as she continued to walk. "Small talk, doctor? That's a first." She heard Jake exhale through his teeth and she chuckled. "All my life. I was born here."

"Really? I didn't know that," Jake said with genuine interest. "And where did you study?"

"I went to school here. Then I went to Mater Spei College and ended up at Virginia Commonwealth University."

"Woah!" Jake was surprised. "You studied in the States? I had no idea."

Oh, it was too easy! Kuda took a deep breath as she tried to come back with a decent reply.

No idea? Really? Why would you have a clue really? It's not like you have my CV for constant reference,is it?

Err… no

No idea? Your magic fairy didn't whisper it in your ear this morning?

Definite no.

No idea? Wow! And here I thought that you were the genie that knew everything about my business. Who knew?

Aaaah!

All she said was, "Yeah. Richmond was a fun place. I really enjoyed it there."

By this time they were almost at Kuda's gate. She had left the lights off and her house was dark. King padded into her yard and went to his drinking bowl. When he was done, he disappeared behind her house, as usual.

"Can I show you something?" Jake asked. At her gasp of pretend horror Jake chuckled. "Nothing to worry about. It's just that I have this picture."

Kuda looked at him with interest as he pulled something out of his wallet. He gave her an old looking photograph but she couldn't see it properly in the dark. She held it up and a glimmer of excitement shot through her.

"I was wondering if you might know the person in that photograph."

Jake watched her as she gasped, this time in surprised pleasure.

"No," she whispered. "Really?" She wasn't talking to him, more to herself and Jake was intrigued despite himself.

"What is it?" Jake asked, moving closer to her.

Without answering, Kuda opened the gate wider and rushed to her door. Unlocking it, she beckoned Jake to join her and he hurried after her. She pulled out a box of matches and lit her trusty gas lamp. Immediate light washed over the small room. He saw her look at the picture again in the light and he swore her eyes shone and her smile blossomed.

She looked beautiful.

Without saying anything, she moved on to another room and he followed. He found her kneeling by a box where she was unpacking paintings and putting them carefully on the floor next to her. He looked at them as she took them out one by one and he was impressed by how good they were.

He saw one of King being chased by a chicken and was amazed by the detail of the picture. It was so good it could have been a photograph.

"Did you paint these?" he asked, impressed.

"Yeah," she answered, distracted. Then, "Found it!"

She pulled out a painting that she took great pains to hide from him while she studied it. Her eyes fluttered from painting to picture repeatedly, making her look like she was watching a Ping-Pong match. Finally, her eyes flew up to meet his.

"Where did you get this picture?" she asked.

Jake shrugged, not sure what was happening.

"My mother gave it to me when she found out I was coming here?"

"Okay. But, why did she have it?"

"Well, she took it. That's me holding the baby. The reason I showed it to you was because I was wondering if you knew who the baby was and if she was still in the village. I know it's a long shot but I figured I would ask. If you don't know, I will probably ask Manini about it."

Kuda's eyes widened and her eyebrows shot up.

"That's you? In the picture?"

"Yes. My parents were based here about thirty years ago. I came with them." Jake frowned, not sure what was happening.

"Well," Kuda said, "I know for a fact that she's still here in the village."

"Really?" Jake moved closer to her. He was excited that he would probably get to meet this mystery child that he had held so many years ago. "Have I met her?"

"You have, actually," Kuda told him dryly. With a flourish she turned the painting she was holding in her hands and Jake saw it for the first time. It was a painted replica of the picture he had just given her.

He slowly walked towards Kuda and the painting and held out his hands to take it from her. He sat down, speechless, staring at it. Finally he looked up and couldn't help but smile at the goofy look on Kuda's face.

"How?" was all he asked.

"That child. The one you're holding. That was me almost thirty years ago. I had the exact same picture."

Chapter Nineteen

Reminiscing and Remembering

Jake and Kuda sat in her living room. She sat across from him and looked at the pictures, upside down. Jake stared at both the picture and the drawing, still not believing it. All this time she had been right here. For now, as they sat in the same room, their hostility seemed to have fallen away. For once, they were just a couple who had discovered that they had an amazing connection. They hadn't said much in the last half hour, almost as though talking would take away the magic of the moment. Finally, however, someone had to break the silence.

"So we have a history," Jake said, shaking with laughter.

"Who knew?" Kuda asked, cracking up as well.

They sat grinning at each other like manic monkeys at a luau. They were relaxed and at ease in each other's company.

"So I saw you in diapers," Jake teased and Kuda actually giggled.

"Unfortunately. I just can't believe that the boy in the picture is you. I've waited a lifetime to meet him. You. Yeah. The boy. Who's not a boy anymore. It's all so confusing."

Jake laughed again. Giddier than a school girl.

"How did your parents end up here?" Kuda asked.

"My dad was a doctor and he came here back then, on something of an adventure I guess. Mom came with him and I became part of the troupe," Jake said with a grin.

"It's still so hard to believe," Kuda told him, her hilarity slowly easing. "How long were you in Jackalas for?"

"We lived here for a year. Unfortunately only a month of that was after you were born and we had to leave when you were still very little." There was a tinge of regret in his voice and that seemed to sober them both up a little. "Dad got ill and they decided the best place to treat him was back in the U.S. We all packed up and flew back." Jake dropped his head a little, his eyes sad. "He died though. Barely three months after we got back."

"I'm sorry to hear that, Jake," Kuda said, her voice soft. "It can't have been easy for you and your mother."

He gave her a small smile. "I haven't thought about him in a while but being here like this just made me remember."

Kuda smiled back. A look seemed to pass between them and Kuda felt her eyes widening. Not this again, she thought as she felt her pulse quicken a bit. Perhaps her conversation with Manini had her seeing Jake in a new light and now, with this mellow moment and sharing of memories, things seemed to be getting cosy. A little too intimate actually. Not good.

She frowned and lowered her eyes. As she lowered them, they fell upon the picture. She stared at it for a while. Anywhere other than at Jake's doleful eyes was good actually. That way she could control her wayward thoughts a little more. Her frown deepened.

"Have you ever wondered what these shadows around us were?" she asked, changing the subject. Jake followed her gaze and then nodded.

"All the time," he told her. "At first I thought it was the angle of the camera and the lighting but they just seem to be…" he thought of a word that would adequately describe what he wanted to express and came up short. "Wrong," he finally said after a pause.

He saw her nod. "When I was painting the picture, I remembered every detail of it but I couldn't bring myself to paint them in. They do seem wrong and somewhat creepy, to be honest."

It was Jake's turn to nod. He looked up at Kuda. Something she had said struck him. "You remembered every detail?" he asked. "What do you mean?"

When he asked this question, he saw her face close up. Kuda closed her eyes for a moment and when she opened them, it was her turn to look down.

"When I was fifteen my home burnt down. I lost everything. I lost the picture as well but I was able to draw it from memory. I had looked at it often enough to be able to." She gave a wry smile but refused to look up.

Jake wondered at her choice of words. "I lost everything" instead of "*WE* lost everything". It implied so many things but from the shuttered look that had just appeared on Kuda's face, he knew not to push for answers. Not tonight anyway.

Taking the picture off the table he stood up and pulled his wallet out of his pocket. He tucked the picture away in it and smiled down at Kuda. She was looking up at him now and decided that perhaps standing up too was a good idea. She took her painting and walked to her room while Jake stayed behind in the sitting room. After she had put the painting away, she came back to where Jake still stood.

"I guess I best get home," he said to her. "It was lovely to meet you, my little African, Blue Blanket Baby."

Kuda burst out laughing at his silliness. She shook her head and gestured with her hand, indicating that Jake should precede her to the door. He crab-walked around the table and headed to the door she had indicated, a small smile on his face the whole time.

He walked to the door, which he opened. Kuda was behind him and indicated that she would walk him out. The two walked slowly to the gate, side by side. King detached himself from the side of the house and joined them. Kuda ruffled his fur and then bent down to give him a big hug for some reason. King nuzzled her neck and Jake was once again struck by just how big the canine was. He looked like he could easily swallow Kuda whole if he wanted to.

Kuda stood up and looked at Jake for a second before her eyes slid away and looked off into the distance.

"Jake, I…" Her voice trailed off and she fell silent. Her body had tensed up and her jaw was locked up like she was holding something back that she wanted to tell him. Like her whole body was revolting against making whatever revelation she wanted to make.

"What is it?" he asked her, his own voice soft.

She frowned, still not looking at him. For a terse minute he thought she wasn't going to tell him what she had meant to, and his own body tensed up. He wasn't sure he wanted to hear what she had to say all of a sudden. She turned to look at him and in her eyes was such sorrow that he almost took an involuntary step back.

"When I said I lost everything when I was fifteen, I meant it. I don't want to talk about it right now but I just wanted to tell you what I meant." Kuda took a deep breath and when she spoke, her voice was a broken sound of shattered emotion that made Jake feel like his own life had been a paradise compared to what she had been through.

"My mother was murdered when I was fifteen and I witnessed the whole thing."

* * *

Jake lay in his bed looking up at his ceiling in the near dark of his bedroom. The lights were off and his window was open, allowing a cooling breeze to flow softly over his shirtless body.

His left arm pillowed his head and for the life of him he couldn't fall asleep. He couldn't get over what Kuda had told him and he hurt for the child who had witnessed the death of her mother.

After she had made that incredible announcement, Jake hadn't known whether to hug her or ask for more detail about what had happened. He remembered making a strangled sound at the back of his throat and then taking her hand in his. She hadn't pulled away. Inadequate as it was, all he was able to say to her was "I'm sorry."

She had nodded in acknowledgment of what he had said and opened the gate to let him out. When Kuda had opened the gate, King had shot out like a bullet and disappeared into the night. Kuda had called after him but he had ignored her. She had shrugged and said that he would be back shortly. He was able to jump over the fence easily, so she wasn't worried that he wouldn't be able to come back into the yard.

Jake had left after that, walking in the night with no fear that anything would happen to him. So unlike life in New York.

Now, he sighed and turned to lie on his side. He tried to think about what could have happened to Kuda's mom, and how she had handled everything afterwards. His heart bled for the fifteen year old girl whose mother had been taken away from her. He could not imagine going through what she had gone through at her age. Difficult would not begin to describe it.

When his own father had passed, he had been too young to fully realise what it meant. He remembered missing his being around as well as his mother crying a lot during that time, but that was it. He hadn't really missed his father until much later in his life, when he realised that other boys had someone they could sit and watch football with; to teach them to drive or chat about girls in a way that his mother probably wouldn't have approved of.

Still...Kuda had been through a hell that very few people got to know.

* * *

He must have fallen asleep. Surely he had because there was no other plausible reason for what he was seeing. He tried to raise his head and his head refused to obey him. His hands failed to rise from where they lay on either side of his body. Although he'd fallen asleep with the light on, his room was almost completely dark. His eyes moved to the globe on the ceiling and he realised that despite the darkness around him, the light was still on. Around him was a wall of shadows that were humanoid in shape. They just stood there and did nothing, surrounding him like a barrier of darkness.

Again he tried to move but again his body denied him. He felt his breath catch in his throat and his lungs rose and fell with each inhalation and exhalation. His eyes darted this way and that, trying to see past the shadows that were all around him. He felt panic set in and he felt like his chest was going to implode, when, just that like, the shadows were gone and the room was restored to full brightness.

Suddenly he had the full use of all his limbs and he jumped up off his chair like he had been poked with a blazing hot pitchfork. He walked slowly around the room but there was no sign of the darkness that had been around his bed like a halo around a giant head.

Something drew him to the window and he looked outside, towards Kuda's home. The chill that he felt hit him all at once.

He couldn't see the building that Kuda called home for the shadows that surrounded it completely.

Chapter Twenty
Shaken

The day had been hard. Try as she might, Kuda had not been able to raise a smile. She had made an effort, however, when she and Jake had helped Manini out again after work. The milking had been done and the cattle were secure in the *kraal.*

"Come," Manini said to Jake. "I will show you how to make some *zengwe*. Perhaps you will learn how to make it quicker than Kuda did. She cannot cook to save her life and were you to marry her you would surely die of hunger."

Kuda gasped and Jake chuckled. Washington let out a full-throated laugh and patted her on the back.

"Don't worry, child," he consoled her. "I've eaten your cooking. It's not that bad." Kuda was starting to feel vindicated when he added, "I mean, if it hasn't killed me yet, it never will."

Grumbling beneath her breath, Kuda marched towards Una. "You have more respect for me than those two," she told him. "And if you say one thing about my cooking, you're the only one small enough to put over my knee." She gave him a warning look as he started to speak. Una grinned and walked to his hut. When he had his hand firmly on the handle, he looked back at Kuda. His face wore the biggest, sunniest smile a face could ever wear.

"It's because of her food that I am currently suffering from stunted growth. I wouldn't touch it if I were you." Una said this just before he disappeared into the hut.

Kuda couldn't help it. She stared at the closed door with her mouth wide open for a few seconds as the other three guffawed around her, Washington literally bent over from mirth. She burst out laughing as well, her hands wrapped around her stomach as tears streamed down her face. This went on for a few minutes until she took a deep breath and let it out slowly.

"That boy will be the death of me," she said.

"Not the other way around?" Jake asked with a smirk.

"Don't you start too. My cooking is not that bad and to put all those rumours to death, I'll invite you to a meal so you can judge for yourself."

"Should I risk it, Manini?" Jake asked, looking at the old woman.

"I don't want to be an accessory to murder, but if you feel like you have nothing to lose, go ahead," Manini responded.

"Oh, come on. My cooking is not that bad. Jake already ate it and he survived to tell the tale," Kuda retaliated.

"Kuda, that is not something I would go around telling people. I mean, they could get the wrong idea and believe you actually tried to poison Jake. Can you imagine? His *muti* must be very strong," Manini said.

"What's *muti*?" Jake asked.

"It's got something to do with powerful medicine," Kuda tried to explain. "Not medicine as in vaccines and antibiotics but as in magic and traditional medicine. Something like that, anyway. Manini believes in it."

"And you don't, Kuda?" Manini asked.

"No, I don't," Kuda said, shaking her head firmly. "*Muti* brings to mind, my mind anyway, visions of people dancing around a huge fire, waving so-called potions and making promises to long dead people who can't even hear them. Superstition is one thing, but belief in black magic is something else. It's all rubbish as far as I am concerned."

Kuda was a bit disconcerted, however, when she looked at Manini and saw the fury in her eyes. Her face was still and she looked as though she had been frozen in time. She turned away from Kuda and mixed the ground millet into the water that she had been boiling.

"Manini, don't tell me that you believe in that nonsense," Kuda continued. "It's all hogwash."

Manini was silent for some time as she stirred the pot which was sitting on the open fire, slowly mixing the millet to make a smooth porridge. The flames licked the bottom of the pot and made their dark mark on it. In the fading afternoon sun, the red heat of the flames on the black of the pot was a beautiful contrast.

"I believe," Manini said finally, softly. "And I also believe that your inability to comprehend things that are invisible to the human eye may, in the future, harm you more than you think. You must always be prepared to look beyond what you see, Kuda, for it is only then that you can make out what lies beyond the superficial things that are in front of you. Remember that."

"You speak as though my life will depend on that statement one day, Manini. I'm not denying that sometimes in life we can be harmed by things we overlook, but I refuse to believe in the idea that our ancestors or dead beings or ghosts are out there watching over us and keeping us out of harm's way."

"Then you have been detached from where you come from for too long," Manini told her.

"I know exactly where I come from and where I am going." Kuda stood with her hands on her hips, looking at Manini. Gone was the laughter they had shared such a short time ago. In its place was an emotion Jake was not sure he could decipher.

"You know no such thing. Despite all your learning, you are still an ignorant child who fails to tune in to what goes on around her. I had given you more credit than that and I see I was wrong." Manini did not raise her voice but Jake saw that the knuckles of the hand she was using to stir her porridge were bone white. If she squeezed the spoon any harder it was likely to crack. He also noticed that Kuda was as still as a baobab tree in a windstorm. Washington stood shuffling his feet behind her, like himself, clearly unsure of what was going on.

"What has gotten into you?" Kuda asked. "I never took you to be such a superstitious, old —"

Manini stood up so quickly that the breeze her skirt created caused the flames to flicker. She turned to Kuda and the wrath in her eyes made the younger woman close her mouth at once.

"Kuda Chilume, go home at once lest I say something I may regret tomorrow. But let me leave you with a thought; if our lives are random patterns that are not guided by unseen forces, why then do you see the things you see in your dreams? Perhaps they are nothing more than random images, but what if they are a warning of things to come? Have you thought of that, child? What if they are preparing you for what is to be? Remember that from now on and don't let your arrogance be your downfall. Be prepared for anything. Perhaps what you see in your dreams are images that your forefathers put there to keep reminding you of what is to be."

The look of horror on Kuda's face made Jake take a step towards her. Her face had tightened and her mouth had opened as though to deny what Manini was saying.

"I never told you about my dreams. How do you know about them?" Kuda asked. Her voice was a whisper, as though afraid that if she spoke too loudly, whatever it was she saw in her dreams would come to life. "And how could you say something like that? Don't you know that what you are saying is worse than anything I have seen in my life?

"Then perhaps you will mark my words, child. Perhaps you will be aware that sometimes in life there are forces out there, other than ourselves, which play a role in our lives."

The two women stood glaring at each other. Both wore the wan expressions of two fighters who had been in a war without understanding how it had started.

"How do you know about my dreams?" Kuda asked again. "How?" Her chest rose and fell as though she was manually trying to get herself under control.

"Perhaps one of those dead people you speak so ill of whispered it in my ear not too long ago." There was a triumphant look on Manini's face that nobody watching her understood. Jake was confused by the expression and the confusion was not untainted by an element of unease. He had never thought Manini would be cruel but the look on her face reminded him of the look he had seen on many young boys' faces as they set beetles on fire with cigarette lighters.

Kuda turned and left the compound without another word. Jake stared after her, not comprehending what had just happened. For a moment his fury at Manini was barely containable. Then, he saw her, saw how the expression that had baffled him had been replaced by fatigue. She looked like she had aged a hundred years in a minute, as though she had taken a heck of a beating from life but was still standing. He looked at her and he felt ashamed. Still, he wanted to know what had just happened. He *needed* to know.

"No, Jake. Please don't ask. Not now. A time will come when you will understand, but for now, please let it be."

Manini looked at him with such appeal in her aged eyes that Jake could do nothing but nod. "Now, go after her. Make sure she gets home alright."

Jake nodded again and turned to go. He was not surprised to see that Washington had moved backwards into the shadow of a hut that was behind him. Kuda was nothing but a shape in the darkness and he said his goodbyes and hurried after her. He jogged up to her, caught up and fell into step beside her.

"Are you alright?" he asked her.

No response came from her and Jake wasn't sure if he had missed it or if she had responded by some means he could not perceive in the near darkness. The moon was just making its light known and its luminosity would soon blanket the land and them. The sun had already beat its lazy retreat beneath the horizon and had it not been for the full moon, darkness would have covered them like a shroud.

Jake touched her elbow and she stopped. Her head was bowed and she stared at her feet for quite a while. Jake stood by her side, allowing her the time she needed to regain her composure. When she started walking again without looking up at him, he simply followed her.

Finally, when he could no longer handle her silence, Jake spoke. "What happened back there?" He wasn't sure she would answer him but he was hoping she would.

"I don't know," Kuda said and Jake released a breath that he did not know he had been holding.

"What's the deal with the dreams?"

Kuda laughed and the sound made Jake's stomach lurch. It was a harsh cackle. It was a sound so alien to her that Jake almost told her to never laugh like that again.

"I don't know why I'm surprised," she said. "Manini has always known a lot of things. I don't know why I thought I could hide the dreams from her. It was stupid, really."

"Kuda, I don't know what you're talking about. What *about* the dreams?"

"The dreams? I'm not sure I would call them dreams, Jake. You've seen how I respond to them. Dreams are fun and sweet and make you smile when you're sleeping. They don't make you scream and wish you would wake up. They don't make you wish you were dead, just so you wouldn't have them anymore. Then, just when you wish you would die, you think, what if I *do* die and I have the dreams and they just go on and on because you can't even wake up anymore. And then you do wake up and pray they never come back again. But you know as soon as you sleep that night, they *will* come back, worse than before. No, Jake. I don't have dreams. I have life altering illusions that carry over into my waking life."

Kuda had stopped to look at him as she spoke. She had not raised her voice but the flatness of her speech made pinpoints of dread mark their way across Jake's chest. There was a fear in Kuda's eyes that belied the lack of tonality in her voice. It was as though she was afraid to let loose any emotion for fear that whatever it was she was afraid of was nearby and would jump out at her if she spoke too surely. As Jake was about to respond to her, he caught a movement of shadow out of the corner of his eye. Kuda saw it too. At the same moment.

They both turned.

Chapter Twenty One

Things That Go Bump

As they stood in the darkness, they saw a miniature hurricane of blackness coming towards them. It twirled this way and that, inflating and deflating like a Halloween balloon that had millions of tiny whirlwinds in it. It stood about two metres high and was about a meter and a half wide across the middle. It funnelled off at both ends and gyrated maniacally towards where they stood. As it got closer, the buzzing sound that emanated from it became louder and louder.

"What the hell is that?" Jake asked and, not sure of how lethal it was, both he and Kuda backed away from it.

The billowing ball of black was suspended in the air, about fifteen centimetres from the ground and, without warning, it shattered before their eyes and was gone. Jake and Kuda stared at the spot where the darkness had disintegrated and then looked at each other. Kuda took a step towards the place where the whole thing had happened and Jake put out his hand to stop her.

"Since we don't know what that was, it might be prudent to stay clear of it," he told her.

"Whatever it was, it's not there anymore. What are the odds that it will come back?" And so saying, she took another step forward. Jake tightened his fingers on her arm but she moved forward before he could get a grip of her arm. He followed her and heard her gasp a few seconds later. On the ground were thousands of dead flies. They lay in little heaps of black, as though someone had deliberately sifted them through a giant strainer and left them there. Kuda moved a pile with the tip of her shoe, expecting them to take off all at once.

Nothing happened.

They were definitely dead. Jake squatted to take a closer look but none of the dead insects moved.

"I've never seen flies do that," he said. "I wonder what caused it." He stretched out his hand but thought better about touching the piles of dead insects. He stood up and brushed off his hands on his pants anyway. "Come on. We should get going."

Kuda backed away from the insectile carnage and brushed her hands off her pants as well, as though she could feel the insects crawling around in the palm of her hands. Although it was not a hot night, she knew that within the next few seconds, her whole body would start to sweat. She looked around frantically, expecting the shadows that she knew would be close.

Memories of dead flies on window sills rushed into her mind but refused to take form. Vague thoughts of little fat-bellied flies lying dead throbbed in her mind, bringing images but not tying them to anything. The feeling of knowing but not grasping that knowledge had her shaking her head, as though to dispel the familiarity of what she was experiencing. She looked around, seeking something, yet not knowing what.

As she turned, Jake's presence forgotten for the moment, her eyes caught sight of a dark figure and she felt a scream forming in her chest.

She took a step back, stumbled and fell butt first into the dead flies lying behind her. Her hands went back to break her fall and she felt the give of a thousand little bodies as her weight landed on them. With a scream, she pushed off the ground and hopped around like a grasshopper on a caffeine fix, brushing the squashed bodies off herself. She waved her hands in the air to try and flick them off but when she saw that the flies were stuck she wiped them off of the front of her t-shirt. She stared down at herself in disgust, at the mess that was left on her chest. Blood and gore were mixed there in equal proportions and she stood still, not knowing what to do next.

Jake saw the dismay on her face and rushed to her side. He started to brush off all the dead insects on her chest and then the seat of her pants. Not sure where to start first, he used one hand for her front and one for her back. When he saw how ineffective this was, he settled for starting with her t-shirt. When that was as clean as it was going to get, he started to brush off her pants. When he heard her gasp, he wondered what was wrong this time. He stopped what he was doing and looked up at her from his half bend, brushing-off-pants position. He followed her stare and saw a dark figure standing not too far from where they were. Jake automatically pushed Kuda behind him.

"Good evening, Kuda," the figure said in Kalanga.

Jake recognised the greeting. So Kuda knew this person. It was probably alright then. He relaxed and made to move back to her side but she gripped his arms and stayed behind him. He glanced behind him and saw that Kuda was deliberately using him as a barrier. Her eyes had that same wild look that they had had when she had woken up from her nightmare and seeing that made him tense up all over again.

"What do you want?" Kuda asked in the same language. Her voice was a panicked whisper. She kept herself safely behind Jake's back.

The old man chuckled. "Is that any way to greet an old man, my child?" he asked.

"I'm not your child. Don't call me that." Her voice was a near scream and once again Jake felt his hackles rising. What the hell was going on here tonight? Who was this old man? Jake was sure that he had never seen him before. But, if Kuda knew him, and they obviously had some history together, what was upsetting her?

Her grip on his arm was applying enough pressure to actually hurt him a little but that was not what was bothering him. Kuda was scared of this man. Terrified would actually have been a more apt word. He could hear how her breath sped up from behind him and the way she had spoken had seriously freaked him out.

"Who are you?" Jake asked the old man.

For a long moment the man did not speak. Then, he turned and looked at Jake for the first time. He stared at him for what seemed like an extraordinarily long time. The old man wore a long coat that covered him from his neck to his ankles, despite the heat. His gnarled hands held onto a cane that looked like a shepherd's hook; almost as tall as he was, with a curve at the end. He wore a hat that was pulled low on his head, over his eyes. His collar was pulled up and all that Jake could make out was a hint of nose and white teeth when he smiled.

"Doctor Dawn," he said. If two pieces of sandpaper had been rubbed together, the sound they would have made would not have been more raspy than the sound that came from the man's throat. "You and I have not met."

"You seem to have an advantage over me, sir. I don't know who you are."

"You will," the man promised, then turned his attention back to Kuda. "Kuda, you and I have some unfinished business."

"I have no business with you," Kuda whispered. "None. Just leave me alone."

"Very well. Tonight is neither the time nor the place." The man looked up at the sky, at the moon. Kuda followed his gaze and a whimper escaped her. The old man smiled and Jake knew right there that he hated this man with a vengeance. He had terrified Kuda, which was bad. What was worse was that there was such *badness* surrounding him that it was palpable. There was also a threat in his gesture, that one movement of looking up at the moon. What the *hell* was going on here?

"Come on, Kuda. I'm taking you home," Jake told her. Kuda refused to move. "Come on," he said softly, moving his arm back and putting it around her shoulders. He moved her, somewhat forcibly, but it seemed to be the only way he was likely to get her feet to take a step.

"Until we meet again, Doctor Dawn," the old man said as they moved off. He docked his hat, a gesture that was somehow mocking and completely menacing in its attitude. Jake felt like throwing a punch but he concentrated instead on getting Kuda out of there. He didn't even bother to respond. After he had taken a few steps, making sure that Kuda did the same, he turned back to check if he was following them. It was more an involuntary response than anything else. When he saw that the old man was not following them, he didn't know whether to be relieved or not.

What did worry him, and it bothered him a hell of a lot, was the fact that he couldn't see the other man at all.

* * *

"Kuda, who was that?" They were back in Kuda's home and Jake felt that if he held back the questions any more he would burst.

"I don't want to talk about it, Jake. Not now. Not ever." Her hands were around the mug of hot tea he had made for her. They shook so badly that she had actually spilt the hot liquid on them a few times. She hadn't seemed to notice though.

"I just want to help, that's all," he said to her.

"There is nothing you can do," she said flatly.

Jake banged his own mug on the table and was satisfied when she jumped. He stood up and headed to the door.

"Alright then. I'm off. I'd offer my services but I know they would be rebuffed so have a wonderful night and I will see you at the clinic." He headed for the door and had his hand on the handle when Kuda spoke. He turned to face her.

"Events were set in motion fifteen years ago and they can't be changed now." She looked up at Jake and the appeal in her eyes was his undoing. He came and sat down beside her. He took the mug from her and put it on the table. Then, he took her hand in his.

"What's going on?" he asked her.

"Things have happened in my life that I have never been able to understand. How could I expect *you* to?"

"If you tell me, we could work it out, Kuda." She laughed out loud at that one.

"It's not that simple. It never has been."

"Then let's take it from the beginning and we'll see where it lands us."

Kuda shook her head. "Now is not the time or the place to go into it."

"There will never be the right time or the right place. Don't you see that? Every day that I see you, you become more and more afraid. I don't know why but I would like to help. Tell me what's going on. Please." Jake continued to hold Kuda's hand and felt frustrated when she shook her head.

"I don't know what's going on," she told him. Her voice was a soft plea. "All I know is that I have these really strange dreams. Every night it's the same dream and every night I wake up with charcoal on my hands. There are drawings…"

"What drawings?" he prompted when it seemed as though she didn't know how to continue.

She stood up, withdrew her hand from his and paced in the small space of her living room. She rubbed her hands in agitation as she walked. She wound her fingers together and released them, squeezing and rubbing all the while. She looked at him, looked away and then back at him again.

"When Manini talked about my dreams, it scared me," she said, changing topics slightly. "I never told her about them because I was afraid to. But, she's got this way of knowing things about me. Ever since I was a kid she's known stuff about me that no one else ever did. So it really freaked me out when she talked about them because of all the things I have hidden from her over the years, she should have mentioned them sooner."

"Have you always had them?" Jake asked. The goose bumps on his arms refused to go away. Kuda shook her head.

"No. Not always. I had them as a kid. Not as grisly as they have been over the past few weeks, but I did dream often about things that came true. Then they stopped for a while when I was at school. When I came back here, after I graduated, they started up again. Recently, though, they have gotten so bad that they terrify me even when I'm awake." Her voice had toned down to a whisper. Her hands were still busy but at least she had stopped pacing. "I … I draw this … this *thing.* Every night for the past couple of months I have woken up and there are drawings of it all around me. Every night it gets closer. And, sometimes, I don't even dream but when I wake up, the drawings are all around me."

She stopped talking and abruptly sat down, as though her feet couldn't support her anymore.

"Can I see the drawings?" Jake wasn't sure he wanted to but he felt that he had to. Perhaps it would help him understand why she was so upset. Perhaps seeing her drawings would help him ease her fears. He was sure she was going to refuse. Instead, she looked at him and nodded.

"They're in the spare bedroom," she said as she stood up. Her voice still had not risen much above a whisper. She stayed where she was for a second, as though gathering her strength. Then, she walked to the bedroom and he followed close behind her. He heard her strike a match and almost immediately the effects of the gas lamp filled the room with white light.

What he saw stopped him at the door.

On the floor were dozens of charcoal drawings. In each one was a face that looked half human and half something else. He took a closer look and realised what the other half was; hyena. The angles were different in each picture but it was obviously the same face.

Jake took a step inside and looked around him. As he looked, he felt the skin around his neck tightening. He felt his throat constrict as he swallowed some saliva.

He bent and picked up the closest drawing. In it the creature was smaller, further away. The features were still the same but there was a distance between himself and the beast in the drawing. He could feel it. He looked around and saw another picture. This time the spit wouldn't go down as he tried to swallow. His mouth was dry.

He bent and picked this one up too. The hairs on his body refused to lie flat. If anything, they stood up even more. In this drawing the creature was almost out of the picture. It was as though it were physically straining to burst through the paper that contained it.

"The one you picked up first; I drew about six weeks ago. The other one was two nights ago," Kuda told him. "From the way you are staring, I guess you picked up on the progression."

Jake stared at her.

"Did you do this deliberately?" he asked. His voice was so hoarse he almost believed it didn't come from him. He coughed slightly to clear it.

"How could I, Jake? I wake up every morning and there is at least one new picture on my floor. I don't even remember how I did them. All I know is that I *did* draw them and they are scaring the hell out of me. This thing is coming and from its proximity in that picture I'd say it was almost here."

"That's impossible," he breathed and the moment he said it he knew it was the wrong thing to have said.

Kuda took a step back, distancing herself from him physically and mentally. Quickly he put the pictures down and moved over to where she stood. He had to step over quite a few drawings to get to her. He grasped her arms but she turned her face away.

"I didn't mean it that way," he told her. She looked up at him. Her eyes were huge in her wan face, making her look lost and hopeless.

"You asked me to show you and I did." Her voice was smaller than it had been before. Jake felt a pang in his heart that had nothing to do whatsoever with physical pain. "This has not been easy for me and I don't know how much longer I can handle it. You look at the pictures, Jake. You look at them and tell me how I could possibly do this voluntarily."

The fear was back in her voice. Jake cursed himself for being an idiot and pulled her to him without thinking. He held her to him and felt calmer.

"I'm sorry. This whole thing is just so strange. I don't understand what's going on here and I'm not sure I know how to react to everything." He held her closer and was pleased when he felt her arms wrap themselves around his waist. He laid his chin on top of her head and sighed. "Why have you kept them?" he asked.

Kuda shrugged. He felt the movement and tightened his arms around her.

"I didn't know what else to do with them," she said. Her voice was muffled against his chest. "It's almost as if by keeping them here I could keep track of this thing."

She pulled back a little from him and looked up at his face. Her irises were large brown orbs in pools of white. "Every night it draws closer and I feel as though if I didn't have these pictures near me, that it would sneak up on me and get me while I was asleep. Or unsuspecting. It doesn't make sense but that's how I feel."

But it did make sense. In a strange way it made a lot of sense. And looking at the pictures scattered around Kuda's room, Jake wished like hell that it wouldn't make sense at all.

Chapter Twenty Two

Weird Becomes Disturbing

When Kuda bumped into Jake the following day at the clinic, she didn't know whether to nod and walk on or stop and say good morning. He had left soon after seeing the drawings the previous night. He had asked her if she needed anything and she had told him no. Somehow, her refusal of his help had changed the mood and he had left soon after. Now, in broad daylight, things were different. The atmosphere was not the same as it had been the previous night and had it not been for the fact that she had walked past the spare room that morning, she would have convinced herself that the previous night had been nothing but a bad dream.

For a moment she stood and watched Jake, not knowing what to say to him. Their relationship had changed last night. Nothing was the same anymore. He had seen a part of her that she had always kept hidden from the world, a part that not even Manini or Aaron had ever seen.

"Good morning," Jake said to her. There was an intensity in his eyes that reminded her of their first encounter. He wasn't sure how she would react to him this morning and somehow that made it easier for her. She smiled.

"Morning. How was your night?" she asked him.

"Fine, thank you. And yours? Any more bad dreams?"

Kuda shook her head. She walked past him and took the coat that was behind him. She pulled it on before she turned to face him. "Sometimes they don't happen every night. I should be used to it by now."

What she didn't tell him was that even though the nightmare didn't come every night, when it did come, the thing would be closer still. As though it had snuck up on her when she wasn't looking. Sometimes, the "not knowing" where the creature would be in the next dream terrified her more than having the dream every night. She looked down and busied herself by buttoning up her coat so that he wouldn't see there was more to it than she was letting on.

"You didn't sleep much last night." It wasn't a question. Jake raised his hand and touched her cheek. "You look absolutely worn out."

"I'll live," she told him and the thought was immediately followed by a hysterical *"Will you?"* that bounded and echoed in her head like a bumblebee trapped in a plastic container. She stifled a wild laugh and bit her lower lip to keep it inside. "I have to go," she told Jake and ducked past him before he could say anything.

She walked out of the room without adding anything more and as she left, she knew that had she looked back, Jake would have been looking after her with a baffled and concerned look in his eyes. He was already in too deep for her liking and she wasn't sure she wanted him any more involved.

It was dangerous out there and something was coming for her. She didn't want Jake around when it finally came because it would mean certain death for anyone near her when it happened. She would just have to keep away from him. Somehow she knew that would be a lot easier said than done.

When she bumped into the second body she thought it was ironic and a small smile came to her face. It was immediately wiped away when she realised who it was that she had collided with.

"What are you doing here?" Her question was sharp and abrupt and she felt her eyes narrowing as she spoke.

"Medical treatment," Timile said. It took a lot of control but Kuda decided that slapping the smirk off his face was not worth the trouble after the satisfaction of doing it had worn off.

"Alright then," she replied with a little smirk of her own. "I'll see if Doctor Dawn can attend to you. I've got more important patients of my own that need me."

The look that dropped onto his face was definitely better than what she had anticipated. She felt her grin grow.

"Do you think you're too good for me?" he snarled and Kuda knew that had she been alone, she would have thought twice about antagonising him any further. Somehow, Jake's presence in the other room bolstered her confidence.

"Don't you know it," she said. "And let me tell you something else, you egomaniacal jackass. If you were drowning in a bucket of water, it would not be worth the clothes on my back to put my hand in that bucket and pull your face out."

Timile's jaw dropped and Kuda's smirk grew.

"I'll make you pay for that, you little –"

"Cut the rubbish," Kuda hissed. She was suddenly furious. She felt her chest rise as it refused to settle. She felt as though she was about to choke on her pent-up emotions. "You have threatened me and followed me and been on my case for as long as I can remember. I have had it with your snide remarks and your insinuations and your leers and everything that you have done to me in the past few years. I will not be intimidated by you anymore, do you understand me?"

Kuda took a step toward him and poked a finger into his chest. Her voice was barely above a whisper as she continued. "I have wasted too much effort and emotion on you and I will not do it anymore. I will not be scared of you nor will I back down from you ever again, Timile. If you get your kicks out of hurting people who can't fight back then it's just not happening with me anymore. I'm not afraid of you. I'm just fed up. You stay away from me. I am not taking crap from you anymore."

The two of them stood facing each other for what seemed like aeons. There was no movement from anywhere and it seemed as though the very air they breathed had come to a standstill. They were in limbo. Timile's face was slack with shock, as though his jaw-bone had been pulled from the lower half of his face. The look on his face should have made Kuda want to cheer but the events of the last few weeks had gotten to her. She didn't have the energy.

As she watched him, however, the slackness was replaced slowly by a sly look. The shock gave way to a grin that crawled its way over his face and made him look like a wolf that had just seen a fawn. His eyes narrowed and he ran his tongue over his lips. Slowly. Suggestively.

"You don't know what I'm capable of, do you?" he said. He pushed his face close to hers and it was all she could do to keep from flinching. She held her ground and raised her chin so their noses were almost touching.

"You try me and I swear you will get more than you bargained for. I'm not running from you anymore. I've run away from you so for most of my life and I'm done."

Their noses stayed so close Kuda could see the sweat beads as they broke out on Timile's skin. His eyes were mud-brown and as she looked into them she knew deep down that she had been right to be afraid of this man. Not by moving a muscle would she betray that though.

His teeth flashed in a sudden grin and she had to bite the inside of her mouth to keep her composure. She tasted blood.

Timile moved closer.

"Didn't you ever wonder," he whispered into her ear, and he was so close his breath caressed the side of her face and her hair. "Didn't you ever ask yourself how your mother ended up at the bottom of that ravine? She was my first little accident. You will be my last. And believe me, for you, it will be worse. Much worse."

Kuda felt as though a hand were squeezing her heart within her chest. She felt as though she would not be able to breathe ever again. But she did. She leaned closer to Timile's ear and whispered into it the same way he had whispered into hers.

"I've known all these years, you sick bastard. All these years your little secret has been our little secret and you never knew it. Now, aren't you asking yourself what other little secrets of yours I know? I know you are. So go to that little hole in your head that no one else can access and think about that one before you make any more 'surprise' revelations."

She leaned back enough to look him in the eyes. The triumphant look was gone and the crazy look she had seen so often of late was back.

"Go home. I don't want you here." She stood her ground, not giving an inch. It didn't matter that he stood a head above her or that he was big enough to squeeze the life out of her with his bare hands. She had had enough and she wasn't about to tolerate anymore. "Go home," she told him more forcefully, the way she would a dog that had soiled her garden.

He looked like he wanted to choke her, to wrap his arms around her neck and squeeze until she lay limp, without breath. He actually took a step closer to her but in the split second it took Kuda to wonder what she was going to do next, he stopped. He looked up, above her head, and the snarl on his face deepened.

"This is not over," he said to her. "Not by a long shot." He spun on his heels, pushed through the swing doors and was gone.

Kuda drew a shaky breath and felt her shoulders slump. She raised her hand, wiped at her mouth and was not surprised to find blood when she drew her hand back. She turned to find something she could use to wipe the blood off her face. There was bound to be something in the other room. But first, she had to make a conscious effort to get her legs to function. She stayed where she was for a moment, feeling the shakiness of her limbs retreat. When she felt she was anchored enough she willed herself to move.

She pushed through the doors and saw that Jake was busy at the computer. *How much had he heard?* She wondered. Probably nothing unless he had been standing right at the door, which he clearly hadn't been. He looked up.

"Are you alright?" he asked her. "You look shaky." He stood up and walked over to her. Kuda quickly tucked in her head and pulled a wad of napkins from the roll standing by the door.

"I'm fine," she lied. Her hand shook a little bit and she put the white serviettes to her mouth. She dabbed at it but it was no longer bleeding as much as she thought it would be. That was quite a nip she had given herself. She looked up at Jake as he stood beside her.

"You would tell me if you were in trouble, wouldn't you?" he asked her.

Kuda looked at him, at the face that had become so dear to her in the short time that he had been there. She saw the concern on his face, the way the creases around his eyes had deepened. A frown had made a resting place on his forehead and the lines there reminded her of chocolate swirls. He did not touch her but she felt comforted.

"Are *you* alright?" she said instead of answering his question. "You look a little pale."

Jake smiled. "I'm alright. I just didn't get much sleep last night."

Kuda nodded, and threw the wadded napkins into the trash can.

"I'd best get back to work," she told him. She gave him a small smile as she pushed open the door and left the room.

* * *

Jake's hands were shaking so he pushed them into his pockets almost violently. He took a ragged breath and tried to calm himself. He wanted to smash something. No, correction. He wanted to bash Timile's face in with his bare hands; cause him as much pain as he seemed to have caused Kuda. And the damning part of it was that Kuda's pain at that man's hands was more than just physical, it was also psychological.

He had been about to leave the office when he had heard Timile telling Kuda about the ravine. The door was slightly ajar and he had seen the two of them almost nose to nose. For a quick second he had wondered what the hell was going on but when he heard Timile's whispered words he had frozen in shock. He had heard everything.

He had also seen the fury in Timile's eyes when Kuda had stood up to him and just as Timile had been about to do something – he didn't know what – he had looked up and seen him standing at the door. Jake had no idea what Timile had been about to do but it would not have been good. And if he had hurt a hair on Kuda's head, Jake would have killed him. Timile must have seen the fury on his own face because he had sneered and stepped down from whatever it was he had wanted to do.

When Timile had left abruptly, Jake had hurried back to the desk, not wanting Kuda to see him standing there. Pretending that he hadn't seen anything was one of the hardest things he had ever done.

Kuda needed to understand that she had stood up to Timile and that he had backed down because of it. There would not have been any point in his telling her that Timile had left because he had seen him.

God help him if the two of them met again. He hoped he would have the strength to not beat the man to death with his bare hands.

Chapter Twenty Three
Growing Pangs

Timile sat alone in the dark.

He liked the dark.

It was always peaceful in the dark.

It used not to be that way, however, but he had since made his peace with that. He had spent so much of his life in the shadows that the absence of light was never an issue with him.

He lay on the floor, on his back, with only a white towel wrapped around his waist. His arms were spread out and his bare feet pointed outwards as he rested on the ground. Looking up at the little he could see of his roof, he dozed occasionally, passing in and out of awareness. At times he was actually cognisant of the fact that he was asleep, but there were times when he wasn't sure. He slipped in and out of consciousness and often his dreams merged with his memories. Sometimes the two became intertwined and his dreams became memories while his memories became dreams.

He scratched at a scar on the outside of his left thigh. It was a deep scar and ran a good twelve centimetres. He knew exactly how long it was. He had measured it often enough. He ran his fingers over it without moving the rest of his body and returned his arm to the spread-eagle position that it had been in before. With his other hand he ran his fingers over the ribs on the left side of his body. These had been broken more than once and it had always been a wonder that they had never punctured his lungs and killed him.

His right arm had healed with only a slight twist in it which indicated that it had been set slightly wrong. He had worn the plaster of Paris for eight weeks. Bathing had been a nightmare during that period and keeping it dry had been hard. He had managed, however, and his recovery had been complete. It was a pity that he had had to wear it for another eight weeks when the same arm was broken again hardly three months into its healing.

He touched the puncture wound in his left shoulder. That one had also taken a while to heal. It had been deep and had almost gone clear through his body. Luckily no major arteries or muscles had been damaged and he had been right as rain within a few weeks. Just in time for the scar at the back of his head to become a permanent part of his scar collection.

He took a deep breath and let it out slowly.

Kuda.

She was never far from his thoughts. Every time he breathed he thought of her. It was as though she was sewn into the very fabric of his being. A second never went by that he didn't think about her. It wasn't even about being obsessed. It was almost as though the very thought of her was what was keeping him alive. She, however, did not seem to believe that he needed to be an integral part of her life. She constantly spurned him and no matter what he did, she rejected him at every turn. She refused to let him into her life and no matter what he did she turned her nose up at him at every opportunity.

He moaned.

It was a sad, lonely sound that sat deep in his throat. His fingers curled and he balled his hands into fists. He felt his fingernails digging into the soft flesh of his palms and he knew that he would draw blood. He always did. He couldn't seem to stop himself, however, and he felt the warm fluid flow slowly over his hands. He finally uncurled his fingers, the only movement that he made.

His eyes rolled back in their sockets and he felt his eyelids flutter. He moaned again as he thought about Kuda. In his mind's eye he saw her brown eyes and her beautiful lips. Her flawless skin was soft and he often wished he could run his hand over the curve of her cheek and down her neck. She never smiled at him and each time she saw him it seemed as though her lips curled with disgust, like he was something that had been dropped from the rear end of an animal and landed on her table top. In her dessert.

All he wanted was to be a part of her life; to be someone that she could smile at and engage in meaningful conversation with. Someone who she could hug and share private jokes with. Someone whom she could hold close and tell that everything was going to be alright. He wanted so much. So very much.

Once again, his memories floated into his consciousness as he seemed to move from one stage of awareness to another.

* * *

He had been sitting by the river, afraid to go to school that day because he knew the other students would laugh at him. They had in the past and they definitely would do so today as well. His breathing was shallow because breathing too deeply hurt something deep inside his body. He had been afraid to take off his shirt, afraid of what he would find underneath it. He was done crying and knew that he would not cry again that day, no matter what anyone said to him.

He had been sitting there for over half a day, certain that school had started and ended, and that no one would care about where he was anyway. In that entire time, he had barely moved. He had watched the birds come and go, drinking their full or taking their morning baths, and he had envied them their freedom; their delight at being alive. He could not remember the last time that he had had a feeling of delight. If ever.

He heard rocks falling to his left and looked up quickly, suddenly afraid. When he saw who it was that was climbing down the bank to get to where he was, he had smiled despite his pain. Then, he had frowned. She had often seen him like this but he still hated it. He never wanted to upset her and she, invariably, would be distressed. Not because she felt sorry for him, but because she hated the injustice of it all. He did too but there was never anything he could do about it. He had told her that so many times and despite her belief that he *should* do something about it, he didn't believe he could.

He felt her sit down next to him and he looked the other way.

"Hi," Timile heard her say. Her voice was soft and it was almost his undoing.

He mumbled a response without looking at her and she didn't say anything for a while. She sat next to him quietly and they both listened to life happening around them; the bleat of the goats in the pasture; the cows lowing not too far from them; the sound of children screaming laughter further down the riverbed.

"You weren't at school today," she told him. It wasn't an accusation. It was a statement which told him that she had looked for him and had been worried when she had not seen him. Jackalas II Primary School wasn't a big school and he knew everybody knew he hadn't been to school that day and why. It didn't bother him anymore. He had more serious things to worry about. Like whether or not he would be alive to even make it to school the following day.

She stood up and went and stood in front of him. He felt her intense gaze on him but he refused to look at her. When he heard her breath catch in her throat, however, he involuntarily looked up at her. When he saw the tears pool in her eyes he looked quickly away.

"It's not that bad," he whispered. "It's been worse."

And it had been. Today was one of the days which hadn't been as bad as it could have been. It was still bad, but at least today he hadn't bled. At least not much.

She took his hand and gently pulled him up. He felt like his ribs would crack and break as she did so, no matter how carefully she assisted him.

"Come," she said to him. "Mama cooked lunch and it should be ready by now. Your plate is waiting for you."

He swallowed the lump in his throat and tried a smile which he was certain came out all wrong. He had been certain he would not cry any more today but the tears formed behind his lids anyway. He blinked furiously and made sure not one wet drop escaped. He would not cry in front of her. He walked with her, her hand in his, as she walked slowly to accommodate his tentative pace. At one point he stumbled and she caught him, never missing a beat. Her arms were warm and gentle around him. Protecting him.

"Thank you, Kuda," he told her.

She smiled and he knew that he would be okay. At least for the next few hours. She tugged gently at his hand and they continued their measured walk. For that moment, with her hand in his and her beautiful eyes urging him on, he thought he truly knew what happiness was.

* * *

Sliding back into consciousness, Timile opened his eyes into darkness. He had not turned the lights on and the darkness was complete. For a moment he was disoriented; not sure what time it was. Not time as in time, but time as in period. Slowly everything came back to him and he felt his face tightening in anger.

It was time to get up.

He slowly stood up with the grace of a leopard about to get ready for its hunt. He stretched and then walked to his bedroom in the dark. He had work to do tonight and he would need to ensure that he did it right. He had no choice. Messing it up was not an option.

Chapter Twenty Four

Clawed Creatures

It started off pleasantly enough.

The day was too pretty, too painfully calm in the promise of a fresh, spring day. The leaves of the trees were emerald green, the flowers bright assurance of better days to come. The sky was a clear, perfect blue, the blue that poets spoke of in hushed, awestruck voices.

Kuda walked amongst this wonder, her heart light with no worries at all to weigh it down. She took in deep, cleansing breaths and laughed gaily. Life was beautiful and she was a part of it.

Then, without warning, the scenery changed. Black clouds rolled over the baby blue blanket that was the sky and covered it in one swift motion, like a magician pulling darkness out of a hat instead of a rabbit. She was no longer in an open field but stood in the woods, with trees that were so tall she could not see the sky anymore. There was something sinister and threatening in the air and she knew she had to get out of there. The woods were a dangerous place. Nothing played fair in the woods.

"Run!" she screamed in her mind but her scream was voiceless. Absolutely silent. However, something must have warned her because her legs started to move her. She started to run. Up ahead was a clearing and from this clearing shone a white light. She knew that if she could reach the light she would be safe. She knew that as surely as she knew that if she stayed in the woods she would die.

Something was coming after her. Something evil. Something that wanted to hurt her. She ran faster, her breath was a sob in the hollow of her throat. Something laughed at her. A hideous, mocking sound which made her heart freeze. She knew she had to keep running, or else it would catch her, and when it did, it would kill her.

Branches broke behind her as it came for her, tearing through the trees and heading straight for her. She ran. She looked down and saw that even though her legs were moving, she wasn't. It was like being trapped in a time warp. It was like running in slow motion up a down escalator. She took two steps forward and fell three steps back. She looked back and the white light was receding, leaving only a large, black hole. With a mighty effort, she pumped her legs harder, and she was suddenly able to move. She ran in earnest now, legs pumping viciously because she knew she was running for her life. Branches caught her hair and snagged her face, leaving welts on her arms and legs: any part of her body that was exposed. She barely felt the pain of the grabbing branches. Her brain was screaming at her to move. To get out of the woods before it was too late.

She looked at her shoulder, and saw a pair of blood-red eyes. Long, white fangs overcrowded a huge, menacing mouth that curled into a malicious smile. The creature had caught up to her and it wound itself up like a spring and pounced, going for her. As it came for her neck, its face changed, became more human, but the fangs stayed and the eyes remained red.

Kuda held up her hands in a puny attempt to protect herself, yet even as the beast pounced, something changed. Instead of attacking her, instead of the expected pain of disembowelment, the creature jumped over her. It landed spryly on its feet in front of her, and Kuda skidded to a halt. Her feet got tangled, and she almost fell over, but she managed to find her footing. She gasped for breath, the air in her windpipe felt as though it was a hard lump.

The thing before her snarled. The sound it made was not human, yet the face of the being before her could once have been man-like. The facial structure was that of a man who had been in the middle of a nuclear disaster with a canine and somehow the two faces had melded together. The eyes were more man than dog, but the rest of it was the merging of the two organisms. The forehead was pushed back as though someone had hit the developing head with a brick, therefore permanently sloping it. The nose too had been pulled back, making the nostrils large and flaring. The lips were raised in a vicious snarl exposing hyena-like canines that looked like they could rip the leg right off a bull in one bite.

Its skin was mottled orange and brown, a cross between the colours of a leopard and a hyena. Tufts of hair grew all over the grotesquely hunched body of the thing before her, and had it not been for the fact that it stood on two legs and had fingers, one would have never assumed that perhaps it had once been human.

It circled Kuda as she stood, still gasping for breath, every cell in her body trembling. She turned with it, afraid to look away, unable to look away. As she rotated, her eyes never left the thing before her. Without looking away, Kuda noticed the dark shadows that formed around her. They were still, yet somehow they seemed to be coming closer. Impossible as it seemed, the trembling in her body became worse. The Shadows had found her again. Perhaps they were the ones that brought the man-thing to her. *They* led it to her. Their elongated bodies stopped a couple of metres from her, forming a solid wall of shadows. She knew that if she reached out her hand and touched one, it would be like touching a brick wall. She shuddered.

"Kuda."

She jumped and jerked as though she had been electrified. The voice had come from the creature. It held out a hand, reaching for her. She stifled a scream and flinched away. The thing pulled its lips back, and the attempt at a smile was gruesome.

"Kuda. It is almost time."

* * *

Kuda awoke with a start. She was wheezing and her blankets were wet from her sweat. She lay in the dark, breathing loudly and hating the sound. She needed some water. Her throat was dry and she could barely get much needed air into her lungs. She got shakily to her feet and dragged herself to the kitchen.

Getting a glass of water she glugged it down and felt her throat open up a little more. Just as she felt her breathing start to even out, she felt a sharp pain in her temples.

"Nonononononononono. Not again." she whimpered.

Falling to her knees she slid sideways to the floor and lay there, unmoving, groaning.

She felt the fear explode in her chest and she screamed.

Outside, King howled right along with her.

Jake awoke with a start as he heard the baying animal and knew instinctively that something was wrong. Grabbing his clothes he pulled them on quickly. He hurried to his front door and yanked it open. Standing outside, the hair on his entire body seemed to stand up straight as King's howling seemed to penetrate his skin.

Without pausing to think he dashed towards Kuda's house.

Chapter Twenty Five

Snapped

Chedza had had a good day at school. Due to the planned school trip that she was going on over the weekend, however, she had needed to come home to pick up a few things that she would need. She was happy though and was looking forward to the weekend. She had made up with the guy at school and they had started chatting properly again. He had apologised to her for everything that had happened and she had admitted it wasn't his fault and that she had been real immature to behave the way she had been.

All in all, it had been a good day.

She hummed as she walked home in the darkening day. The encroaching darkness did not bother her as she had walked this path many times. She felt a smile bloom on her face as she thought about him. His eyes. His smile. His dimples. The way he had held her hand as they had walked down to study hall the previous day.

She giggled unexpectedly and did a little skip as her heart seemed to grow in her chest. She had never been happier.

She heard a sound; like a stone being kicked. She glanced behind her, not worried at all. Probably one of the villagers walking home as well. She frowned as she realised she had dawdled longer than she should have. It was full dark now and she still had another kilometre or so to walk before she got home. There was a slight drop to her right, caused by months of fruitless water-pipes fitting that should have been completed before the school year started. Ah, Bots. What can one do?

She saw a lone figure, walking in the same direction she was. A man probably, judging by the height and gait. She continued her walk, humming as she went.

She heard the sound again and that was when she realised that something was wrong. She turned in time to see a man throw a punch at her. She ducked but she was not fast enough and the blow glanced off of the back of her head rather than missing her completely. She couldn't see who it was and she didn't want to.

Her breath caught in her throat as she fell to the ground. She tried to crawl away but the man stomped her in the middle of her back. She collapsed onto the ground, all the breath leaving her body. Pain filled her lower back and she gasped. Rolling onto her back she stared up at the figure that stood above her. Her eyes widened as she recognised that body that had an arm raised.

She uttered one word before the arm came down and a long, sharp object pierced her body.

"Why?"

* * *

Kuda moaned as she felt a sharp ache in her chest. It happened again and again. Over and over again, she felt a piercing pain in various parts of her body. Her head felt like it was going to split in half. She heard a shriek in her head and then silence. Then, just like that, the pain was gone. She lay on the floor trying to get her breath back.

Just then a pounding on her door and Jake calling her name made her get quickly to her feet. She unlocked the door and saw Jake's eyes open in alarm at her tear streaked face.

Outside, King had stopped howling.

"Chedza," she screamed at him. "Chedza's in trouble.

Without waiting for him, she grabbed her shoes, ran out the door and Jake followed close behind her.

* * *

The man took the young woman's body and threw it over his shoulders. In his head, a single phrase repeated itself over and over again.

"This is the only way. He said it was the only way to get her to love me again."

He had been given very explicit instructions about what he was to do. And he had followed them down to the letter.

* * *

Kuda raced ahead of Jake and he followed close behind her. King ran by her side, moving silently, like a shadow beside her. She stopped by a house and pounded on the door.

When a groggy Susan opened it, concerned, Kuda shushed her and grabbed her arm urgently to get her attention.

"Get Chose and go get the police. NOW, Susan. Meet us by the river. Tell Chose they must go where my mother fell. He will know where. Hurry."

With that, Kuda was off again, leaving Susan with an open mouth and saucer sized eyes. Jake and King raced beside her.

The three of them sprinted through the night. Jake didn't know where Kuda was heading but he sped beside her, no questions asked. He didn't know what was going on but he knew that whatever it was, it was something that was beyond his comprehension.

* * *

Kuda knew deep in her heart that she was too late but hope refused to die. She experienced a sense of deja vu and denied it. This was not going to happen to her again. It couldn't. She would not be able to deal with it a second time. So she ran. Faster than she had ever done in her life. She ran.

King and Jake continued to run beside her. Neither made a sound. Then, as they got closer to the river, King growled deep in his throat and ran off, speeding ahead of both her and Jake and sprinting off. Kuda wanted to call him back but she knew he would not listen. Something dangerous was up ahead and she wanted him to rip it to shreds.

Not long after, she and Jake reached the river bed. Looking frantically around her, she searched. She didn't know what it was she was looking for but she knew she would recognise it when she saw it. She heard Jake trying desperately to catch his breath beside her and she ignored him. In the darkness, she could hardly make anything out. The light of the half moon was barely enough to illuminate anything. But she didn't really need to see. She knew exactly where she had to go. She was just fighting the inevitable.

She paused for a split second and then slid-ran into the riverbed. Once at the bottom she started running again. She heard Jake doing the same behind her but she did not stop. Running on the thick sand, she made her way forward. Above her, on the bank, somewhere, she heard KIng barking furiously.

She had never heard King bark like that. Goosebumps marred the skin on her body with their sudden appearance.

She didn't break her stride, however. She trudged on.

Then, she stopped so suddenly Jake almost ran into her.

Fear clutched at her heart and she felt tears prickle in the corner of her eyes. A solitary tear escaped her left eye but she barely felt the moisture as it trailed a trip down the side of her face.

Jake saw it at the same time. He tried to hold Kuda back so he could go and investigate before she got there. She brushed him aside and sidestepped him. Before he could galvanise his aching muscles to move, Kuda had sped past him and was racing off again. She reached the lump lying on the ground before Jake could catch up to her. However, he heard her sobs even before he got to her.

Kuda held someone in her arms. When he reached her he looked over her shoulder and his horror was instantaneous. He took an involuntary step back and almost fell. Then, he dropped to his knees and put his arm around Kuda's shoulders. He rocked with her as she moved back and forth, her tears wetting his hand.

"Dear God," he heard a hoarse voice mutter. He didn't realise it was his for a second.

In Kuda's arms lay Chedza. Her body had been stabbed repeatedly with a sharp object and her throat had been slit.

* * *

King ran after him. It was the figure that had been by the river; the scent that had been hanging around Kuda for the longest time. He finally caught up to him and the man turned around and picked up a stick. The stick would not deter King. He was going to rip his throat out. Before he did, however, he stopped and barked at the man. Loud, furious barking, as though yelling at him.

Then, King got ready to attack. As he jumped towards the man, however, another body slammed into him knocking him away. As King rolled on the ground and got to his feet, the creature that had attacked him snarled at him. King snarled back. The two circled each other and the man ran away.

The tall, man-hyena creature bared his teeth and extended his claws, getting ready to attack. As did King.

Then, King bared his own teeth and tilted his head as though listening to something. He visibly shook his body as though to collect himself. He stopped snarling and sniffed, as though in disdain.

The creature stood still, confused. The dog was not afraid. It was almost as though it had been told to step down. As though to confirm this, the dog raised his leg, released a string of urine and then turned and sauntered away. Infuriated, the creature growled and got ready to attack again. However, King had already nearly disappeared from view.

The creature turned and looked in the direction the man had run. It turned and faced the river. From where it stood, it could hear a sobbing woman and see her cradling something in her arms.

Satisfied, the beast loped off into the night.

Chapter Twenty Six
Sorrow

Kuda stood alone on the rocks. Her heart felt as though it could not hold any more grief. She felt as though she was drowning and didn't know how to come up for air. She stood there, trying to hold back the tears that had somehow not fallen yet. Nothing in her life had gone right for as long as she could remember. She should have known better by now. Every time she thought things would work out all right, something really bad would happen.

She hadn't thought that Chedza would end up dead. She could have done something. She could have done something, yet she had not. She could have done something to help her. She didn't know what she could have done, but there must have been something that she could have done to prevent the death. A tear trickled down her cheek and the wetness infuriated her. She wiped it away, removing any trace that it might have ever been there. She had cried enough to last a lifetime. She didn't want to cry anymore. She wouldn't cry anymore.

As another leak escaped her eyes, she scrubbed it away with the back of her hand. She sniffed and shook her head, denying more than the tears. She denied the life that had so far brought her heart-ache and pain. She denied the fact that she would ever be happy. She denied the assumption that there was a light at the end of this particular tunnel.

"Why?" she thought, and didn't notice that she had actually said it aloud until Jake spoke behind her.

"It was just her time," he said.

Kuda spun around, her anger immediately transferring itself to Jake.

"How would you know who's time is up, Jake?" Her voice was soft, hopeless. Angry. "Do you have a direct connection to God? Does He tell you who's going to die, Jake? Who's next? You? Me? Manini? Who, Jake? Because somebody is going to die, Jake. One of us will die very soon."

"You don't know that, Kuda. You can't tell the future," Jake told her.

Kuda laughed. It was a horrible sound, and Jake hated it.

"No, Jake. I can't tell the future. I just know things, and sometimes they happen. Not all the time, but a good portion of the time. The way I know that one of us will die, Jake. The way I knew that my mother would die."

"Hey, I'm not going anywhere." Jake moved closer to her and pulled her into his arms. She resisted for a moment, but then let him hold her.

Her voice was muffled against his shirt as she spoke. Her words chilled him anyway.

"There's something really evil out there, Jake, and it wants me. It will get me. Whether it keeps me, or not, will be up to the three of us. Are we strong enough to fight it?"

"Kuda," Jake said. "You're upset about Chedza. We both are. Don't let that scare you."

Kuda pulled away. She took a few steps away from him and turned her back to him.

"I've felt this before. It's happened before."

"What's happened before, Kuda? I don't understand." He moved closer to her. Close enough to touch her, but he didn't.

"That's your problem, Jake. You don't understand. You refuse to understand, but it's really obvious. Something is conspiring to get me. It failed once, but it has regrouped, and it is here again. It's just a matter of time. I turn thirty in two weeks, and that's when it will happen. It's a cycle that I've never been able to break, and I'm not sure how much more I can take."

"Kuda, I don't know what you're talking about." Now, he did reach out. He shook her gently, trying to shake some sense into her, because she was scaring the crap out of him.

"Don't you? Don't you really?" she laughed again, the same laugh that made him want to rip his ears off so that he would not have to hear it. "Well, let me explain it to you, Jake. The same thing that killed my mother is here in this village, and guess who's on its 'To do' list. I am, Jake. I'm what's for dinner." Kuda's voice rose, becoming hysterical as she spoke. "It killed my mother fifteen years ago, now it's coming for me!"

Her voice rose and became a wail. She pushed away from Jake, almost making him fall. He tried to hold onto her, but she broke free and took a step backward, almost hobbling over the edge. Jake made a mad grab for her, and grabbed a handful of her shirt. For a moment, he was afraid it wasn't enough, and that she was going to fall over the brink anyway. Their eyes met in that instant, and they stood there for a second, neither body moving. Perhaps if she had struggled or fought against him, she might have fallen, but she allowed Jake to pull her into his arms. He held her, and she began to cry, and he knew why she cried. Not for the near miss, but for what she thought was waiting for her ahead. For what she had already lost. She had reached her breaking point and he wasn't sure how much more she could take.

As she sobbed into his shirt, he stroked her hair. He didn't know what else to do. After a while, her sobs subsided, and he urged her to sit down. They sat side by side on the edge of the rocks. Slowly, Kuda composed herself and dried her tears. She wiped at them with the back of her hand, wanting to get rid of the wetness there.

"Now," Jake told her. "Calm down, and tell me what's going on."

Kuda was quiet for a while, not knowing how to start. Memories flooded her and she felt overwhelmed. She remembered everything that happened to her that day. To her and her mother. It was not something that she would ever forget. She started to talk and her voice was soft, barely a whisper. It was as though she was afraid to talk loudly, as if, by raising her voice, the monsters would hear her and come after her. Had they not been sitting so close, Jake would have had to strain to hear her.

"Mom and I shared a birthday. Somehow, that alone seemed to forge a bond tighter than that of a normal mother daughter relationship. It's not that we did everything together, or anything like that. It was more like the bond that twins talk about. The bond of knowing and feeling what was going on with the other person even before they said anything. It was the strangest thing. Like, when I was eight, I was at school. My mother had gone to the river to get some water. She fell down a ravine and badly twisted her ankle. She couldn't make it out alone. I was in class, Jake. It was nine o'clock in the morning, and I didn't know what my mother was doing, but when she fell, I felt her pain. I felt her fear."

Kuda's voice dropped to a whisper. She turned her face away from Jake's, not so he wouldn't see her, but so that she wouldn't see the disbelief in his face.

"I heard her cry out in my head. I heard her screaming as she tumbled to the bottom, and I saw where she had fallen. As quickly as the pain and the vision came to me, they disappeared, but I knew she needed help. There was only one person who would have believed that something like that would happen, and that was Manini. I ran from class. Needless to say, everybody was astonished."

Kuda made a small sound in the back of her throat. It could have been a laugh or a sob. Jake could not tell what it was for sure.

"Manini wasted no time. She found Washington and they asked me to lead them to where my mother was. We found her.

She was a little scared, but apart from the ankle, she was fine. That was the kind of bond that existed between my mother and I, Jake. That was how close we were. What was worse, however, was that she told me that she had been pushed. That someone had done that to her on purpose. She never knew who it was but I saw it. It was Timile. He pushed her down the ravine. To this day I don't know why."

Jake was quiet for a moment, processing what she had said to him. He knew by now that whatever Kuda said to him was not impossible, even those things that seemed incredible, or really tall tailed. He chose his words carefully, focussing on what he felt was more important right then.

"With such a close bond I can understand why her death was so devastating to you," Jake said.

Kuda turned to look at him. "No, Jake" she said to him. "You cannot possibly understand what devastation is unless you saw what I saw and felt what I felt." She turned away from him again. When she spoke, her voice was as toneless as a broken church bell.

"The day she turned thirty, I turned fifteen. We stayed home, had our evening meal. We joked, laughed. It was just the two of us. Aaron had gone home to the States: his son was graduating from college and he wanted to be there. Mom was a bit edgy, but she tried hard not to let it show. I just took it that she missed Aaron. Maybe I didn't want to know why she was so upset because, in a way, I was scared too. I had been having really bad dreams. She had as well. Sometimes she was in my dreams, sometimes she was alive, sometimes not. Something told me that she and I had been having similar dreams, but

I thought that if I didn't talk about it, then it wouldn't come true. Many times I had started to ask her if she saw what I saw in my dreams. Many times I stopped before I asked. Maybe if I had, she would still be alive today.

"Kuda, you were a child. You can't change people's fates," Jake told her.

"Don't you think I know that? Do you know how many times I've lain awake at night and told myself that over and over again?" Kuda took a deep breath. When she spoke again, her voice was even wobblier than it had been before. "After I went to bed that night, I heard her pacing. She was restless. Had been for a few days. When she finally went to bed, I thought that it meant everything would be alright. As soon as I fell asleep, the dreams started again, and this time it wasn't a dream. It was a premonition."

Jake squeezed her hand again, more for his benefit than hers. A trickle of fear was tying a knot around his chest, and he didn't like the feeling. When Kuda continued, his grip tightened around her hand until he felt her knuckles crack. She didn't even appear to notice.

"I saw her go outside. I saw her standing and it seemed as though she was standing right under the full moon. She held a large knife in her hand, and I knew that she was expecting someone. Something. She was waiting for something to come at her from the night and it did come. It was the creature from my dreams. It was the hyena-man that had appeared in my nightmares over and over again. This time, when it attacked in my dreams, I heard my mother scream outside. It was *her* scream that woke me up. That and the pain I felt as it attacked her. I felt every strike it made at her, every time it slashed her skin with its teeth or claws, I felt it. It debilitated me, made me unable to go to her until it stopped

"By the time I got to her, it was all over. She lay in a pool of her blood, with this thing over her, doing something to her body. It saw me as I came and it stood up and looked at me. Then it laughed. And I remember saying, 'Animals can't laugh, what are you?' And the funny thing was that it *answered.* It answered my question."

Kuda laughed, and although the hysteria had gone from her voice, the lack of tonality was even more unsettling.

" 'You know who I am,' it said, and it was right. I did know. I have always known. And then it came to me. It came to me and stood right in front of me and held out its paw. It wanted me to go with it, and I think I would have had a woman not arrived at that particular time. She was there, suddenly, and she stood by my mother's body. Her arms were held out in front of her, and in each hand was a pile of beads. In her right hand, the beads were black, and in her left hand, they were white. They were glowing as though they were luminescent.

"This beast gazed at her for just a second, and then ignored her. It turned back to me and beckoned, and I remember taking a step towards it, wanting to give it whatever it wanted. Then the woman spoke. She said 'Dikhutso, I bind you from doing harm to this child. The damage you have done will be reversed. You will not have her.' As she spoke, she mixed the beads in her hands, and they seemed to float above her palm. They revolved and they spun and they moved over to where I stood with this thing she had called Dikhutso. They encircled us, moving faster and faster, seeming to increase in number. Then, suddenly, the three of us were within this circle of moving beads, and I don't think we were at home anymore. It was as though we were in a completely different place. Behind Dikhutso was a wall of blackness, and behind the women was a wall of pure light. I stood between them as though I was a prize in some kind of contest that I didn't even know I was in.

"Then the thing said, 'Gabedi, you have tried to stop me before, and you have failed. What makes you think you can do it now?' And it grinned. Then, the woman, Gabedi, she said, 'I have never been able to do it before because I was always alone. Now, I have the ShadowChild to help me, and you will never defeat me again.' And the grin just left his face like it had been slapped off. 'She is young and she can still go either way,' he said, and Gabedi smiled and said, 'Go home. Tonight the child will not be yours.' Then they stared at each other for what seemed like an eternity. Finally, Dikhutso smiled again and said, 'What I have taken tonight will last me for a while. We will meet again, sister. Take her, for now, but she will be mine one day.' And just like that, I was back at my mother's compound, and her body still lay where it was. I was alone again. I walked over to where she had been murdered, and I closed her eyes… Manini found me there when she came by not much later. "

Kuda hadn't realised that she was crying as she spoke. She had thought that she was all cried out. She pulled her hand from Jake's and wiped the wetness away.

"I've never told anybody what happened that night. I told the authorities that a hyena had attacked her. I couldn't tell them anything else!" She looked at Jake, saw his dear face, and wanted to weep. She sniffed, "That's why I blame myself for Chedza's death. I felt it when it happened, when she was attacked, and whoever did it is still here, and he will kill again."

"Is it the same person who killed your mother?" Jake questioned carefully.

Kuda shook her head. "No, but I can't shake the feeling that there's a tie somewhere. Something is happening, and whatever it is, you, me, Manini, and this *thing* in my dreams are all tied up in it. But you need to understand something, Jake. 'Dikhutso' refers to being cursed and 'Gabedi' means twice "

Jake frowned, feeling like there was a connection he was missing. "Cursed twice? Like having two negative things happen at the same time?" he asked.

"I don't know," Kuda whispered, her eyes still moist.

Jake wanted to ask more, but he didn't know what to ask. Something was going on, and Kuda was right in the middle of it. He knew that much for sure. He just didn't know what he was going to do about it. He stood up and pulled Kuda to her feet.

"Come on," he said, "I'll take you home." As they walked to her place, he knew for sure that at least one person would have the answers.

Manini had to know what was going on.

Chapter Twenty Seven
Knowledge and Knowing

Jake found Manini seated in her *segotlwana.* She was alone and Jake presumed that Una had already gone to sleep. The old woman was staring into the fire, as though searching for something deeply profound in the glowing red embers. Jake called out her name and she looked up.

"Hello, Jake. Come on in," she invited.

Jake bent at the waist and walked into Manini's small cooking area. He sat down across from her. The lamp was off and although he couldn't see her face well, he saw enough to see that she was not surprised to see him.

"I need to talk to you," he told her. Manini nodded, her face still turned towards him. "It's about Kuda."

"I wondered when you would come," Manini said. Leaning forward she stroked the coals with a stick that she held in her hand. After a few pokes, the flame reared up and licked at the stick in her hand. Manini pulled the stick out before it caught fire and laid it by her side. She sighed and looked back at Jake. "What do you want to know?"

Jake didn't know where to start. He had so many questions and he knew that Kuda would refuse to answer any of them.

He had tried to ask her a number of times and she had always neatly side-stepped the questions he had posed. It was only recently that she had opened up but he knew there wasn't enough time for him to wait for her to tell him everything.

"What is happening to her?" he finally asked.

Manini continued to look at him without saying anything. After a moment she turned back to face the fire. The flickering flames drew mobile shadows on her face as she sat as still as one of her huts. Jake wasn't sure she was going to say anything and opened his mouth to add onto what he had already said. Manini raised her hand, motioning for him to keep quiet. He closed it again.

Moments passed. Manini said nothing. She continued to look in the flames, as though seeing something in them that only she could see. After what seemed like a very long time, she looked up. The smile that was usually a part of her visage was lacking. She looked sombre, more serious than Jake had ever seen her.

"You are a good man, Jake," she finally said. "I have known that since I first saw you. Kuda knows it too. Yes, she is afraid. She has very good reasons to be. It has nothing to do with you but I believe you may be able to help her. However, in order to do so, you need to know … some things."

Manini sighed and poked at the fire again with her stick. She seemed to be weighing what it was she wanted to tell him, as though she had to say it just so or something bad would happen. This time she thrust her stick so deep into the coals for such a long time that it caught fire and the end burst into flames. She pulled it out and stuck the end into the sand beside the fire. With a small fizzle, the blaze died.

She opened her mouth to speak. No words came out and she closed it again. She closed her eyes and breathed deeply for a few seconds. Once again she opened her mouth and this time she was able to speak. Her voice was low and thoughtful, as though she was thinking about every word before she spoke it. The result was a halting narration which, despite its hesitation, still gripped Jake's attention.

"Kuda was born on the night of her mother's fifteenth birthday. She was a very healthy child. In fact, she was so healthy that in all the time that I have known her, she has never been physically sick. Not a sniffle, not a cough, not even the usual childhood diseases that other children suffer from all the time. No, not Kuda. She was special. Her mother knew it and I knew it. We discovered it at quite an early age but we should have known earlier. I should have noticed it earlier."

Again, Manini was quiet, as though unsure of how to go on.

"How?" Jake asked, unable to tolerate the quiet much longer. "How was she special?"

Manini looked at Jake as though to gauge his reaction as she prepared to tell him what she was about to say next.

"Kuda was a Dream Child," she said. Jake didn't understand.

"What do you mean she was a Dream Child?"

"Kuda saw things. Sometimes she saw them when she was awake but usually she saw them when she was asleep. She dreamtd things and they would happen exactly as she had dreamt them."

"You mean she would dream things and they would happen?" Jake asked, striving to understand.

"Yes. And no. Kuda saw the future. She saw things as they would happen and they would happen exactly as she had seen them. She didn't make things happen. She could just foretell the future. She could see it. Unfortunately she saw other things as well."

Jake was not sure he wanted to know what kind of things but he heard himself asking anyway.

"What things?"

Another silence greeted his question. From outside, the lowing of the cattle reached them and Jake found himself grabbing onto the sound as though it would encourage Manini to speak sooner than she seemed inclined to. He shifted where he sat, his lower body starting to go numb because he had been sitting on the floor for so long. In the dark, something bit his neck. He flicked it away and then scratched the spot absentmindedly.

"What things, Manini?" he asked again.

"Kuda could see the Shadows and the Light," Manini eventually said, her voice lower than it had been previously.

Jake noted Manini's wording and once again he wasn't sure he understood. "The Shadows" and "The Light" as opposed to shadows and light. This was more than just a reference to darkness and illumination. There was more to it than Jake could figure out and he waited for Manini to elaborate. However, when she continued, it was from a different angle.

"From the beginning of time, people have believed in the power of good and evil. The two are locked in a continuous battle and always will be until one triumphs absolutely and completely over the other. More often than not, people would like to believe that good will triumph over evil. Sometimes it happens that way, sometimes not.

"Both sides have emissaries and through the years these forms have changed according to circumstances and situations. Different people call them different things, but whatever they are called, they are always around us. They see us at all times. They interact with us and sometimes they determine our behaviour. Under certain circumstances they can make us do things that ordinarily, we wouldn't do. They can help us or they can cause mischief. They can heal. And they can kill."

The fire had died down again and Manini used her stick to revive the embers. When they didn't produce as many flames as she would have liked, she added some kindling. After a few seconds they caught fire and the reddish tongue of the fire stretched its fingers and brightened the *segotlwana.*

"Kuda could see some of the forms. From what she described to me, what she mostly saw were the dark forms. She said they were like shadows, that they were dark and elongated; like our shadows cast by the evening sun. When she was younger she could talk to them. They told her things but they never bothered her or tried to harm her in any way.

But then, a few months before her fifteenth birthday, things started to change."

Manini went quiet. Jake shifted where he was sitting. He wanted to shake her, to tell her not to stop talking. He knew from experience, however, that she would not be rushed.

"Kuda started to dream. The dreams were harbingers of things to come. Some say premonitions. Some say forewarnings. Whatever the case, it terrified her. She became...quiet. A ghost of her former self. Her mother… her mother was like her. She too could foretell the future."

Manini suddenly stopped talking and her eyes shot up and looked at Jake. Her eyes seemed to blaze with the same fire that burned near her feet.

"You, Jake. You were different from them. Yet you were the same."

Jake stood up suddenly, his head nearly hitting the roof of the hut they were in.

"What do you mean?" he asked when he finally found his voice. There was such a strong tremor in his voice that it sounded like he was stuttering.

"You were touched by the same power that touched them so many years ago, when you were a child. When you were here the first time."

Jake felt his mouth fall open and he forced it shut with an audible snap. "How do you know about that?" he asked. Then felt stupid. Kuda had warned him that Manini had a knack of knowing things. Besides, he didn't know whether he was asking about her knowing about his being there thirty years ago or about the weird power that had "touched" him.

"Jake," Manini said as she reached out and touched his hand. Her hand was warm. Perhaps because his hand had suddenly gone cold.

"You know. That is why you came here tonight. Not to get answers to what you didn't know. But to remember what you had forgotten."

Chapter Twenty Eight
Concealment Revealed

Jake didn't quite remember the walk back to his house. What he did remember was standing by the gate to Kuda's house and wondering whether or not to go and check on her. He had decided against it and had decided to go home instead. Once there, he threw himself on the couch and looked up at the ceiling. His thoughts were whirring sand devils in a congested mind. He couldn't focus on anything. It was as though he had had a drum load of confusion dumped directly into his brain.

He couldn't stay on the couch. Standing up, he headed to the kitchen to get a glass of water. As he took a step, he heard a voice in his head.

(wait)

Startled, he stopped and looked around to try and figure out where the voice had come from. He was alone.

(think)

There it was again. Why did it sound like Manini's voice?

He thought his heart would speed up because this was highly irregular. Instead, his heart did the reverse; it slowed down. He felt the thudding in his chest stop for a couple of seconds before it started to beat again.

Another couple of seconds.

Another beat.

Three seconds.

A beat.

Four seconds.

Another beat.

Then, the voice whispered again.

(remember)

Jake felt like a switch had been turned off in his mind and all the thoughts that had been doing the hustle in his brain disappeared. He knew he was awake and yet he wasn't sure. He tried to frown but he wasn't even sure if he could do that. His mind had become a bubble of blackness.

Then, he saw a small pinpoint of light ahead of him. The light grew and he saw himself, a five year old boy playing with a baby girl wrapped in a baby blue blanket.

* * *

She was lying on the floor and he was lying next to her, making faces at her and giggling as she tried to put his finger in her mouth and suck on it. She stared myopically up at him, a spit bubble forming at the corner of her mouth.

He continued to play with her, unmindful of the adults who were a few metres away, occasionally throwing glances in their direction but for the most part having their own conversation. His mother was there, as was the baby's mother and another woman. Her name was Manini Chipo. She was usually around, helping with the baby.

He thought he heard a noise from outside the room they were in. He stood up, making sure the baby was fine and went and peeked out the window. He saw nothing but darkness. After a moment, when his eyes had adjusted, he thought he saw a huge dog sitting at the corner of one of the rooms in the yard. The dog sat in a funny position and looked bigger than normal dogs. It was almost as if it was half standing on its hind legs.

As he watched, the beast bared its teeth and he took a step back from the window, suddenly afraid. Curiosity fought within him and won. He went back to the window and looked outside.

There was nothing there.

"Jake? You okay, hun?" his mother asked.

He didn't answer, eyes still searching the night. Whatever he had seen wasn't there anymore. Maybe there had been nothing there in the first place.

Turning away from the window he went back to the baby. He stopped. There was something around her, surrounding her like a dark, transparent wall. Frowning, he walked towards her. The translucent wall opened up for him and allowed him to get to the baby. He held out his hand and touched one of the humanoid shapes that had made a circle around him and the infant. It was like touching a bag of rice. He laid his hand on it for a second and then dropped his hand. Shrugging, he went back to playing with the baby.

When his mother took out a camera and took a picture of him, after placing the baby in his arms, he totally forgot about the dark shapes which now formed a semicircle around them. Besides, playing with Kuda was more fun.

Looking up, he saw Manini looking at him and the baby. There was an expression that the five year old did not recognise.

The thirty-five year old Jake, however, who was watching everything as though he were at a drive through, recognised the look. Her eyes were opened wide, and all colour had left her face. It was a look of pure terror.

Jake blinked and just as quickly the scene changed.

* * *

There was a young girl, a teenager, playing with her friends by the river. Someone was watching them. He could not tell who or what. All he could see was that they were carefree and full of life. The being that was watching them kept its distance. It was never far, yet it never got too close. It had been watching the young girls for years now. Fourteen years now to be exact. Fourteen years and three months.

It was time.

That night, it followed the young girl home. That night, its intention had become very clear. That night, while the young girl's parents were asleep, it snuck into their room and killed them while they slept. The scent of blood filled the night air and their screams pierced the calm night.

But it wasn't done yet. After it had killed the young girl's parents, it went for her. It did not kill her, however, for its plans for her were more insidious. Her screams, when it went for her, were not those of the dying but death would have been a more welcome reprieve.

Her child was born nine months later. On her fifteenth birthday.

* * *

The moan that escaped Jake's lips died quickly in his throat. He realised that his heart was still beating too slowly. This defied logic. He could not explain it. He felt his eyes roll in their sockets and he thought he was going to fall. He swayed but kept on his feet.

(remember)

* * *

The rain poured down harder than it ever had on that night. Lightning snaked across the night sky repeatedly like electricity gone mad, lighting everything below it as it streaked through the heavens. As if in direct competition with it, the heavens increased their deluge and seemed determined to cause a repeat of the floods of Noah's time.

High above a small village, in a set of caves that were hidden from the easy view of the village, a woman looked down and screamed. The scream pierced the night air and was drowned out by a roll of thunder so loud that even she couldn't hear her scream. She howled out again in pain, rage and frustration. Over and over again she screamed, crying out until her voice was hoarse and her throat was raw. Then she screamed some more.

As her water broke she howled in agony. She walked slowly over to where her pot was set on the fire to boil. She felt wave after wave of pain as contractions swept over her body, preparing her body for birth. She fell to the ground on her hands and knees and she felt the urge to push. Her breath caught in her throat as the contractions continued. Listening to her body, she pushed and pushed and finally, the baby was born. She picked it up and her tears continued.

Then, the urge to push came again. She whimpered as the pain increased. And she pushed. Exhausted, she gave a huge push and finally the pain stopped. She lifted her daughter from the blankets. She looked at both children and her crying continued.

As much as she hated how they had been conceived, she could not hate her children. Still, she had to name them.

Dikhutso. Gabedi.

Cursed. Twice.

* * *

(there is more)

But he didn't want to see more. He had seen enough. He had seen things he could never unsee. He felt like his brain was going to implode, the blood rushing through the veins in his temples like a high pressure valve. Falling to his knees, the sudden pain rushed up his legs and that seemed to free him from whatever held him.

He gasped as he felt his heartbeat speed up and return to normal. Falling forward, he collapsed onto the floor and then just lay there, not moving save for the rapid rise and fall of his chest.

What on earth was he up against?

Chapter Twenty Nine

What's Thicker Than Blood?

Manini was tired. She always was, these days. She sat looking into the embers of the dying fire and wondered which direction her life was going. She had thrown her beads over and over again but had seen nothing clearly. She knew there was danger coming but she could not identify where it would be coming from and this was unusual. She could only guess but she knew her guess was more of a feeling of foreboding than anything else.

One thing that she was sure of was that she would be dead before the new moon appeared. She had been alive for way too long and her soul was exhausted. She never understood why people wanted to live long lives. All it did was make you aware of how infinitely sad life was. She had seen so many things in her life and she had had enough. It was time to move on.

She had some regrets in her life. Who didn't? To err is human and all that. Her biggest regret, however, was that Una's mother, her great great-granddaughter, had died before she could see her son grow up to become the wonderful young man that he was now. It was painful to bury your daughter. And your daughter's daughter. And her daughter too, while death skirted around you as though *you* were the plague.

The second major regret she has was the fact that Kuda too had lost her mother when she was a teen. She had always wondered if she could have done something to change that. In her heart of hearts she knew that she could have stopped the murder, but sometimes turning a blind eye to one's failures was the only way of coping.

She tightened the shawl around her shoulders. It seems that the older she got, the colder she seemed to be most days. She sighed. Kuda had told her about her cancer the previous year. That wasn't a problem for her really. The risk of cancer increases with age and God knew she was about due for it. She had lived a really long time. Very few people lived as long as she did.

She was just so tired.

Reaching down, she took a bottle of a concoction that she had mixed the previous week. In the bottle was a dark liquid that was thick and looked like it had the consistency of curdled milk. She wrapped her slightly arthritic fingers around the bottle and then twisted the top off. Reaching out she held the open bottle over the fire and watched closely as she waited for the viscous liquid to drop into the embers.

When it did, smoke curled its wispy fingers upward like a lost wraith.

Jake had come to her tonight and she had known it was time for him to know the answers. They were not strangers. They had met the first time he had come to the village. She had known who he was when he first came. She had never forgotten him. She had always known he would come back.

Washington found her looking into the fire when he arrived barely five minutes later. The liquid had revealed nothing to her. It was as though her sight was being blocked. She sighed. She had been expecting that as well.

"What do you see, old woman?" Washington asked her. The smile that was a constant on his face was gone. His features were sombre and questioning.

She did not look up. "Nothing."

Washington nodded as though the answer was not surprising.

"Does he know?" There was no need to ask who the "he" was.

"Yes. Some of it."

Washington nodded again. He set his long frame on the ground next to where Manini was. They both sat by the flames, neither speaking for a long time.

"I have known you a long time and I have never seen you this distressed," Washington said quietly. Manini's eyes didn't leave the fire. After a minute or so, she sighed. Her shoulders hunched down as though to ward off something that she didn't want to touch her.

"I have made decisions that I have not been proud of. I have taken...lives. All for what I thought were the right reasons but now… I am not sure."

"You have never doubted yourself before."

Another long pause.

"Remember when I sent you to Washington all those years ago?"

Washington chuckled. "Of course, I remember. How could I not?"

"There was that girl child. The one you met. The one you gave the necklace to."

Washington was looking at her, waiting for her to finish.

"I killed her."

Washington frowned, his hand reaching down to take hers in his large ones.

"I know," was all he said. "And I know it had to have been for a good reason. You have always done what you do for good reasons. I have never questioned it, nor have I had reason to. I am sixty years old now, Manini. And you were significantly older than me when I was a child. I remember stories of a woman who didn't age the same way as we did. I believe you are what you are for a reason. I also believe you have done all you have done for good reasons.

"When you sent me to America nearly ten years ago, I knew it was because it had to happen. And when you told me I had to give Sharon that necklace, I knew there was a reason for that too."

"Do you know why she had to die?" Manini asked. She pulled her hand out of Washington's and continued to stare at the fire.

He shook his head. "I have never needed to understand your rationale for doing what you do. You gave me a task and I did it. I have not lost sleep over it."

"She would have kept Jake from coming back." She spoke as though she had not heard Washington's response. "She would have married him and kept him there. Jake needed to come back to Jackalas II. Everything depended on his being here for Kuda. Had he not come, there would not have been any hope for us. We would never be able to defeat...him."

Washington nodded grimly. He had never known who "him" was. He had just always known that there was a "him", lurking in the shadows like the bogeyman unchained. Always in the periphery of one's mind but never coming all out. Because if he were to come out, then who knew what other horrors would follow close behind him.

"What happens now?" he asked.

Manini finally looked up from the fire and into Washington's eyes.

"Now? We wait. There are two weeks before Kuda's birthday. Whatever is going to happen, will happen then."

Washington stood up. He did not want to leave her but he knew a dismissal when he heard one. He looked down at this woman who had looked after him for most of his life. She had found him when he was an ailing teenager and she had healed him. She had disappeared for a couple of decades and then had returned to Jackalas II. When she came back that time, she had stayed. There had been whispers about her; about her looking exactly the same. She had allayed the fears by claiming that it was her mother who had been there before, not her. Some people believed her. Others were sceptical but they minded their own business. Only Washington was aware of the truth.

He didn't care. She had trusted him with that knowledge and he had not abused her trust.

And now, because of the time he had spent with her, and after all the things he had done with her and for her, he knew her well enough to know that something was coming to an end. It had been a long run and it would be over soon. Sighing, he said his good night and left.

He met Kuda at the gate and the two of them greeted each other. She gave him a tired smile and he smiled back, his heart breaking at the thought of what might be waiting for her in two weeks.

"I will see you tomorrow?" she asked him, her brown eyes guileless.

"Without fail, young one. Without fail."

She nodded and he left the yard while Kuda headed to where Manini was still sitting. She greeted her too and sat down opposite her. Manini was sipping on what looked like tea and she poured Kuda a hot mug and handed it to her. Kuda smiled her thanks and took a sip.

"How are you holding up?"Manini asked her.

"I don't know. I'm all shook up. Confused," Kuda told her.

Manini nodded. "It is to be expected. A lot has happened over the past week."

Manini took a sip of her tea and Kuda did the same. The two sat in silence for a while, neither inclined to break it.

"Do you want to talk about it?" Manini asked her. Kuda downed her cup and placed it on the ground. She raised her eyes and gazed at Manini, her eyes contemplative. Finally she spoke.

"After my mother died, and I was committed into the psychiatric ward, I never thought I would ever get over it. Even after I was released it took years for me to feel safe, most of which was because of you, Aaron and Washington. But now, it seems like it was all for nothing. That all those feeling of fear that I had thought I had gotten over were nothing but a faux feeling for all those years."

Manini looked at her and nodded, encouraging her to speak.

"And now, Chedza is dead. I will die too. As will you. We will all die the way that my mother died. It is just a matter of weeks before that happens."

Kuda looked down at the cup on the ground. "What did you put in my drink, old woman?" she asked, not unkindly.

"Something to loosen you up. I needed to understand what was bothering you without having to pull it out of you," Manini said, taking a sip from her own cup.

Kuda nodded, as though what she said made a lot of sense to her. She looked up at the woman who had been such a pivotal part of her life for most of it.

"When Aaron left for the States fifteen years ago, I could never dispel the feeling that he never should have left. That had he never left, my mother would never have died. That's why I have resented him for so long. It is an irrational feeling and I have no concrete justification for it. All I know is that after he left, everything got worse. The dreams, the fear, the sense that something was coming. It was almost as though he were a buffer, holding back the monster."

Kuda cocked her head and looked at Manini, who in turn was looking at her.

"Now, Jake is here and I have the feeling that he is my buffer. That he is here for a reason. Almost as though he needed to be here to stop whatever is coming. Like Aaron had deliberately sought him out even though they had never met. I felt like all our lives had been orchestrated by someone, drawing us to this pont."

Again Kuda watched Manini, as though expecting her to say something, but Manini gave nothing away, her face as calm as it usually was.

"Go on," she said instead.

Kuda said nothing for a moment, watching Manini as she took another sip of her tea.

"I remember things but they disappear and I get snippets of them, almost as though they are being hidden from me. I remember Timile. How he and I used to be close. How he changed after his mother died. It was almost as though he became a different person after that. We no longer hung out and he became obsessed with me. It never made sense to me. I also remember my life being in danger, like something was coiled around me and could kill me if it wanted to. But it's so distant. Like I'm looking at it through a thick fog. Do you know anything about that, Manini?" Kuda asked.

Manini said nothing.

“The other night, I woke up and there was utter darkness around my and Jake’s houses. That is not something I should have forgotten but I did. For some reason I am remembering it now. Is whatever you put in my tea making me remember?” Kuda asked when Manini failed to respond.

Manini finished her tea and put the cup down. She looked at Kuda and sighed.

“When the Shadows find you, Kuda, they are there to guard you against the one who seeks to harm you; when his plans are nefarious. However, it seems they had guarded you against other dangers as well. I suspect that the snake was one of those.

“That night, when your homes were surrounded by the Shadows, he had gone after Jake but it seems like they protect him as well. Life happens for a reason. Things in life happen for a reason. Whatever the reasons, their truth comes out at a time when it is needed. Go home, Kuda. It will all be over soon.”

Kuda stared at the woman she adored more than any other and nodded, standing up to leave.

“Tomorrow then. Sweet dreams,” she said as she headed out.

Behind her, Manini sighed.

As Kuda left Manini’s compound, all elements of the discussion that they had just had slowly seeped from her mind like brewed tea through a sieve.

* * *

As Washington walked home, he looked up at the moon. It looked like a clipped fingernail that had been tossed up into the night sky. In two weeks, Kuda would turn thirty. So much was going to happen then and he wondered what the outcome would be. It worried him. It worried him a lot. Manini had gone through so much to ensure that they stood a chance of winning. When he has sent her to America a few years ago to attend to Sharon, Jake's finance, he had never questioned it. All he had known was that it was necessary. It was for the greater good.

In all his years, he had never questioned her plans and he was not about to start now. Her planning was advanced and he prayed that her plans would go well. The only problem was; Manini was not the only player in this game.

He stopped. He had been so lost in his thought he had not been mindful of his surroundings.

Up ahead stood a lone figure. It was a man. He wore a long coat that covered him from his neck to his ankles. His gnarled hands held onto a cane that looked like a shepherd's hook; almost as tall as he was, with a curve at the end. He wore a hat that was pulled low on his head, over his eyes.

Washington knew exactly who it was. It was the "him" that Manini had always whispered about. He knew it as surely as he knew his given name had not been Washington.

He did not even think about running. There would be no point.

The two figures stood looking at each other for a while. Then, faster than Washington would have thought possible, the man attacked in a flurry of movement and a blur of motion. As sharp claws ripped out his throat a random thought blipped through his mind; So this is what death feels like.

As the blood flowed from the open wound in his neck, he raised his hand in a futile attempt to piece his shredded skin and oesophagus together. He took a step, then another before he fell to his knees, then flat on his stomach.

As a large hand grabbed him around his waist and threw him over broad shoulders as though he were a bag of feathers, another thought, one that wasn't his, whispered in his head.

(Death is just the beginning)

Chapter Thirty
Nowhere to Hide

When he was eleven, he started to hear the voices in his head. He had been playing, alone as usual, with a piece of wood that he had been using to draw shapes in the sand. The voice *(Hello, Timile)* had greeted him. He had spun around, sure that someone was behind him. There had been nothing there. He had shrugged and gone back to his play. When the voice had spoken again *(Hello, Timile. Do you want me to play with you?)* he had frozen in mid play.

This time he had been scared. He had looked wildly around, sure that someone was there, hiding in the bushes and playing some kind of evil trick on him. He knew all about evil tricks. He had been the victim of many bad jokes. Like the time he had been locked inside a chicken coup with three mother hens. He still had the scars to prove it.

When The Voice had chuckled, he had run screaming into the house. His mother had taken one look at him, raised her hand and brought it down on the side of his head. Timile felt the impact reverberate throughout his skull and his teeth rattled against each other. The slap sent him crashing head first into a wall, momentarily blacking him out. He shook his head to clear it and the blood that had spurted out of his nose when his head hit the wall stained his shirt.

This infuriated his mother even more. She picked up the closest object, which happened to be the long-handled broom she kept behind the door, and brought it down on Timile's back. Timile had whimpered in pain, knowing from experience that if he howled through the pain that wracked his body at the impact, the punishment would be worse.

"Hey, *wena*! See that blood you are getting all over the place," his mother had screamed as she brought the broom down. "Get the cloth and clean it up. Now!"

Timile had gingerly stood up, cradling his injured body, and gone to find the cloth that his mother used to clean up spills. All this time, his parent had stood glaring at him, waiting for him to do something wrong again so she could clobber him with the stick in her hand. Not that she needed an excuse. Dragging himself across the room, Timile had squatted and wiped at the mess, only succeeding in smearing the red globs over the floor.

"Look at the mess you are making!" his mother had screamed as she brought the broom handle down again and again on his small body. She beat him until he passed out and then she kicked him into the corner so that she could clean up the mess herself.

When he came to, perhaps seconds, perhaps minutes later, his mother's broad back was turned to him. He dared not move so he stayed where he was, feeling his body throb with so much pain it was like a living thing that was trying to muscle itself out of his body. He stared at his mother as she finished what she was doing and stood up. She cast an eye in his direction and when she saw that the boy was awake, she scowled.

"Next time I will kill you if you do something like that, boy," she snarled in her son's direction.

Timile wanted to ask what he had done but he could barely breathe because of the pain in his ribs, never mind talk. Besides, asking would have earned him a second bout of pain, so he kept quiet. He had lain where he was, trying hard to wrestle each breath past the anguish that surrounded his body like a shroud.

(Get up)

This time, when The Voice came, he could not flinch. Numbness had started to settle over his body, making the pain a dull throb.

(Get up, boy!)

No, Timile answered in his own head, it hurts too much.

(Look at her) Timile looked at his mother. The way she continued with her duties as though she had done nothing wrong; as though she had not caused him so much pain that he would be peeing blood for the next week.

(Look at her. She expects to see you on the ground like this. She thrives on your pain. She relishes it when you're grovelling and crying because it gives her power over you. Don't give her the satisfaction. Stand up, boy.)

I can't.

(STAND UP, BOY!)

The Voice became a boom in his head and Timile winced at the noise. His mother turned to look at him, clicked her tongue, and went back to what she was doing. Timile stared at her and perhaps it was that tongue click that made up his mind. He could do it. He knew he could. He had done it before.

With a whimper, he urged his battered body to move. Slowly, he unwound his body from its foetal position and straightened his legs. He pulled his hands close to his chest and used them as levers to push himself up. He dragged his feet to his chest, forcing himself to get onto all fours. He got painstakingly to his feet, swaying as a wave of dizziness forced him to support himself against the wall.

(Good boy. Now go to the well and clean yourself off.)

Timile made his way to the front door, his feet dragging as he tried to minimise the movement in his upper body. It hurt worse than the time his mother had used the metal pot to cause him harm.

(Keep your head up)

He unconsciously straightened his back and raised his chin. It took him a while to get to the well. He had left some water in a bucket earlier in the day and he was grateful. That way he would not need to draw any. He got a cup and got some water. He washed his hands and then rinsed his mouth out and spat into the dusty earth. He cupped his hand and poured some water into it. He raised his hand and washed his face. He did this a number of times until he felt his face was clean.

He raised his face to the sun and breathed in deeply. He stopped when pain rippled across his torso.

(Stay out of her way for a couple of weeks; until you are feeling better. I will show you how. We will manage her. Nothing is broken. It's all just bruises. You will heal.)

Timile didn't question what he heard. He just accepted it.

Over the next few weeks The Voice became his constant companion. It knew things that he didn't. It guided him when he didn't know what to do. When his mother was looking for him, it told him where to go to avoid her. When she was away, it told him what to do to ensure his healing was faster. It told him how to mix certain herbs that it had him go look for so he could get better quickly. He lathered it on his body and his recovery was swift.

Seven days later he was healed.

(You are ready now.)

He was waiting for his mother when she got back from wherever it was she often went to. She wasn't drunk exactly but she had been drinking. She smelt like fermented wheat. She had not seen him for a week and when she did she stopped for a moment. He looked...different. More assured. Her eyes narrowed and the usual spiteful leer sprouted on her lips.

"Come here, boy." It had been years since she had called him by name. Not since his father had left him with her for another woman. He had been a constant reminder of her loss and she had never let him forget it. As Timile walked towards her, she stood watching him, her grin growling larger.

A few seconds later, he stood in front of her. She looked startled for a moment. She didn't remember him being almost as tall as she was. With a sudden movement of her hand, she brought her open palm down to slap his face. This time, however, it never landed. Timile caught her wrist in mid-air and held it.

"Never again," he said to her.

For a moment she looked at him with her mouth open, not comprehending what had just happened. Then, her usual cruel look reappeared on her face and she pushed him back. She raised her hand again to strike him. Timile struck first.

(Hit her between the eyes with your fist)

When she screamed and grabbed her face after Timile punched her, he reached back and took the spade handle that he had left next to the door. He twirled it in his hands as he circled his moaning mother.

(Hit her in the back of her neck)

Timile swung the spade handle back and took careful aim. He brought the handle down and heard a sickening sound as her neck snapped and she crumpled to the ground. She started sobbing quietly, tears streaming down her face as she lay on the ground like a discarded doll.

He wanted to take another swing, wanted to take out years and years of frustration on her. He raised the spade handle to do just that.

(No. You cannot raise suspicion. Once is enough.)

He realised he was breathing heavily and that his heart was beating super-fast. For a moment he thought about going against the voice but a quiet growl in his mind stayed him.

(Lift her and carry her outside.)

He threw the handle away and raked the back of his hand across his mouth. Turning back to his mother, he bent and lifted her. She made an incoherent sound, which he ignored. He strained under her weight but he knuckled on. Heading outside while he half carried and half dragged his mother, he was not worried that anyone would see him. The Voice assured him that it was all clear.

(Keep walking. You are almost there.)

He kept his head down and kept walking.

(Just a few more metres.)

The incessant mewling of his mother disgusted him. She could dish it out but she couldn't take it. How many times had she told him to stop his crying after she had brutalised him? How many times had she caused him to make the same sounds that she was making now? One time. *One time* and she was a whimpering mess. *How many times had he had to endure it?*

He gritted his teeth and trudged on. When he got there, he bent his knees, and heaved his mother over his shoulders. He watched as the woman who had borne him went down the well. He heard a "plomp" sound as she hit the water; heard the sounds she made as she cried at the bottom.

(It won't be long now.)

And it wasn't. He sat there and waited until the sounds stopped. It took over an hour and he waited. He waited for her to be quiet. He waited until the sounds stopped. He waited until she died.

He reported her missing after two days. When they found her body in the well it was after another two days. They ruled it an accident. People had seen her drinking that night. The conclusion was simple. She had tripped and fallen into the well. Simple.

It was after that incident that The Voice became a constant in Timile's mind.

Chapter Thirty One

Saying Goodbye Again

The morning of Chedza's funeral was depressingly beautiful. The sun had mellowed its fierceness and harnessed its anger. Kuda barely heard anything that was said. Her heart was in a hole that was so dark that she didn't believe it would ever see the light again. It had been ten days since the attack and she had been struggling to function over the last week and a half. She raised her eyes as the priest offered words of comfort to the mourners. She saw Chedza's mom weeping into a white handkerchief and her dad with his arm around her. His eyes were staring at nothing and he looked gaunt. Both had lost weight and looked like they had not slept in weeks.

Beside her, Jake squeezed her hand. She did not squeeze back. She stared straight ahead. Out of the corner of her eye she saw a familiar face. His eyes were fixed on her and she felt her chest hitch in a sob. Aaron looked back at her. He gave her a small smile, to let her know that he was there for her. She refused to acknowledge him. She could not. She dropped her eyes and stared at her black shoes.

The priest was taking forever. She needed to get out of there. She squeezed her eyes shut and thought about the happy girl child that she had loved so much. A life that had been cut short by such senseless tragedy.

The police had investigated the murder but had not come up with any suspects. This was what made it even harder; knowing that the murderer of one of the village's beloved was still on the loose. There was no trace of anything to guide the police's search. It was almost as if there had been a supernatural clean-up of the scene.

Kuda focused on what was going on and saw that the coffin was being lowered into the ground. She could no longer hold them back and the tears coursed unchecked down her cheeks. She tried to block out her ears to Chedza's family's weeping but their cries burnt through her wall. When the first spade of dirt hit the top of the coffin Kuda turned her face into Jake's chest and sobbed openly. It took barely five minutes before the coffin, along with Chedza, was buried.

Turning, Kuda pulled herself from Jake's arms and hurried away.

* * *

Aaron sighed as he saw the truck drive off. His ride would be there in a few minutes. He walked inside the empty house, memories drifting in his thoughts as he remembered events that had taken place over the twenty odd years that he had lived in Jackalas. So many beautiful memories that were now overshadowed by the not so beautiful ones. Still, he had loved his life in the country, in this village. He had loved his wife. And his daughter.

He was supposed to have left weeks ago but he had not been able to. There was one door that he had not been able to bring himself to close. It was still wide open. He had not been able to let Kuda go despite his knowledge that he could not hold on forever. He had waited, hoping she would come to him; to talk to him one last time before he left. She had not. And now, tragedy had struck again. He had wanted to be at Chedza's funeral. For Kuda. Yet she had not even acknowledged him.

It was only now that he would admit to himself that their relationship truly was dead. Aaron knew that she would not come to him, especially during this time. He didn't want to break the news to her, today of all days, but he knew he had no choice. He closed the door behind him, the one that lead to the empty house, and he climbed into the car that just pulled into his yard.

"I need to make one last stop before we head to Francistown," he told the driver. The driver nodded, and Aaron directed him to Kuda's house. Once there, he knocked on the soft wood of her front door. The house was dark, but the door was ajar, so he knew she was in there somewhere. When she came to the door, Aaron's heart crumpled in his chest. Her red eyes were striking in her face, her face drooping like melting wax, and her once lush hair was matted and uncombed. Aaron could see that Kuda was straining with the urge to not shut the door in his face.

"Kuda." He wanted to say more, but he couldn't. His throat defeated him, and he sat there staring at her like a gaping fish.

Her face didn't move an inch. No expression. Nothing. "May I come in?"

Her hand dropped and she walked away, throwing herself onto her couch. The curtains were closed and it was dark in her living room. Aaron stepped over her heels on the floor and her black headscarf before sitting across from her. Her eyes bored a hole straight into his chest, looking like dark lumps of coal sitting in her face.

"Why are you here, Aaron?"

"Kuda, I'm –"

"Save your sorry for someone who needs it. Tell me what you want, and then get out."

"Kuda .–"

"No, Aaron!" She forced herself out of her seat and glared at him, a fire blazing in her eyes. "I've needed you to be there for me once before and you betrayed me by leaving!" Her eyes glossed over, her voice softening. "Do you know how much it hurt to suffer through that alone, Aaron?" She coughed, her voice hoarse. "You left me when I needed you the most, and now I don't need you at all."

Aaron stood from his seat, his head shaking in disbelief. He took Kuda's limp hands in his, and she didn't pull away. She had no energy left. She couldn't pull away from him. Aaron pulled her into a hug, but her body was lifeless. Her energy was gone. She stepped back warily, and Aaron let her slip out of his arms.

"Tell me what it is that you need to tell me." Aaron heard the honk of the car outside, and his eyes snapped to the window. Kuda's gaze followed, and she recognized the insignia on the side of the car. Her eyes flickered with recognition. Aaron felt something break inside of him. He started to speak, but it was too late. "So you're leaving? You're leaving me again?" She chuckled humourlessly, already having accepted that the people closest to her were always going to leave her.

"Kuda, I have to go back. I'm old, and I wish to die at home."

"At *home.* So this isn't your home anymore?"

"You know what I mean."

"It doesn't matter, Aaron. Your ride is waiting for you." She turned to her bedroom and walked away from him the same way he would walk away from her.

She heard him sigh and then his footsteps headed towards the door. He stopped. Then he said something, not turning to face her as he said it.

"You will always be my little girl, and no distance will ever take that away from me."

Then he was gone.

Kuda fell to her knees, as tears broke out from beneath her closed eyes and fell onto the floor. She punched the floor once and sprung to her feet.

"Aaron!" she screamed. She raced out of the house and sprinted after the vehicle that was carrying Aaron away. She screamed his name again and ran after the car that was speeding away. It didn't slow down. "Aaron," she cried, her voice hoarse. She fell to her knees and sobbed, her tear filled eyes hiding the moving vehicle from her. She dropped her face into her hands and cried uncontrollably. She didn't know how long she sat there but when arms wrapped themselves around her she looked up.

"I'm sorry," she sobbed, her words breaking around her tears. "I should never have blamed you. It was never your fault. Now it's too late. You hate me –"

Aaron shushed her and held her close to his chest. His own tears joined hers and the two sat in the dirt and hugged.

"I could never hate you." He dried her tears with his thumb. "You're my baby. I love you more than you will ever know."

"And you're the only father I have ever known. And I never told you how much I appreciated that. I have been so angry at you for so long, and it wasn't even your doing. I'm sorry, Aaron. I'm so sorry. You were there for me after mom was killed. You made sure I recovered, took my meds, got over my psychosis. You held my hand for years, comforted me and helped me recover. You buffered me from the world when the world beat me into the ground. I could never have gotten to where I am without you. And I behaved like a brat and blamed you for so many things when all you did was love me and help me grow. Forgive me, Aaron. I'm so sorry."

Aaron held her face in both his hands and looked into her eyes. "There is nothing to forgive. I will always be there for you, no matter what." They sat there for another minute, not saying much, just revelling in being father and daughter again after so long.

The hooting of the horn of Aaron's ride had them laughing self-consciously as they untangled themselves from each other's arms.

"I know you have to go but I want to say I'm so sorry for all the lost time that I wasted. I should have been a better daughter and I –"

"Kuda," Aaron shushed her again. "It's water under the bridge. I'm leaving tomorrow but I'm only a phone call away. Call me if you ever need me."

Kuda nodded, her lips quivering in a little smile.

"I love you, Aaron. And I know my mother did too."

Aaron gave a wobbly smile in return. "I know," he whispered, before kissing her on the cheek and walking back to his car.

Kuda took a deep breath and then let it out slowly as she watched her father close the car door behind him.

"Godspeed," she whispered.

Chapter Thirty Two

A Guest in the Night

Kuda had taken a long walk and stayed out until the orange flame had left the evening sky. Tired, she sat down on a rock that was still warm from the afternoon sun. King stayed by her side as though he sensed her need for comfort from another being. Occasionally he nuzzled her hand, whimpering as though to let her know that he was there for her.

"Oh, King," Kuda said softly, her voice a low sound in the quiet of the night. "Why do things have to be so difficult? It's my birthday tomorrow and I feel like I won't even live to see the day end."

King, of course, had no answer. He whimpered again and then licked her hand. Kuda smiled. She scratched the back of his huge head with her fingers and then held his face up, next to hers, so they were facing each other. She looked into the canine's eyes as though searching for answers that had eluded her for a long time. Not seeming to find them, she asked some more questions of her own.

"What is happening to me? I don't even know who I am anymore. Why is this happening to me? *Why*?"

Unable to find the answers she sought, she let the dog's face go. King stayed where he was for a moment. Then he woofed. Once. Kuda chuckled as she looked at the dog's earnest face.

"As if you would have answers for me," she said. King woofed again, as though he knew more than he could communicate. Kuda took a deep breath and stood up. "Come on, pooch. Let's get home. It's getting late."

In the darkening day, the two made their way home. The near full moon cast enough light to make their trip home an easy one. Tomorrow would be a full moon and the feeling of dread in her stomach would not dissipate.

Kuda was tired. She didn't want to think anymore. Not about Jake, not about Manini. Not about anything. It was hard enough trying to sort out her own thoughts without trying to solve other people's problems at the same time. She felt as though if she could get through the next few weeks she could get through anything.

If she survived her thirtieth birthday.

By the time she reached her house, the moon had fully risen and was lying in the middle of the sky like a beacon for sinking ships would at sea. King immediately ran to his water bowl and, as she unlocked the door, she could hear him slurping noisily from it. Kuda dragged herself into the living room, leaving the front door ajar. In the brooding darkness, she walked across the room where she kept the matches. She groped around for a moment before her reaching fingers found them. She opened the box, took out a stick and struck it. A wavering light brightened the darkness and she held the matchstick for another second, watching as the flame ate away at the short piece of wood. She then opened the lamp with one hand and set the burning wood to the wick. The room brightened immediately and she shook out the match.

Leaving the lamp where it was, she went into her bedroom and repeated the ritual of turning on the lamp in there as well. When that was done, she went into the kitchen to get something for King to eat. She opened a can of dog food, emptied it into his bowl and carried it outside. King was waiting for her and she could hear the swish of his tail as he swept the ground with it. She carried his food to his usual feeding place. As she put his bowl down, she thought she heard King growl from behind her. She turned, surprised.

"What's the matter, boy?" she asked softly. "You don't want your food today?"

His tail was no longer making the swishing sound and she could see that King had stood up and was glaring through the half-open door and into her living-room. Kuda called to him but King failed to respond. That same low growl was coming from his throat but it seemed as though the sound was coming from his whole body.

"Come eat, King," Kuda called again, louder. The dog stopped growling and looked at her. Just as quickly, it turned back to look at the house. Because of the light that came from the living-room, Kuda could see that King stood very still and that his ears were as erect as floppy ears could be. She walked over to him and patted his head. When the dog failed to respond in any way, she walked over to the door and opened it wide. She didn't see anything.

"See," she said. "There is nothing there. Now go eat."

King remained where he was for a moment. Turning his head, he looked at Kuda as though to ask if she was sure.

"Go eat," she repeated.

Apparently appeased, or perhaps his hunger called to him louder than whatever it was that had gotten his attention in the first place, King turned and trotted to where his dinner was waiting. Kuda went and picked up his water bowl, refilled it at the tap, then went back inside. This time she closed the door behind her.

She flopped onto the sofa and stared at the ceiling. Flickering shadows danced above her and she closed her eyes. She opened them again because an image of Jake had suddenly come to her mind as soon as she had done so. She didn't want to think about Jake. Not now.

Instead, she concentrated on watching a self-destructive moth that had found a way into the house while she had been outside with King. The moth kept making a Kamikaze attempt to reach the flame and was continuously thwarted by the glass. Its suicidal attempts became annoying after a while and Kuda stood up. Her bed was calling her and she couldn't resist its appeal much longer. She stood up, picked up the lamp and took it with her to her bathroom.

After brushing her teeth and washing her face, she stripped down to her t-shirt. She blew out the lamp and took it back to the living room in the darkness. The lamp in her bedroom was still on and she turned that off as soon as she had climbed into bed.

Darkness surrounded her like a warm blanket and as soon as she closed her eyes she fell fast asleep.

* * *

Timile waited until all the lamps in the house had been blown out. Then he waited another hour or so just to make sure that Kuda had fallen asleep. His position behind the sofa made his legs cramp but he welcomed the pain. It meant that he was getting closer to his goal. He felt the hard handle of the knife digging into his side. He shifted and moved it to ease the discomfort and then he continued his watch.

It had been close when she had come home. He had had to wait longer than he had expected and he had fallen asleep. When she had opened the door earlier, he had almost given his position away with the unexpected snort he had made. Kuda had not noticed but the dog might have. He had been sure the dog could smell his excitement and that it would sniff him out. The Voice had taught him to make a concoction that would mask his scent, so he had not been worried that the dog would smell him. He had heard Kuda asking the dog what was wrong. As though that useless mutt could answer her questions. However, he had been worried and had only relaxed when Kuda had closed the door behind her as she prepared for bed,

The sounds of her getting ready for bed had excited him more than he would have thought possible. The idea that she was undressing while he was right there in the same house made him dizzy with delight.

Outside he could hear the buzz of nocturnal animals as they kept their vigil in the night. Closer at hand, a cricket made its incessant *ri-ri-ri* sound, close enough to be annoying but not close enough to reach. The sound faded in and out of Timile's consciousness as he faded in and out of sleep. With the cap-naps that he took, his mind wandered, and sometimes his sleep became deep enough for him to have dreams. Fantasy and reality became an intercourse of images. Some of these images confused him while he rejoiced in others.

Images of him and Kuda playing together as kids. Of her hugging him. Of her rejection of him. Of how she had threatened to sic the cops on him if he persisted in his courtship of her. He felt the same fury he had felt when she had repeatedly rejected him. She had constantly spurned him, as though he wasn't good enough for her. As though she was too good for him. Well, tonight the last laugh would be with him. Tonight he would make her pay for all the times that she had made him feel worthless.

He writhed uncomfortably as thoughts of what he would do to her crowded his mind. He wanted to make her submit to him. To degrade her. He wanted to see her squirm and plead and beg for mercy. Tonight, she would know who was boss. Tonight, she would finally see the truth that he had known all along. Tonight, he would show her that he had the power of her life in his hands. If he didn't get what he wanted he would slit her throat.

The night aged. Still he waited.

Chapter Thirty Three
Pain and Darkness

It was close to midnight as Jake headed home. The stars above him looked as though they were a whisper away. He had never seen stars like these in any other place in the world but tonight the awe they usually inspired in him was muted. So much had happened in the last few months that sometimes he wondered if he was really living his life or if it was all a strange and distorted dream. And, to top it all off, the things that Manini had said to him had increased that sense of being in a badly scripted nightmare.

In a way, everything she had said to him explained a lot of things. However, the feeling of being in some kind of unreality stayed with him. Kuda had said so many things to him and he himself had seen a lot that somehow defied explanation. Yet, having it all spelled out for him had increased his disbelief.

He wasn't a closed-minded man but how was he supposed to put all these things together and not head for the loony-bin? How could he hope to have Kuda in his life without wondering what new little surprises would pop up in their future? Was he just supposed to forget all the things he had learnt about her and still try to make a life with her or would it be a futile attempt at normalcy?

He didn't know what to think. However, he knew he had to see her. If not for anything else, to see if she was alright. Manini had said the forces had gathered and whatever was going to happen would happen soon.

Unmindful that it was almost midnight, he headed for Kuda's home.

* * *

Tonight her dreams were just that. Dreams. They were not premonitions or warnings of things to come. They were just the random illustrations of a resting mind.

However, she awoke immediately when a muffled thud reached her ears, dragging her from her restful sleep. Her eyes flew open and, for a moment, she lay in bed listening. Perhaps King had inadvertently bumped into her door. He did that sometimes when he decided that he wanted to sleep right at her doorstep. She smiled in the darkness at the thought and then snuggled down for some more shuteye.

When another bump reached her ears a few seconds later she sat up and got out of bed right away. With all the things that had happened in the last couple of weeks, she wasn't about to stay put. If, somehow, someone had managed to get into her house while she had been away, that person was going to pay dearly. If whoever it was had had good intentions, they would have made themselves known the second she had walked through the door. Whoever this was, they were up to no good and Kuda would be prepared for them when they got into her bedroom.

Moving quickly, she picked up the heaviest object she had in her room. It was the wooden carving of the elephant that she had by her bedside. Holding it in both hands, she moved as quickly and quietly as she could. If she got under the bed she would be at a disadvantage although it would be a good hiding place. So she moved behind the half opened door and raised the statue over her head.

She did not know how long she would have to stand before the intruder showed himself. She hoped not too long because the elephant was heavy and she was not sure how long she could hold it up. As that thought crossed her mind, she heard the soft rustling of someone who was trying very hard to be quiet but was not succeeding as well as they probably thought they were. Kuda's hands tightened on the carving and, even as she tried to stay calm, she felt her heart beat faster.

This is crazy, she thought. It hadn't seemed as insane as it should have when she had contemplated it a few moments ago. Anyway, it was too late now to do anything about her situation.

She felt the bedroom door move as whoever it was that was outside her room pushed it open, slowly. Kuda felt the breath stop in her throat and she had to consciously get it moving again. Then, nothing else happened. Fear started to beat a steady tattoo in her chest and she felt pressure squeeze her chest tightly.

This wasn't craziness, it was insanity. What the hell did she think she was going to do if the guy outside her door had really cruel intentions? She wasn't the biggest or the strongest person in the world. Heck, sometimes King pushed her over when he jumped on her. What if this person was huge? What if he really wanted to hurt her? He had obviously planned this and suddenly Kuda was extremely scared. King had obviously known that something was wrong earlier and she had ignored him. Why, oh, why?

She felt her arms start to tremble from the exertion of lifting the carving and she didn't know how much longer she could hold it up. She was bound to brain herself at this rate if her uninvited guest didn't show himself soon.

The silence was huge. It crowded around her and made it difficult for her to breathe. He was there, though, waiting. Perhaps, despite the darkness, he could tell that she was no longer in the bed.

Without warning, the figure crashed against the door, shoving it against her, pinning her between the door and the wall. She cried out and almost dropped the elephant. She held on, just barely, and tried to push back against the weight pressing against her. It was a futile attempt. Again the door was rammed against her and she felt her strength going all at once. She dropped the carving and somehow it fell to the side, away from her head, without doing any damage to her person.

When the elephant bounded on the floor, a large hand reached around the door and grabbed her wrist. She was yanked forward at the same time that the door was slammed shut and an involuntary scream pried itself from her lips. She was tossed across the room like a rag doll and with a sickening thud, her head hit the closet. She thought she would pass out from the pain but she didn't.

She moaned, not wanting to move. Not able to move. She felt herself being turned over by a large boot, then being kicked in the ribs like a dog that had just soiled its master's favourite rug. The pain was so unbearable that she could hardly breathe. Panting, she lay still.

She heard laughter. It was Timile.

"Who's the loser now?" he asked. He laughed again. It was the same maniacal laughter that had scared her so much before. She could not speak, however. She was not sure she had the ability to try. She lay on the ground, facing the ceiling, feeling the pain as it washed its way across her body. She wondered if she had broken a rib and decided she had not. She probably would have passed out by now if she had. Or, worse still, the broken rib would have pierced her lung and she would be drowning in her own blood.

"Who's the loser now? Who is the loser?"Timile chanted this over and over again. It was a litany of madness. A pathetic attempt to dominate an indomitable spirit. With each complete sentence, Timile delivered a blow to Kuda's body. He kicked her legs, her arms, her sides. Pain racked Kuda's body and she wanted to scream; to scream so hard her voice box broke and the pain killed her. She wanted to rant and rave in the craze-filled way that Timile would probably scream if he lost control of the thin rein that held his insanity in check.

She wanted to die.

She wanted to kill him.

Then, just as suddenly as they had started, the kicks stopped. There was no movement from either of them. Kuda could hear Timile panting in the dark, a jackal that had over-exerted itself. She could also hear her own breathing; the shallow breathless gasp of a wounded impala. Her body spasmed and she did cry out. It was a breathless convulsion of sound that seemed to come from something that was not human.

From above her, Timile chuckled. "That's right," he said. "Cry. Beg me to stop because what I am about to do to you is going to be a lot more painful than what I just did. You will beg me to stop, Kuda. You will beg me the way that Chedza did. You will pay for everything that you have ever done to me."

That was enough to make Kuda bite down on her bottom lip to stop any more sound from escaping. She would not give him the satisfaction. She would rather die first. Then it occurred to her that she probably would die here and the situation struck her funny bone. Morbid though it was, Kuda started to giggle. It was a thin reedy noise that was like the hissing of a kettle that had been boiling too long. It slipped past her throat increasing in volume like an approaching freight train. Slowly the crescendo became a full blown roar of laughter that just wouldn't stop.

She lay, doubled over in pain, on the floor. Her body throbbed with a pain so fierce she wanted to disown it and give it away to somebody else. She lay there, hugging her body and laughing hysterically. Outside, King started to bark. The sound was so unexpected that she stopped abruptly.

King's fierce barking shook Kuda out of her hysteria and she stopped and listened to what was going on outside. She felt relief as she heard him raking at the door. It meant that he knew she was in danger and wanted to help her. This thought bolstered her courage and without giving much thought to her battered body, she forced herself to her feet and attacked.

Timile, who had been listening to her wild laughter, and then to King's unexpected barking, was caught off guard. She smashed into him and the two of them tumbled to the floor. Timile recovered quickly, however, and the two of them rolled over and over again until they hit the edge of Kuda's bed. Being stronger than her, Timile quickly gained the upper hand and pinned her to the ground.

"It seems as though our little play will have to be cut short," he snarled. In the darkness, Kuda felt him moving to get something from his shirt with one hand. The other went around her throat. She wasn't sure what it was she was reaching for but she was sure it would hurt her more than the kicks had. She ran her hand over the floor, hoping to find something that she could use as a weapon. Her hand landed square on the elephant carving that she had dropped earlier. She clutched it while Timile's hand closed around her throat and squeezed.

Desperate, she grabbed the carving, managed to lift it somehow, and swiped at the air in front of her. It was too heavy for her to aim accurately with it but she was rewarded with a thud as the elephant connected with Timile's head. It could only have been a glancing blow because she didn't have enough strength to really do damage, but Timile groaned anyway. He released her throat and now used both hands to dig at whatever was inside his shirt. Finally he retrieved it and raised his hand to attack.

Kuda screamed.

And screamed and screamed. Her scream was choked off as she felt a pain in her shoulder as though something sharp had been driven into her body. She heard a sick, sucking sound as the object was withdrawn. In the dim light she saw Timile raise his arm to stab her again. Helpless, she waited for the pain that would signal her death.

Chapter Thirty Four
Breaking Through

Jake heard the scariest sound in his life when he was about seventy metres away from Kuda's place. For a moment he wasn't sure what it was and he froze in his tracks. It was the fierce barking of a large animal and for a random second he wondered if lions had taken to barking. The realisation that it was King made his blood run cold. Either the huge canine had gone crazy or Kuda was in trouble. Although the thought that King had somehow lost it kept him still for a moment, the idea that Kuda was in some kind of danger galvanised him into action.

Adrenaline pumping, he raced towards the house as though the hounds of hell were at his heels. What if whoever it was that had attacked and killed Chedza had gotten to her? King's incredibly savage roar, which should have been a bark by normal standards, assailed his ears again. No wonder the dog rarely barked. It would have scared the hell out of any sane, living creature.

Reaching Kuda's gate, he didn't even try to open it. Instead, he hurled himself over it and sprinted to the door. King blocked his way.

The huge animal was throwing itself at the door as though it were made of something other than wood. Then, suddenly, King swirled around and snarled at him. Jake's breath died a cold death in his chest and he almost passed out right then. King, however, realised who it was and stopped snarling. Jake felt the cold air in his chest slowly warm up again and he breathed. He wasn't sure what to do next but when a blood-curdling scream erupted from inside the house he didn't waste another second.

He threw his shoulder against the door and smashed right through it. King had already done most of the work and as he felt himself flying through the wood he prayed that Kuda was alright. As he landed, he immediately sprang to his feet and raced to her room. He was on time to see a dark shape raise a sharp object and prepare to plunge it into the prone figure of the woman lying beneath him.

Without pausing to think, Jake hurled himself at the dark form. As the two bodies impacted, Jake's breath was knocked out of him. At the same time he heard the other man grunt in pain as they smashed into the wall behind them. They fell to the ground with Jake beneath this other figure. The man raised his arm, the arm with the weapon, and Jake realised it was a knife. As the knife came rushing towards his head, he twisted out from under the other man's weight and the blade dug itself in the floor with a metallic thud.

With his right hand, Jake struck out and felt his fist connect with the side of the man's head. The crazy freak bellowed and, without much surprise, Jake realised it was Timile. Timile jerked the knife out of the floor and raised it high above his head to strike again. Jake grabbed the knife-wielding arm with both his hands and held on. By shifting his weight at the last moment and twisting to one side, he managed to throw Timile to the side.

Both men immediately sprang to their feet like hot-wired jack-in-the-boxes, Jake, fuelled by the fear that Kuda may be dead, brought his clenched fist up. He struck Timile on the nose with all the fury that was in him and he heard a resounding crack. Timile gave a bellow of pain and grabbed his ruined nose with both hands. Jake went after him and punched him again, this time in the gut. Timile fell against the wall behind him and Jake followed.

He continued to apply a steady flow of unrestrained blows at Timile. If Timile had killed Kuda, he himself would die tonight, so help him God. He would kill the black-hearted bastard if it was the last thing he did.

A groan from behind him might actually have saved Timile's life. Jake stopped the brutal punishment he was administering and spun around. He heard Timile slide down the wall but ignored him as he hurried to Kuda's side. She moaned again and he fell to his knees beside her. He raised her head from the cold floor and cradled it in his arms. She was alive, just barely, but she was still breathing.

Jake heard a deep growl coming from the door and he looked up. He saw King's large frame. The darkness somehow accentuated the huge shape of the dog. It took a step into the room and, not sure what was about to happen,

Jake carefully but quickly picked Kuda up and carried her to the bed. He set her down gently. Behind him, King had entered the room.

"Get that dog away from me," Timile snarled.

"You're not in any position to be making demands," Jake spat back. "I should sic him on you, you crazy bastard. I should let him rip your throat out."

King continued to advance, heading for Timile, the low growl still coming out of him. The dog didn't advance in a straight line. It circled. Like a wild dog circling its prey.

"Keep him away from me!" Timile screamed and the little sanity that he had held onto for so long seemed to desert him at that point. He bolted and King was right there beside him. The two figures disappeared from view. Jake heard Timile scream once, then again before he turned all his attention to Kuda.

Jake stood up and went to look for some matches. He wanted to see how badly Kuda was hurt. He felt around on her nightstand and found a box almost immediately. He struck a match and lit the lamp by the bed. The flame reared up and sucked hungrily at the paraffin-soaked wick. He turned towards Kuda and almost fell to his knees.

She was lying so still he feared she might be dead. He reached out and felt for a pulse, wanting to make sure that she was still alive. He found it and almost wept with relief. He felt that tingle in his nose and the wetness in his eyes and knew that he would weep at any moment.

Kuda's face was a mass of bruises. Her eyes were swollen shut and her lips were the size of fried sausages. Her cheeks looked like someone had stuffed boiled eggs under the skin there. Her whole face was discoloured. Blood seeped from a wound on her shoulder and as carefully as he could, he ripped her t-shirt so he could see the wound. He was relieved to see that although the wound was deep, it was clean. No main arteries had been cut and although she would sport a scar for the rest of her life, it was not a life-threatening wound.

She needed immediate attention, however, there was no way to get her to the hospital quickly. Chances were she had a concussion and he wasn't sure what other damage she had sustained.

He continued to examine her, tears streaked unnoticed down his cheeks. When he was done, he bundled her up in the comforter that lay on her bed and carefully carried her out of the house. He needed to get her to the clinic immediately.

* * *

A shuffling of papers. A soft rustling like dry leaves on the forest floor.

In a picture that lay on the ground in Kuda's room, a charcoal face seemed to turn slowly and look out into the guest bedroom. The charcoal face, with eyes as black as obsidian and teeth as white as porcelain, seemed to be deciding what to do. The drawn image from within the picture slowly pushed its misshapen face against the white paper and the paper bulged outward; the way a child, who had been playing hide and seek and hidden behind a curtain, would have pushed against that curtain.

The A5 piece of paper bulged obscenely as though getting ready to deliver a giant, mutant baby that had no intention of ever being good in this world. The shape of a wolf-like face pushed slowly against the inside of the sheet, testing the world beyond before it finally came forth. The paper-covered face turned slowly, as though studying the contents of the room, before it withdrew. All was still in the room for a moment.

Suddenly, a hairy arm with claws like daggers and gnarled fingers tore through the paper from the inside. Slowly, an elbow appeared, followed by a shoulder. Another arm burst through and the creature from within the drawing started to claw its way out.

Chapter Thirty Five
Clashed

As Jake carried Kuda towards the clinic, where he knew he could attend better to her while he waited for an ambulance to arrive, he kept glancing down at her still features. She was breathing but his fear that something was seriously amiss started to cause disquiet in his mind that he could not dispel.

He caught sight of the face of his watch and it showed 00:01.

It was Kuda's birthday.

It was at a moment that he was glancing down at her that he hit a solid wall where there should not have been one. Confused, he looked up and his eyes widened, his mouth opening in shock.

A solid line of dark shadows stood in front of him for as far as his eyes could see. He looked to his left, then to his right. There was no way that he could go around it. He felt anger rise up within him and he threw his shoulder against the wall of shadows. It did not budge. He could not put Kuda down and he knew somehow that he would not be getting through that wall of shadows at all. Desperate now, he wondered how long it would take him to walk around it. He turned to his left and started walking. He had taken two steps before he realised that the shadows had moved. In the blink of an eye they were no longer in front of him but had formed a tunnel of blackness that extended to his left.

It was clear what they wanted him to do.

He had no choice.

He wanted to rave and rant but somehow there was an urgency in the air that made the hairs on his body stand straight.

Time was running out.

He turned and walked down the tunnel of shadows. It took him only a moment to realise where they were leading him.

* * *

The beast stood in Kuda's guest room and looked around. Growling softly, it went and stood in front of the picture of Manini that Kuda had been drawing for such a long time. It put its nose right next to the picture and its growl grew louder. Then, with a sudden twirl, it leapt out of the room. It stopped just as suddenly when it smelt blood in the air. Lowering its nose, it headed towards the knife that Timile had stabbed Kuda with. A howl of rage burst forth from it and quicker than was humanly possible, it sped out of Kuda's house.

* * *

Timile screamed as King jumped onto his back and wrestled him to the ground. The dog didn't bite him, however. It bounded off his back and sprung in front of him. Timile lay on the ground for a second before he scrambled to his feet. King growled at him and approached. It was as though he wanted him to see him coming. With deadly intent, King tensed his body and jumped.

* * *

Neither Timile nor King had seen the creature approaching. As King pounced, the creature too attacked and hit King while he was mid-air. King, not expecting the blow, wasn't able to move out of the way. The knock sent him rolling in the dirt after he landed hard. He got up slowly and shook his head. The creature stood impossibly large, taller than a grown man.

King bristled and his hair seemed to stand on end. The rumbling in his chest increased until it stopped suddenly when he attacked, going for the creature's throat. The beast moved at the last moment and punched King, causing the large canine to plummet to the ground. Not giving up, King immediately got up and launched himself at it again. The two met in mid-air, claws and teeth gnashing and ripping. King got his teeth into its shoulder and the beast howled as it punched him over and over again. Finally, King let go. The creature threw a punch that caught King on the neck and, with a small whimper, he went down and didn't get up.

The beast went to stand where Timile was cowering on the ground. Timile stood up, an uncertain look on his face. He dusted himself off and stood and faced it. As he watched, the beast grew shorter, its snout growing shorter until it became a human nose. The teeth shortened, becoming less sharp, the lips more human.

"You hurt her." It wasn't a question.

"She deserved it," Timile responded, his chin jutting out.

"I told you not to touch her physically. You had Chedza to satisfy your bloodlust," Timile was told.

"I needed her –"

Timile didn't see the blow coming. Before the words were out of his mouth the creature had shifted and its sharp teeth had sunk into his neck, ripping through his spine. Its jaw snapped three of four times before Timile's head separated from his body and fell to the ground. His body spasmed a few times before it fell to its knees and went still, blood spurting from the severed neck.

The beast turned to go and finish King off. Its eyes flickered in the near darkness, searching.

The dog wasn't there.

Raising its snout, the creature sniffed the air. Strange. It could not smell the dog. It was as though there was something blocking him from getting a sense of where the dog was. Its lips curled in a sneer as it turned and loped off into the night.

There was somewhere it needed to be.

* * *

When Jake arrived at Manini's compound, she was waiting for him. She hurried him over to the middle of her yard. He stopped, confused, when she directed him to a space in the middle of her yard.

"Lay her on the ground," she instructed.

"What --?"

"Don't question me, Jake. Just do it."

Jake did as he was told, carefully laying her on the cool earth. Manini moved quickly and laid three black crystal-like balls around her; one a metre from her head, another a metre from her right foot and the third a metre from her left foot, creating a triangle in which Kuda lay.

"Jake, stand between her head and the stone," she told him. "There is no time for questions. Do it now."

Jake did as he was told and watched as she stood in a similar position by Kuda's left leg. Manini looked around frantically. Washington should have been here by now. Where was he?

She saw a movement at her gate and breathed a sigh of relief. The relief was short lived as she heard a deep laugh.

"Expecting someone?" a voice asked. Manini froze. "Someone other than me, that is."

Manini seemed to recover and she smiled at the visitor. "You're early. I was expecting you a little later than this."

"Oh, you should know me better than that, sister."

"Sister?" Jake whispered. "He's your brother?"

Manini nodded. "Unfortunately, there are some things that we cannot change."

Kake circled Manini and Jake, keeping his eyes on Kuda.

"She was not meant to get hurt tonight. Timile got a little… carried away," Kake said,

"You turned him into what he was. You took an innocent child and turned him into a killer," Manini accused.

Kake shrugged. "There are things that we have both done in an attempt to further our cause. Like, for example, the death of a young lady in a car accident in America." Kake smiled and continued to circle the three people. "Did you ever tell Jake that you were the reason for the death of his beloved?" Kake chuckled again as Jake whipped his head to stare at Manini. Mannini did not take her eyes off her brother. "Or that you could have saved Kuda's mother but you chose not to. You let her die yet you could have stopped the killer. Coined another way, you could have stopped me but you were too afraid."

"It wasn't like that," Manini said, her teeth clenched.

"Oh, really, dear sister? How was it really?"

Manini went quiet. Jake felt a fury rising in his body. He felt hot and he wanted to grab the old man and beat him to a pulp. As though reading his thoughts, Kake grinned.

"Please do, American. It would make everything so much easier."

"Jake, don't step outside of the triangle," Manini warned.

"Ah, your triangle. Seems like you are one person short." Kake sneered and continued to walk around them. "I believe Washington was supposed to be your third but he had an unfortunate incident. I believe he's communing with the dead as we speak."

"How did you keep his death from me?" Manini asked.

"I've learnt a few things over the last hundred odd years or so. Let's just say the man you have been consorting with for the last couple of weeks wasn't who you thought it was. This was child's play." Kake stopped moving and looked at Jake. He was a few metres away from him and Jake believed that he could take him.

The old man continued to talk, his old cloak hanging around him like a lifeless silhouette. "You seem to have been learning too, dear sister. Three stones. Power in threes. Three represents Past, Present and Future. Or Birth, Life and Death."

"Or Beginning, Middle and End," Manini told him. "And I believe this is the end for you, *dear brother*."

Kake laughed. "Not until I'm ready to go," he suddenly snarled.

It was then that Jake moved out of the triangle and attacked.

Chapter Thirty Six

Darkness Comes Calling

The second that Jake set foot outside of the triangle, Kake began his transformation. By the time that Jake had taken a step, the creature from Kuda's pictures stood before him. Jake froze as he saw the face that was melded between the features of a man and a hyena. The forehead that was pushed back, the eyes of a rabid wolf-like beast, the flaring nostrils and the hyena ears. The mottled orange and brown skin and the clawed arms made Jake's breath leave his body in one quick exhale.

The Kake-hyena-beast grabbed him by the neck and snarled. Throwing Jake against the wall of Manini's hut, he went for him. Somehow Manini managed to beat him to it and placed herself between Jake and Kake. As Kake's claws slashed downwards, they caught Manini on the shoulder and she fell to the ground with a moan. Kake howled and as Jake watched, claw marks appeared on Kake's right shoulder; almost at the same spot that Manini had been mauled. Jake fell to his knees and examined Manini's injury.

Kake moved back and howled.

"Get me back into the triangle, Jake. We must get to our previous spots. Immediately." Without questioning it, Jake lifted Manini's slight figure and hurried back into the triangle.

By the time Kake had gathered himself, Manini stood shakily by Kuda's foot and Jake by her head. Kake attacked again. As he threw himself at Jake, a wall of shadows suddenly materialised in front of him. Kake stopped as though he had hit a brick wall. He howled in rage.

The sound made goose bumps appear on Jake's arms and he turned slightly as he heard a sound behind him. Kuda moaned again.

"Don't move, Jake," Manini warned. He thought about ignoring her but something warned him not to.

Kake slashed at the darkness in front of him, his howls getting louder and louder. Then, from the side, King appeared. He was limping. The canine stood still for a moment, as though listening to something. Then, with a sudden spurt, he raced past the Kake creature and headed to where Kuda lay. As he reached her right foot, a force field seemed to appear in a dome around the three people and the dog. Manini fell to her knees. She started a chant.

"With the Power of Three, I call upon thee.

With the Power of Four, I call out for more.

North, East, South and West, I call on the best.

Oh, Mother Earth, put this beast to rest."

Kake stopped howling. He growled and a bright light flew from the top of the force field and struck him in the chest. For a moment the beast seemed to be lifted off of the ground before the light disappeared and he fell back to the ground. With a loud scream that seemed to come from something surreal,

Kake started morphing again. His limbs started shrinking, as did his face and body. Like a clay doll that had been thrown into fire, Kake's body distorted continuously for a few seconds before it finally settled.

When the distortions stopped, he was back in his human form.

"What did you do to me?" he screamed at Manini.

"I stripped you of your ability to change into the beast," she told him. Her shoulder was bleeding freely now and the blood flowed down her arm. Jake stood where he was, too petrified to move. King stood docilely at the third end of the triangle, as though he understood what was going on.

Manini wasn't done chanting.

"For decades and decades we've taken lives

Extended our own and without care who survives

It's time to give back all the souls we have taken

And to free them so they're no longer forsaken.

I give to the ShadowChild to pass on what's not ours

Through her I strip my brother and I of our powers"

Jake watched as Kuda started to rise with Manini's words. She floated in the air as the old woman completed her chant. Then, a black light broke through from Kuda's torso, heading straight up into the sky. Kuda screamed as wave after wave of black light left her body. After what seemed like an eternity, the pulse of black ceased. Kuda floated gently back to the ground and lay still.

Jake hurried over to her and lifted her head. She was breathing steadily. Her eyes fluttered open and she looked at him. Then, her eyes closed again.

Jake looked up and saw Kake lying on the ground. Laying Kuda down again he sprang towards the old man. With a cry, he grabbed the old man and lifted him off the ground. He punched him in the face over and over again. He only stopped when he heard Manini cry out. He looked over at her and was shocked. Her face was a bloody mass, as though he had been punching her. Horrified, he stopped. He rushed over to her.

"What's going on?" he asked her.

She smiled at him. "He is not yours to kill, Jake. He has a different fate. As do I."

"I don't understand," Jake said softly.

"You will. Jake, I'm sorry. I killed her. I killed your fiancé. I had to."

"How is that even possible?"

"There are things that transcend time and space. You should know that by now."

Jake heard a sudden growl and turned in time to see King attack something behind him. He ducked just in time to see the dog launch himself at Kake. Kake held a knife in his hand. King sank his teeth into his wrist and both Manini and Kake screamed. King held onto the old man's arm and refused to let go.

"King!" Manini whispered, and astoundingly, the dog let go.

Kake dashed off, his hand cradled against his chest. Jake made as though to put Manini down and go after him but Manini stayed him. "No. Let him go. Kuda needs you."

Jake reluctantly let her go and headed over to where Kuda lay. Checking her wounds again he gasped.

The bruises on her face as well as the stab mark on her body had disappeared.

* * *

Kake ran off into the night, the pain in his body flaring like a thing alive.

She had betrayed him. The one person who had been with him since conception had turned her back on him. He had had it all figured out too. This would have given him immortality. They had been alive for a hundred and ninety nine years. This would have been his two hundredth year. He could have lived forever. They could have lived forever.

The night he had killed Kuda's grandparents, he had poured his essence into her mother. She had conceived a pure child born of the darkness. For years he had killed his selected targets, knowing that he could use their spirit or whatever it was he took from them. And yes, over the years he had taken and taken and taken. He had also experimented, sought ways of extending his life. Nothing had worked. His children had all died. All except Kuda. And that was when he knew that he had tapped into his immortality. He knew that when he killed her and swallowed her essence, hers would bring him eternal life.

Manini had killed all hope of that now. And he knew why. She had told him years ago that she was tired. He should have managed her better, but when she left him to live her own life, he should have guessed that she was preparing for their end. Now, it was too late. She had stripped him of everything that he had worked so hard to build. No matter.

He was still alive.

He would start again.

His wounds would heal. As would his twin sister's. They had another hundred years or so to go on. He was not ready to leave this world yet.

He had stumbled out of Manini's yard and rushed away. He wasn't aware that he was running past her *kraal* until he saw the large shape of a cow loom ahead of him. Startled, he stopped. Why wasn't she in with the rest of the cattle? No matter. She was just a dumb animal. Moving forward again, he started to run past her.

He wasn't aware of the cow running towards him until it was too late. The last thing he saw was a huge head which slammed into his body and sent him flying. This was followed very quickly by hooves which hit his body over and over again.

As pain descended on his body and he felt his ribs and other bones break, he suddenly realised that he was not coming back from this one.

Around him, a wall of shadows was standing. As the cow continued to stamp and gore his body, the wall of shadows closed in on him until all he could feel were the wounds inflicted on him by the animal and the claustrophobic feeling of being surrounded by a wall of blackness. He thought the feeling would pass as he felt the life drain out of his body, but he was wrong.

It was then that he started to scream.

No one heard him, however, because the wall of shadows had disappeared, along with him and the cow.

Chapter Thirty Seven

Shadows and Light

Kuda came to, slowly. She thought she would feel pain from Timile's stab wound but there was none. Opening her eyes, she realised that something wasn't quite normal. She was surrounded by pure white. Everywhere she looked, she saw white. Even her clothing was white. She wasn't scared but she was curious. She didn't understand what was going on but she didn't feel like she was in any danger.

She blinked and Manini was by her side, also dressed in white.

"Hello, Kuda," she said.

"Where am I?" Kuda asked her.

"Nowhere. Everywhere. You are between space and time."

"How did that happen?"

Manini grinned. "A spell here, a spell there. No one ever really knows what will happen when all the spells come together."

"Timile stabbed me."

"Yes. He did." Manini's grin had disappeared.

"And I think the creature from my pictures finally came out. I don't know how I know but I think it wanted to devour me. Not my body but my spirit."

Manini nodded.

"He won't bother you again."

Manini pointed to Kuda's right and Kuda turned. What she saw scared her. A lot. Kake was in a chasm of black, being continually gored and stomped by Mmantshadi.

"Where is he?" she asked.

"He created his own purgatory. He will not ever be coming out of it."

"He killed my mother." Manini nodded. "Where's Jake?" Kuda asked, turning away from the image. As she turned, she saw Jake holding her in his arms. Next to them, King stood, whimpering softly.

"Am I dead?" she asked.

"No," Manini told her. "Far from it. But you have to go back now. Jake needs you. The way you needed him. If he had not been here, we would not have been able to strip Kake of his powers. He needed to be here. Now, you must go back. Please look after Una for me."

"Where are you going?" Kuda asked, frowning.

Manini simply smiled, a smile so serene and peaceful that Kuda smiled back in response. Manini, however, did not respond to Kuda's question.

* * *

With a start, Kuda woke up in Jake's arms. She sat up like a Jack in a box and the first thing her eyes landed on was Manini where she lay on the ground. The second thing was the wall of shadows that surrounded them.

She hurried over to Manini, ignoring the shadows, with Jake behind her. She cradled the old woman's head in her lap. Blood was coming from her ears and mouth.

"What the heck happened?" Jake asked. "Nobody touched her. She shouldn't be bleeding."

"Kake was her twin," Kuda said. "I think they shared more than just the same womb for nine months."

Manini squeezed Kuda's hands. Her voice was low and broken as she spoke. "I'm sorry, Kuda. For everything. There are so many things I wish I could do differently." She took a deep breath. "I have waited decades for this. Kake is dead. And soon I will be too."

She took Jake's hand in hers and put Kuda's hand in his. "Look after each other," she said with a smile. Kuda nodded and looked at Jake. When she looked down, she saw that Manini was still smiling. It took a moment to realise that the light in her eyes was starting to fade. As Kuda started to sob, Jake wrapped his arms around her and King sat by her side.

All at once the wall of shadows disappeared. As they did, Manini's body seemed to fade until there was an emptiness in Kuda's hands that hadn't been there before. Then, it was just Jake, Kuda and King sitting in the moonlight.

With a loud mournful howl, King said his goodbyes to the woman who had created him to protect Kuda.

* * *

Kuda didn't want to spend the night at her place so Jake offered her his room. As they sat in his living room, they barely spoke. King was snuggled at Kuda's feet and Jake sat opposite her.

"I think it's finally over," Jake said quietly. He had looked for Kake after Manini had disappeared and he had not found him. Washington was nowhere to be found and neither was Timile.

Kuda dared to believe that it really was over. That she actually did have a future after all.

Jake looked at Kuda and smiled. She smiled back.

"You know, I was going to ask you out on a proper date but I got the feeling that you would turn me down. Now, after everything that has happened, asking you out on a date doesn't seem so scary anymore.

Kuda laughed. "Really? Perhaps you should be scared. After all, I'm still the same girl you met three months ago."

It seemed so much longer than that. So much had happened and both of them had the feeling that they had changed in a way that was deeper than they could imagine.

And yet, sitting here together, both of them smiling goofily at each other, they could hope that there was a future for them. As Jake moved and sat down next to her, he twined his fingers with hers.

Tomorrow was another day. There was much to look forward to.

Epilogue

Kuda woke up before Jake did. Not wanting to disturb him, she snuck out of the house and left for her place. The broken front door shook her a little but she stepped into the house with King beside her. Walking to her bedroom she saw her blood on the floor and walked past the room.

She headed to her guest room and stood frozen by the door. On the floor was sheet after sheet of blank paper. The drawings that had terrified her for months had disappeared off of all the pages. Squatting, she picked up a few and shook her head as she turned them upside down. There was nothing on the back either.

Standing up, she headed to Manini's portrait and stood in front of it. She looked at it for a long time before she picked up her paints and started working on it. Hours later, she smiled in satisfaction. The portrait was complete. It was Manini the way she had looked the previous night, when they had been in the white space.

Content, she stood back, happy that it was finally finished.

"Goodbye, old friend," she whispered.

As she walked past the mirror in the room, her eyes went to her image. She smiled involuntarily.

Then froze.

For a second, just a split second, she could have sworn her pupils had not been round at all, but had been the slitpupiled eye of a hyena. Just as quickly as she had thought she saw it, it was gone.

Her heart sped up and refused to slow down.

No, it was over. It was all over. Kake was dead. Manini was dead. There was nothing to tie her to them.

Except maybe, blood.

www.ingramcontent.com/pod-product-compliance
Lightning Source LLC
La Vergne TN
LVHW041143150826
845673LV00001B/61

* 9 7 9 8 8 8 9 0 9 9 7 8 9 *